The Actor

Beth Hunter McHugh

RIVERBEND
PUBLISHING

The Actor
Copyright © 2015 by Beth Hunter McHugh
Published by Riverbend Publishing, Helena, Montana
ISBN 13: 978-1-60639-088-7
Printed in the United States of America.

1 2 3 4 5 6 7 8 9 0 VP 22 21 20 19 18 17 16 15

Riverbend Publishing
P.O. Box 5833
Helena, MT 59604
1-866-787-2363
www.riverbendpublishing.com

For my grandfather

BOOK ONE
A Nice Home

1.

For a time we lived in a very nice house. This was when we still lived in town, four blocks from the university, and when Franny and I were young enough to be close friends without bothering each other too much. As sisters went, we were perhaps unconventionally close, due in part to the way we had been raised. We spent a great deal of time alone.

In 1967, we were eleven and thirteen years old, respectively, and we lived in Montana with our mother and father. I remember Montana during the years in the nice house as a very fertile sort of place. In later years, after almost all memory of the house had been abandoned, that impression would shift for some reason, and the state would recall itself in a dry and suffering way. As a grown woman, I would think about my childhood and feel the need to squint, to brace myself against something, the way one feels walking home in a determined and dusty wind, and every place of respite assumes a seemingly permanent distance.

During its reign, the nice house was a respite of sorts, a place sequestered away from most violence or confusion of the world. Our parents, Nora and David Birch, were educated and informed people, yet they chose to keep most external turmoil just outside the front door of our home. Franny and I were children produced by parents of simpler times. Our school clothes were unfashionable, our record collections outdated, our wildness defined by a stolen cigarette or swear word; we had heard of the Beatles and loved them, we stared after girls in mini-skirts with faces full of envy, and we kept a secret pact that one day we'd run away from home and hitchhike to San Francisco. All of these curiosities were subdued by our own household that, while sheltered, was certainly not dull.

Our mother and father had been independent and rebellious in their youth, and as adults and parents they did not lose much of their tenacity. It was for this reason, perhaps, that Franny and I did not feel the need to rebel much. We had freedom enough. Our mother and father's inner life might have had its complications, but on the outside they managed to hold tight to some vestiges of a remembered and youthful existence, and by the 1960s, after the greatest challenges of work and childrearing and marriage seemed to have been met, they had created for themselves an unbound, creative, and comfortable life.

In the summer of 1967, life in the nice house began to change. The weather was unpleasantly hot. It would be the first summer of a five-year drought that spread across most of the state, its least effect upon our family, since the town where we lived together was a river town, and whose economy depended more upon the local university's draw than on the success of wheat or cattle. Beyond the city limits there were farms that lost an entire year's crop to three months of heat; there were ranches and mountain homes badly burned in wildfire, but in town, the only world Franny and I had ever known, the heat only posed problems of wardrobe, crowded swimming pools, sticky underarms and listless, unending afternoons spent draped in the dim, curtained living room of the nice house, trying to think of ways to pass the time.

The flowers that Mother had planted in half-moons by the side of the front stoop did not do well. The dried petals gave off a kind of brightly hued dust that hovered momentarily before falling to the ground. If we caught the petals early enough, just before their disintegration, Franny and I could grind them between thumb and forefinger and make a sort of rouge that could be spread over cheeks and eyelids. This interest lasted a single day. After that, we took to gathering the petals off the wild rose bushes that grew in the alley and stewing them in jars of boiling water. The water turned pink and smelled sweet, but after a few days the petals began to mold and the whole mess had to be thrown out. We walked to the library and read *National Geographic* and *Life.* We spent our entire allowances on penny candy. We cut pictures from magazines and pasted collages to our bedroom doors. We attempted brownies and lemon mousse. Our favorite activity, by far, was to rifle through the old boxes of photographs that were kept on the shelves in the den behind the television set. We could spend hours studying the younger versions of our parents found in these pictures; the slight suppleness of their youth, seen even in black and white, was strange to us, distant and unfamiliar. There was a photo of our mother in a long canoe with three other girls, their hair sleek and waved against their cheeks, their expressions dark and distracted. Another showed our father with his shirt off, standing in the sunshine in front of a wooden railing, a hammer slung through his belt loop while a second man, a stranger, stood with his arm draped over our father's thin shoulders. Often, after sorting through these pictures, Franny and I would not speak for an hour or two. We felt the need to settle ourselves somewhere to read quietly, patiently, as if proving our capacity for diligence and reflection.

There was a sunroom at the west end of this house. In this room, Mother kept the collection of ferns she had had since her law school days, plants that were so overfed and confident it took two men to lift them. This was her favorite room in the nice house; evenings she would sit there when the light came through the translucent panes in streaks of grey or gold and drink a cocktail. If Father were home and not working he would join her. They sat on the brown wicker chairs they'd found at a garage sale long ago and drank quietly, not speaking. Neither thought to bring a book or the evening paper to accompany the ritual. The idea was simply the sitting, the silence, the feel of the alcohol slowly taking hold and numbing any worry or sadness that the day had brought forth in them. They might sit like this for twenty minutes or so, and it was understood that sound was to be kept at a minimum during that time. Franny and I intuited this and respected it. In the early days of the nice house, my mother held her cocktail with slender, polished fingers.

Our father worked at the university in town. As such, our family did not have a large amount of money, but certainly enough to be considered 'appropriate' tenants of our manicured, middle-aged neighborhood. The nice house belonged to the school, and was rented out at a discounted, faculty rate. A professor of mathematics at the university had built the house when the school was only a crop of buildings in a wheat field. He had been an eccentric man with no family. In the living room and upstairs office, behind the posy print wallpaper that Mother had glued up when we'd first moved in, were rows of equations that this professor of mathematics had worked out in neat, feminine scrawl. None of us were of the left-brain, so we could not make much of the equations, but regarded the mural of numbers as only the curious nature of a lonely man. Father, especially, found the numbers slightly haunting, even when papered over, and bestowed the upstairs office to Mother. He moved all of his work to his campus office, where he spent endless days sitting on a cracked leather couch, glasses perched on his nose, ankles crossed, every empty space hidden in a sea of scripts and books and loose paper. Even months after the equations had been hidden from sight he would not—when he was home—spend much time in the rooms that held the secret of the numbers, and at the time, I felt a kind of pity for him over what I imagined to be a deeply ingrained fear of anything formulaic. My father was an artist and not close to the parents who had tried to push more practical professions on their son. I imagined that his inability to compute the numbers on the walls sent him back in time to afternoons when he would come home to his mother and face her disinterest in the story he was writing or the painting that had been hung in the school hallway. These were a child's imaginings, of course; my father's parents had died before Franny and I had been born. The truth was that my father was simply not comfortable in any room of the nice house, save the kitchen, perhaps, and the sunroom at cocktail hour. I was a careful child, and I watched my father carefully, and I knew that it was a deep restlessness and devotion to his work that kept him away so long that I would sometimes not see him for days on end. From my bedroom upstairs, I could hear his coming and going through the floorboards as I woke in the morning or fell asleep at night. At thirteen, I forgave my father a great deal, enough to invent elaborate and sorrowful, life-long excuses for his absences.

He was an actor. At the university he taught acting to students he deemed 'inadequate leading men and rebellious debutants.' It was the rare student that caught my father's praise or attention. Three afternoons a week, Franny and I would walk over to the theater where our father taught Intermediate Stage Acting and watch the inadequate performers attempt to impress him. They were handsome men and women, built like wires with long arms and legs. The women wrapped themselves in skin-tight, kaleidoscope colors. They exposed pale, knobby knees beneath black miniskirts and pressed false lashes to their eyes. They all moved like dancers, with their chins up and backs straight. Franny and I revered them. We walked home from campus with pointed toes, our backs so straight our muscles ached, always feeling a little less sure of ourselves than we had when we'd first arrived at the theater. The male actors carried an air of European sophistication—at least, what Franny and I imagined to be European sophistication—in their manner and dress. They wore tapered slacks and matching jackets, their hair falling long and disheveled over their brows. It was all in fashion, to be sure. Not a single one was actually European, but to Franny and me they were perfection, acting out a role we found intensely romantic, as far away and fleeting as we could get from our own reality.

For all their success at fashion, they found trouble on our father's stage. I felt like taking them aside and telling them humbly that my father paid most of his attentions to his own work, that no one, not his daughters or even his wife, could capture his greatest interest. "You're fighting a pointless battle," I would imagine myself telling them, taking them into my confidence, laying a kind hand over their skinny, black-clad shoulders. "Why don't you try law school?" I would suggest. My mother taught at the law school.

Afternoons watching our father teach were some of the best that we spent growing up. The final spring and summer in the nice house, we would walk to the campus drugstore, where the boy working the counter would compliment Franny's white-blond hair. We would buy bottles of 7-Up and candied cigarettes and cross to the theatre, its vaulted space dim and cool after the sun, and sit high in the balcony of the auditorium, the sea of empty velvet seats around us and our father down below, yelling or laughing or waving wildly up at the stage. We came to know an empty theater as a kind of tucked away oasis; outside the day might be blazingly hot or gray and frozen, but inside the theater, a thick-walled space like a secret, underground cave, the air was always expectant, cool and open. In such a space it would be criminal not to create great things, a belief that our father clung to fiercely. If his direction ever grew unforgiving, it was only because the room expected it of him. The smell of makeup and shoe polish and ladies' wigs filled the dressing rooms; the heavy velvet curtains that swept across the stage in a rush were old, moth-eaten and patched in places. The stage floor, its wood warped and worn, bore the greatest traces of what went on in the theater, the truest beatings and false steps. Even the most amateur actors considered their craft important and didn't lighten their movements, however unsteady. In socks, after rehearsals, Franny and I would take running slides across the stage, flying headlong into the musty folds of the curtains.

The actors had been taught their conviction; our father had drilled it into them. His belief was that every gesture was a performance of sorts. In life, he felt, there must never be any faltering or doubt, there must simply be decision followed by action, done swiftly and without regret. Doubt, my father believed, bred weak actors and weak lives. The actors—boys and girls, really, not one of them past the age of twenty-one—could not have imagined more desired advice. This was the allowance they'd always longed for, living in the back bedrooms of their parents' houses, forced to work weekends at their fathers' body shop or feed store. No one, they believed, had truly seen them as they now saw one another, as they believed my father might see them if only they could be loud enough, unique enough; if only they could inhabit their given roles as they now performed their daily lives—without the slightest admission of cowardice.

At rehearsals, because we were our father's daughters, Franny and I were granted a kind of star status. Franny fed on the role more than I did. At eleven, she was shaped like a colt, all arms and legs like the actors themselves, only on a smaller scale. Her white-blond head was like a bulb in the darkened theater. She was brave, telling rude jokes or doing imitations for the students that crowded to her after class. At thirteen, I was five foot seven with thick, unruly hair and braces. While the students teased and admired Franny, I would help my father gather his books and papers together. "Do you like this play?" my father would ask me. I would tell him yes, but that the female lead needed to be louder, more courageous. It was a practiced response, but it drew a slow and approving smile from him, an appraisal that I bathed in and clutched to for as long as it remained.

After rehearsal, Franny and I walked with our father to the law school, where we would sneak to Mother's office window and tap on the glass until she looked up from her desk, her glasses cinched at the end of her nose, her shirtsleeves rolled up exposing tawny, freckled skin. When she worked, her hair came loose from its bun and her face flushed with concentration. She did not like interruptions, but when she would look up from her desk to find us peering in at her, she made her smile resolute and relieved. She would smile as if she had been waiting for such an interruption all day long.

Most evenings, Father would leave me and Franny with Mother and go to a work related dinner, or to run lines for extra rehearsals if a play was about to open. If it was a Friday, or had been a hard working day for Mother, or if Franny or I had done well on an exam in school, we would walk to the Felix Diner across the street from campus and drink malts and eat bowls of chili for dinner. The chili would invariably give Mother heartburn and when we got home she would have to put herself to bed with a cocktail and a wet rag across her chest, keeping still in the dim room with her eyes closed, periodically bringing her glass to her lips.

I loved these afternoons and evenings, even with heartburn and Father gone. There remained the knowledge that at some point in the night, we would all be together under the nice roof, in our nice beds. I was not a popular girl at school, so to leave those unwelcoming halls and find myself accepted by three people I knew by heart was a kind of miracle. I know that I took them for granted; they were my family and I was born to them. Even so, I recognized a certain luck-of-the-draw feeling in myself sometimes at night when I went to bed. Lying in the dark, I would forget why I had ever hated myself for bushy hair and braces. I would see these facts of myself as temporary and unimportant burdens, burdens made lighter because they did not prevent me from being loved by those I loved the most. During the last summer we lived in the nice house, I went through each hot day forgetting I had ever known such adult truths, but when night came and I was between cool sheets, with the windows open and the clean smell of well-kept lawn falling through my mother's embroidered curtains, the feeling of random luck would engulf me again. I would bless every night of the past and the future that I could not see, every moment that had led to my conception and emergence into such a world, every moment that would carry me onward.

2.

The battle for our father's attention was a daily ritual; Franny and I watched our mother begin each morning seeking some glimpse of recognition from him. Sometimes it would come if the coffee was good or if rehearsals had gone well the night before, but our mother was an independent woman, and if after a few minutes Father had shown little promise of emerging from his mood, she would resolutely turn herself inward. Franny and I were sometimes less daughters than friends to our mother, drawn unknowingly into a silent alliance, and many nights we slept alongside her in the big bed when Father would return home drunk from the actors' parties and collapse on the couch in the den.

I do not know that my mother was ever a very happy woman, but if she was not, she hid her sorrow well, and when I think of her, I think of a woman expansive with hope. The nice house gave her hope, because she finally had enough space in which to be alone. Her office was at the end of the second-floor hallway. It was a wide room with its own washroom and two enormous, double-paned windows that looked out onto the backyard where there grew a scattering of flowering trees. In late spring and early summer, these trees were flush with color and saturated the air with a sweet, heavy scent. Mother loved them, their smell and color, and she wrote poems about them when she was distracted from her work. These poems were surprisingly sensual; they seemed to recall a past of longing that I had trouble connecting to my mother, who for the most part had always appeared quite staunch and sensible, even in moments of distress. She would sometimes slip these poems, written on scraps of lined paper, into our lunch sacks. I kept the poems clipped together in a shoebox at the bottom of my closet, along with an assortment of torn and forgotten paper dolls. I would recall the poems at strange moments—when my mother came home late, for example, and I would hear her calling out softly to my father, in her voice a kind of weakness that made me cringe. I once made a promise to myself that I would never long for someone I could not have, the way my mother seemed to do the last summer in the nice house. So far as I knew longing, it meant simply wanting, wanting, wanting, every minute of the day. My mother moved carefully around my father, as if she were afraid she might lose her balance and fall upon him.

Franny had developed a bad case of insomnia that last summer, a strange ailment for an eleven-year-old, but she made the most of it by sometimes sneaking out and walking around the block in her nightgown, listening to the conversations coming out of the neighbors' open windows. The gossip gave us something to focus on, something to do. In June, it was Mr. Sparton, our neighbor to the east whose wife raised dachshund puppies, who was having an affair with a waitress at the Felix Diner. Franny and I went to the diner every day for a week to watch the waitress who belonged to Mr. Sparton—a rotund blond woman with penciled eyebrows and a slight limp. She was flirtatious and earned good tips. At the end of June Mrs. Sparton came home from a dog show in San Francisco. The waitress stopped visiting Mr. Sparton, and her service at the diner became slow and distracted.

After the Spartons there were the Trays. On the first day of summer vacation, the Tray teenagers—Ellen and Clem—who lived around the block in the red bungalow, threw a party when their parents were out of town and used up all of their father's liquor supply. After that, Ellen Tray, grounded for one month as punishment, took to sneaking out her window to meet her boyfriend in his parked car at the end of the block.

Ellen and Clem Tray were of particular interest to us. Clem was eighteen, clean-cut and quiet. He liked bicycles. On summer evenings he sat in his driveway surrounded by an assortment of tools, taking apart his bicycle only to put it together again. Sometimes Ellen kept him company, sitting cross-legged in the driveway, the bottoms of her bare-feet black with dirt, passing a cigarette to her brother now and then. They were good friends, the Tray siblings, and united in their survival as their mother's children, who was a cloistered, nervous, and pious woman. None of us, not Mother or Father or Franny or me, had ever heard Mr. Tray speak, though he walked past the nice house every morning and evening on his way to and from work wearing a pressed brown suit.

Ellen Tray would be a junior at the high school where I would start as a freshman in the fall. Ellen was a wild girl. She wore her hair in long, flat sheets that skimmed the small of her back, and walked everywhere either barefoot or in a pair of scuffed leather boots. She smoked and skipped classes and went parking with her boyfriend who had dropped out of school and now worked at a pawnshop on Belmont Avenue. The most curious thing about Ellen Tray though, was the fact that she was a nice person. She did not belong to a clique at school, though she was more stylish than any of the most popular girls. She was kind to everyone. She smiled and waved at Franny and me when we rode our skateboards up and down the sidewalks; she brought casseroles and cut flowers from her mother, who seemed to have decided that we were a family that needed some looking after. One night, sneaking out of her window, Ellen caught Franny in her nightgown on the sidewalk, off on one of her late-night insomnia strolls, and offered her a cigarette. Franny took it and brought it home where she put it in a box of assorted things she kept hidden under her bed.

The neighborhood gossip sustained us through the first few weeks of summer. Then, at the end of June, just when we'd been feeling the dark shadow of boredom at our heels, Ivan arrived. Ivan was an actor who had come to study with Father during the spring semester, and wanted to stay on for the summer Shakespeare festival. He was in need of a place to stay. His arrival at the house, in the last week of June, suitcase in hand, was not an unusual thing. We had often put up visiting actors before; they stayed for two weeks, maybe three, perhaps a month. They slept in the den and took their meals with us. They were either dramatic or morose—any personality in between seemed rare—and when they were present we scuttled about the house as if trying not to wake a sleeping beast. Some were funny and told jokes; others wept and tied up the phone lines. The actresses were invariably the messiest, leaving tissues blotted with lipstick and wrinkled panty hose strewn about the bathroom. They all ran their lines in the sunroom, Father sitting on one of the brown wicker chairs, watching them with a furrowed brow, chin in hand.

Ivan was different. He was neither sullen nor emotional. He was a person who exuded an almost unnerving amount of calm. His voice was low, at times one had to strain to hear him, and he had a nervous habit of ruffling then smoothing the hair on the back of his head. He was not someone who demanded attention; he was of average height, average build. The most noticeable things about him were his eyes; they were a kind of mottled grey, changeable with mood and light. Ivan resided in his eyes; had it not been for this feature, it may have been difficult to recognize him at all, for in all other ways he was a reserved and unobtrusive person.

Mother's reaction to the advent of Ivan was startling. She had been warned of his impending arrival one evening in June, when Father had come home from his office earlier than usual, making a dramatic showing of the groceries he'd brought for dinner, a cut of lamb and fresh mint for mint sauce. He was in buoyant good spirits, a mood that made Mother wary, and she must have had three glasses of wine before the meal was finished. At the dinner table, she listened to Father explain Ivan's situation with a tired, sarcastic face; he was from the east, upstate New York, and had ended up out west with an acting troupe. He had done very well in Anything Goes that spring. "Don't you remember him?" Father addressed the table. "He came here for the after party."

In fact, we did remember him. He'd played cards with Franny and me at the kitchen table while the rest of the cast and crew drank in the living room, rising into raucous choruses of show tunes. We'd all been there for opening night of Ivan's springtime play; we'd all seen him prove everyone wrong; they'd thought him too calm, too invisible to fill the role, but he'd pulled it off without a hitch, his voice hitting the last row like a sledgehammer. "I saw it in him all along," said Father. "The first time I laid eyes on him I knew."

At this Mother cried out. "Oh please," she said, slamming her wine glass to the table, the red liquid sloshing onto her hand.

Father stared at her, the excitement draining from his face in an instant. Between them, on either side of the table, Franny and I looked back and forth, determining alliance. "Nora," Father began, but she cut him off.

"You're excused, girls," she said.

Franny and I left the table slowly, regretfully, though we knew that any coming argument would not begin until we were up the stairs and out of sight. There was the familiar pull between wanting to be a part of the action and wanting to hide from it entirely; arguments between our parents started out fascinating but quickly became frightening, so full of anger and sorrow they seemed to be. Upstairs, in Franny's bedroom, we left the door ajar and lay together on the bed.

The argument was this: Father wanted to let Ivan stay in Mother's office when he came to stay, but Mother wouldn't hear of it; she was crying, undone by too much wine and some sense of timeworn upset, a hurt that Franny and I intuited but did not fully understand. "All that old business," we heard our mother cry. "I thought it was done with! I thought it was gone!" I stood up and shut the door when I heard the shattering of china against the kitchen wall. I turned on Franny's radio and pulled out a deck of cards. Beneath us, after a time, we could sense a silence coming over the argument; we heard the dull movement of feet on the stairs and then in the master bathroom, Father helping Mother out of her clothes and into a bath. She would be silent now, exhausted, holding on to him.

While Mother was in her bath, I crept down the stairs to the kitchen. Father was sweeping up the remains of the gravy boat that Mother had smashed. I stayed just around the corner, watching my father as he worked, then as he shrank to the floor, his head in his hands. I went from my hiding place and sat beside him. He put his arm around me and we stayed there, breathing in the June breeze that came through the screen door. I had always felt that there was a great deal of promise in an early summer breeze, but tonight I did not feel that way. The dustpan sat between us, full of chards of ash-blue china. I picked up the biggest pieces with my fingertips, examining the map of cracks and breaking points that now ran throughout the clay. "Don't cut yourself," said Father, his eyes closed. I felt that I could have stayed on the kitchen floor forever, the weight of the argument still resting heavy in the air, the beginning of summer making its way into the house, my father's body very close and warm beside me. I would go to sleep that night thinking of my father with his head in his hands, how the veins that ran from his knuckles to his wrists had stood out in a way that made him look older than I had known him to be. I would think about my mother's smashed gravy boat, the dust from the wreckage still stuck in crevices on the kitchen floor where any cleaning could not reach. The china dust would remain there forever; it would get caught on the soles of our feet and would be carried with us all, wherever we walked in the world.

3.

Even though Ivan caused a shift in the house, he was not entirely unwelcome. He was a cheerful person, in a kind of quiet, permeating way, and it may have been this alone that endeared him to Mother. If he had been a bitter person, angry or flamboyant or even just a shade too self-important, she would have found a thousand reasons to send him away. It came as a surprise that she let Ivan stay on longer than a few weeks, but the gravy boat incident seemed to have startled even her, pushing her into a mood of cautious good behavior, and by mid July Ivan was as much a part of the house as any of us.

He was prone to planning fancy meals and cleaning areas of the house that Mother pretended did not need cleaning. He would spend his mornings on campus with Father, rehearsing and building sets for the festival in early August. In the afternoon, he would walk home, timidly making his way down the tree-canopied streets, contemplating what he might do to earn a sense of belonging in the house. Franny and I waited for him. We liked him. With Ivan, we had formed a new daily routine. We made our usual rounds about the neighborhood in the morning, taking our skateboards to the drugstore at the edge of campus and crossing the footbridge where the river that divided the town in two moved languidly between dry, dusty banks. We met Ivan walking home for lunch, and in the afternoons went with him to the ethnic market on Ticker Street to shop for dinner. Ivan had befriended the owner of this market, Mr. Selini, a man with dark skin and full lips who wore an apron spattered in blood and olive juice.

The ethnic market was on the first floor of an old river house. These houses lined the northern bank of the river and were set parallel to the train tracks. They had once been quaint and cared for, but were now mostly forgotten, and had begun to fall in upon themselves. Poor families lived there, or single men who worked for the railway or the paper mill. There was a broken sidewalk that ran beside the river and connected the houses, and the riverbank was wilder there, shaded by cottonwoods and willow branches and the stretching shadows of the houses themselves. Before Ivan had come, this had been a part of town that Franny and I rarely visited. For one thing, the sidewalk was too mangled for skateboarding, and there was nearly always the heavy, gaseous smell from the paper mill, whose tall, bricked towers could be seen jutting above the waiting train cars. We did not admit to one another that the primary reason for avoiding the river houses was fear; we had never been directly told to stay away, but we had heard gossip: women so fat they couldn't raise themselves from their own beds, thirteen and fourteen year old girls getting themselves pregnant, men who didn't bathe and put out their cigarettes on their girlfriends' legs. All of these people—real or imagined—came from the river houses, and now Ivan, with his air of calm, was taking us with him on his daily walks to Mr. Selini's house, the last in the row of decrepit buildings.

The first floor of this house contained, from floor to ceiling, metal racks lined with any type of spice or pickled thing one could possibly imagine. Mr. Selini lived alone in an apartment above his store, and he was a lonely but successful man. He had nicknames for Franny and me. I was 'the girlfriend' and Franny 'the light'. The first time we visited the market, Mr. Selini looked up from his butcher block and pointed at me with the flat edge of his cleaver. "You've gotta girlfriend now?" he asked Ivan, a grin spreading over his oily face.

Ivan looked over his shoulder at me and I shrank back between the aisles, pretending to study a foggy jar of mushrooms. "I should be so lucky," he said, turning away and counting money from his wallet. Franny was glaring. Mr. Selini saw her and laughed.

"You don't worry girl," he said. His accent was thick. "You be the light."

Ivan placed his money on the counter and Mr. Selini went back to his cutting.

We walked home by the river houses, the late afternoon light cutting patterns through the lines of laundry and rusting lawn ornaments that scattered themselves across the brown grass. Ivan swung his cloth sack of groceries over his shoulder, the ragged edge of a garlic braid standing skyward. He pointed at the skimming water bugs that crowded in the still pools along the river and whistled verses of show tunes, testing our knowledge. We answered him and followed him, watching him. We knew every song he sang. That summer, he could not have been more than twenty-five years old.

Franny had decided to dedicate her summer to the close observation of Ivan. She did not believe that he was only in town to study acting. She explained this to me one afternoon in the backyard.

We were sunbathing. We had just returned from a walk to the grocery store, where we'd purchased a bag of oranges, not very ripe. Now Franny sat cross-legged, her limbs glistening with baby oil, and spit seeds through the gap in her front teeth. "I've been doing some close watching," she said. She leaned back on her bony elbows and rolled her neck around in a languid, knowing way. "I've been looking at the way Ivan watches Daddy."

"How's that?" I asked.

Franny let the question dangle for a moment, looking me up and down. Then she sat up and leaned in close. "Like he wants to grab his face and kiss him!" she hissed.

I leaned away from her hot, citrusy breath. "You're crazy," I said.

"I only tell truth."

"You'd better keep quiet, Franny. You don't know what you're talking about."

Franny considered for a moment. "But men can love other men, can't they?"

I stared at her. Franny had one of those pretty, pointed faces that only the very pale seem to have in life. I had inherited our mother's olive skin and rope of black hair. No matter how much powder I tried to put on, I would never have Franny's fragile face, and even though I loved my sister, I hated her a little bit too. "Keep quiet, Franny," I said again, softer this time.

Franny squinted at me, the sun making her eyes very dark. She tilted her head, thinking. "Remember that play we all saw? The one we all went to see the night Mother burned the peach pie?"

"What of it?"

"I got to thinking about that one man that everyone kept talking about. That Skipper man?"

"Well?" I was growing impatient.

"Well, wasn't the Skipper man someone special to the other man?"

"Brick."

"Right. Well, this Skipper everyone kept on yelling about. He went and died and after that Brick was an old drunk because of it."

"So?"

Franny took another orange from the bag. She slit the skin with her teeth before continuing, licking the juice from her fingers. "The way I figure," she said, "you have to really be in love with someone to turn drunk after they die."

"Those are men in a *play*," I said.

"Well where does stuff in plays come from? Real people, that's what. Real stuff." I watched her peel the orange and put a slice in her mouth. "This orange tastes like puke," she said, throwing the rest of the sour ball into the hedges and rolling back onto the grass. "I think Ivan's why Mother's so bitchy all the time."

"That's a mean thing to say."

"It's only true," said Franny. "Yesterday, she caught me and Ivan in the den watching *Lawrence Welk* and she called me into the kitchen and told me I wasn't to be in that room with him ever again."

"But Mother likes *Lawrence Welk*."

"Sure she does. But she doesn't like Ivan hanging around her husband all the time."

I sprang from my spot on the grass and grabbed the hose from beneath the plum tree where Mother had left it running. "When I say keep quiet, you better just keep quiet," I said, aiming the hose straight at Franny.

Franny just laughed. "Do it Gracie!" she cried. Her whole beautiful face was lit with laughter. "I'm so damn hot I'm dying!"

I pressed my thumb over the face of the hose so that the water spurted out in a high, arching stream that rained over Franny's body. She screamed and rolled around in the grass until her wet hair was plastered in ropes all along her cheeks and neck. Finally she jumped up and chased me. She grabbed the hose and shot the spray skyward, up towards the impossible heat, where the drops fell back to us in a fine, blessed mist. "I only tell truth!" she shouted, facing the fall of water. She opened her mouth and shook her soaking head. "I only tell truth!" Squinting up through the spray, I saw someone watching us from an upstairs window. A man. Not my father.

4.

The last part of July, Mother and Father threw a party. Our parents threw lovely parties. They made great spreads of food: tomatoes with asparagus cream, hearts from artichokes, finger-sized samosas, cherries stuffed with soft cheese. Father commanded the music, and Franny and I loved to watch the dancers. On every face there seemed a sudden release of long caged happiness. Mother and Father were especially good dancers, though they rarely danced with anyone but each other. They were unfailingly kind to one another at a party, a blessed eye, that summer, in the storm of their quietly growing struggle.

The guests represented their respective niches at the university; Mother invited her colleagues from the Law School, middle aged or very old men and a few women who loved the neatness of law but hated the practice of it. Father came with his actors, many who—like Ivan—were only in town for a month to understudy a role, or to audit a playwriting workshop. These strangers were usually the most interesting guests, because they were brave and stylish, and because they carried with them traditions not known to our small town. At more than one party, Mother had found herself barefoot and numb after drinking some new cocktail the actors had introduced. The actors hummed around my mother; she was David's wife, she was beautiful, and in the presence of people she would never meet again, she became the kind of person one might peg as frivolous or irresponsible. She sat on laps, stole lit cigarettes from the mouths of young men, and made a fuss over fixing her hair and lipstick, using an empty serving platter as her mirror. There was too much drinking, too many dark corners filled with cigarette smoke, too much commotion up and down the hallway, back and forth between kitchen, living room, and lawn, for any uptight guest to have enough time to judge bad behavior. My mother let herself get lost at parties.

Old friends came too. Mr. and Mrs. Tray, who regarded the more unusual guests with an air of humor and shock, respectively; Mr. Sparton, without his wife; a few people from the older, bohemian neighborhoods of our parents' past who didn't drink anymore and left early. When Franny and I were younger, a man named Jack Leroy would sometimes come to a party. Jack and our father had grown up next door to one another, and had gone all through high school and college sharing textbooks, dorm rooms, and beer tabs. Though he was a welcome, comfortable guest, Jack's presence at parties caused a distinct but subtle shift in mood between my mother and father. This shift had to do with an accident that had happened many years earlier, a car accident involving Jack, my father, and Jack's late wife Alice. Alice Leroy had been killed in this accident. This story was not a secret in the household, but neither was it openly discussed. I understood what had happened because my mother had told me, but in my mind the memory seemed a collection of vague, technical details; there had been a car, my father at the wheel, a redheaded woman beside him. "What season?" I had wanted to know when my mother first told me this story. She had studied me; she found the question odd.

"Summer," she said. "Just before you were born."

"What did he look like?" I asked. My father, I had meant.

"He looked the same as now," said my mother, "only younger." She had found a picture. In it Father was twenty-five and slender as a boy, his arm slung lazily over the shoulder of another man. They stood in front of a falling-down or coming-up building, and held hammers in their hands.

I pointed at the other man.

"Jack," my mother said, and tucked the picture inside her blouse.

For a time, when Jack still came to parties, he would bring his daughter Susan with him. I can close my eyes and picture Susan's white, freckled legs following me in some game, though I do not recall a greater friendship at that time, beyond our thrown-together times during parties when we were to stay out of the way of the adults. I can recall that Jack was the only guest at parties allowed to scoop me up and joke with me, and that once he had spent nearly an entire evening with my father in the den, the noise of the party sweeping in waves past the door while the two of them, crouched on the floor, carefully snaked a line of dominoes around the perimeter of the room.

One year they didn't come to any parties, and then it seemed that Jack's name was simply never mentioned again. It was not a falling out; it was simply a falling away, a quiet turning from one another that perhaps was long overdue. Mother's parents had died around this time, one right after the other, in a sequence of clean though surprising death: one suffered a heart-attack while cleaning rain-gutters, the other a brain aneurism in her sleep. These events were distractions enough, and by the time I was old enough to comprehend such a thing as memory, I found that I could remember few details about Jack and Susan, save the picture that Mother had once shown me and the feeling that Jack Leroy was somehow an important person, pivotal even, in my parents' lives.

The party that Mother and Father held that July, during their final summer together, was to be a celebration of the beginning of the Actors' Studio. The Studio was a two-week affair, with plays showing nearly every night and dozens of dinners and impromptu gatherings in between. Franny and I were familiar with the frenzy of the Studio, and the corresponding change that it offered our routine; this was a time when our father would very nearly disappear, Mother accompanying him to events, acting her part as gracious and interested wife. There were smaller parties she would not see, random sessions at the tiny houses and rented rooms of the actors, where cheap beer and hand-rolled cigarettes were abundant and Father was regarded king. These were weeks when Mother would take off from her own work, and stay home during the day with Franny and me, thinking up adventures for the three of us. In her secret way, Mother regarded the July parties as a kind of offering to Father; she made sure to make herself lively and loving, never sullen or mean; she gave him her full self, the girl he had discovered when they'd first met, and he did the same for her, in unspoken agreement.

The Friday of the party, Father came home early from campus, a box of clinking bottles under one arm. He mixed himself a drink before tying on an apron and joining Ivan at the kitchen counter, where a cutting block had already been bloodied by cut lamb from the market. I was at the kitchen table stuffing olives; Franny was perched on a stool in her bathing suit, an overlarge apron tied double around her waist. She was rolling pastry around tiny sausages and she was questioning Ivan, who'd had a letter from his mother that afternoon. "What does she do?" asked Franny.

"She used to be a singer," Ivan said.

"Is she rich?"

"A bit."

"Famous?"

Ivan laughed. "No," he said. He slid the lamb into the oven. "She lives on Long Island in a big house. My father's money." This was how Ivan spoke to us, to everyone. There was little to no regard of decorum; what he knew, Ivan told.

"And what does she do there?" Franny asked.

"Plays tennis. Drinks gin."

"All alone? Don't you have a brother or sister?" asked Franny. She ignored Father's frown of disapproval at this line of questioning.

"I had a sister," said Ivan. "She died when I was in high

school." For the first time since I'd known him, I saw Ivan
turn shy, as if he'd finally realized what he'd been divulging.
He studied the contents of his drink, swirling the melting
ice around the bottom of the glass. Through the floorboards
above came the sounds of Mother walking around on high
heels. Franny watched Father slicing an onion. She did not
fear him, the way I did, and she kept on.

"Was it a violent death?" she asked.

"Franny," Father said swiftly, laying down his knife. He
raised a hand to place on Ivan's shoulder, but the sound of
laughter and car doors made him turn; the first guests were
arriving. "Get dressed," Father commanded, turning from
Ivan to rinse his hands. Franny slid from her stool and walked
backwards from the kitchen, watching Ivan all the way. Ivan
would sometimes finger the back of his hair when he was
nervous or angry, right where the neatly cut line met the nape
of his neck. He stood now in the kitchen doing this, staring
into the contents of his glass until Father reached a hand up
and held his still.

Mother came into the kitchen then. "Is everything
alright?" she asked, looking at Father and Ivan, then to me
sitting at the table. No one spoke. I caught Franny peaking
around from the hallway and shook my head at her. Mother
followed my gaze. "Franny! Dress!" she called, then sighed
heavily. The doorbell rang again. "David," Mother said, and I
saw that she was warning him. She glanced at Ivan, then back
to my father. Then she smiled. A bright, false smile. She met
Father's eye once more before turning on her heel and clicking
down the hallway.

Mother was in fine form as the party slowly unfurled itself,
the conversation growing to a syncopated hum as more and

more people filled the front hallway and living room. Later in the night, the more they drank, they would spread further, gaining comfort in the house. They would help themselves in the kitchen and find private corners for their arguments and intimacies. My mother knew her part well; she laughed and asked questions and I saw her tighten only slightly when Ivan came near her.

Father filled and re-filled glasses. Out of a sense of responsibility, some hosts might have restrained themselves from drinking as much as their guests did, but Mother and Father had never been that type. They were never immune to drinking, no matter the occasion, and the good parts of their personalities expanded the more they drank. Father became brighter, kinder, his whole lithe frame knowing exactly how much liquor to inject until he reached the pinnacle of his charms. He could never be called an outright drunk—he carried himself too well; one hand in pocket, shirtsleeves rolled up, the other hand around a cocktail; he never slumped or laughed too loudly.

He was cordial early in the evening, greeting guests with his instinctual wink and side grin, letting each one believe a secret alliance. Halfway through the evening, he was quick to breathe life back into the crowd by circulating a new drink, starting a new record, and dancing with the most somber of female guests. This generosity would make all the other women look upon him kindly, and would remind the men of their luck to be escorting more attractive women, which would prompt them to request their own dances, and the whole thing would be lit again.

Franny and I hid in corners and snuck champagne. We liked the dancing the best. When I watched my mother and father dance, I felt that I could understand something about the power of familiarity, how it could bind things together unknowingly, only the diligent step of time navigating its course. There was a secret between my mother and father, and when I watched them dancing I could believe that secret was nothing more than the accrued knowledge of all the years they had passed through together.

Ivan watched them dance. For the party he had changed into a pair of black trousers, and the tie over his white dress shirt was narrow and shorter than most of the ties worn by the other men. He did not dance, though he discussed records with Father. When others danced, he stood in the door of the living room, swirling his cocktail, watching as Father hooked Mother up by her waist, her dress bunching under his grip.

When the evening began to slow, I left Franny asleep in the den to sit on the bottom step of the staircase and spy. It was my favorite time, the dimming third act, and there were only two or three couples on the floor. Most had settled themselves at bridge games, or were out on the sun porch, their cigarettes tiny glowing bulbs against their darkened profiles. The air was thick with smoke and people. Father was over at the row of windows behind the piano, struggling to loosen the frame of one that had been painted shut months ago. He was drunk; I could tell from where I sat. He laughed as he fought the window. Out of the dim corner beside him, at the piano's curved end, a figure appeared, a man loosening his short tie. He reached in front of Father and gave the window frame a sharp, inward jab with his palms. There was a crack that split the air as the window loosened, and the bridge players looked up from their cards. A woman giggled. Someone blew a long stream of blue smoke, and the clapping of cards being shuffled wove the periphery of the room.

I watched my father and the figure lift the window

together, the curtains billowing in the sudden expanse of air. Then my father lifted his hand and reached for the face of the man beside him; he cupped the cheek and jaw line of the man's face, letting his thumb linger on the curved tip of the mouth. In a moment they had parted, leaving nothing but empty space beneath the shrinking and ballooning curtain, a perfect place, when one thought about it, to hide.

5.

I decided that I would forget. If I went back to the night of the party, to the polished surface of the piano beneath the open window, to the white curtain in the breeze, I began hating. I hated my father, first. Then I hated my mother, out on the lawn in her bare feet, laughing too loudly and doing nothing. I hated dancers and card players and women who blew their smoke as if they owned the air. I hated Franny for seeing early what I hadn't seen. I hated Ivan most of all. I hated him for not having a job so that all he could do was take walks around town with us, pretending camaraderie, pretending an understanding. I hated that this understanding was not false; he was with us when our mother and father were not. He knew best about our small daily worries, our minor bruises, our boredom and loneliness. I knew that I could not hate him for these things, but I did anyway; it was all mixed up with a strange feeling of pity for him. There was another feeling, too, one that I couldn't name; something foreign in the lower part of my stomach that burst to life like a quick flame whenever I watched Ivan's steady mouth or veined hands.

During the day, I found it easy to distract myself by dragging Franny away from the house and venturing further than we had before, daring to spend afternoons wading the riverbanks by the railroad houses where all peripheral worry was drowned by the stiff attentiveness of fear. After a time, I found forgetting as easy as hating; no matter what I might now know, the habits of the household remained the same. Father continued to go to work and take a glass of bourbon in the evenings; Mother still spent her days upstairs in her office, typing a rhythm on her typewriter. Franny was Franny. July went along.

The first days of August were defined by two large events. To begin, Franny fell in love. I don't know that it could be called real love, but Franny made a big enough deal of it that it seemed real enough, and there were times when I was secretly jealous of the drama that Franny could create for herself, of the self-indulgent obsession that Father took pleasure in teasing her about.

Franny fell in love with Harvard Sharp, the star of a television series called *Those Boys,* which aired every Friday evening at half past seven. The show was about five brothers living on a ranch in Texas. Harvard Sharp played the youngest of the boys; he was the wild one who was always winding up in a fistfight at the end of each episode. He won every fight, even if he was fighting someone very big, and his common refrain was I ain't afraid of livin', brother! Sometimes he would mix it up and say, I ain't afraid of dyin', brother man! Father found these lines very funny and would go around the house when he was in a good mood shouting things like, "Time for dinner, brother man!" and, "where your Mama, brother man?" all of this in a syrupy Texan drawl. When Ivan said that Harvard Sharp sounded more like a black man from Harlem than a Texas cowboy, Franny fixed him with an austere glare and said, "Harvard is a complex being."

It did not help matters that Ivan had once known

Harvard Sharp. They'd been in the same acting troupe that had traveled from New York to California and had ultimately delivered Ivan to our house. No one knew the true nature of their friendship, its history or ramifications, but there was a subtle sense of bitterness that came with any mention of this part of Ivan's life, and as was the case with most of his past, he was purposefully vague when Franny pressed him for details.

Inadvertently, in her quest to expose his feelings for Father, Franny had developed a friendship with Ivan. They were always working on crosswords or puzzles together, they made up funny handshakes and accents, and it was Ivan who first got Franny interested in Hollywood. He had a photo album filled with pictures from the year he had lived in Los Angeles trying to make it in the movies. In the photos he was very bright and tan, someone younger and somehow more comprehensible than the man we had adopted. No one ever said outright that he had failed at his Hollywood endeavor, but the fact that he was in a small Montana town, acting in small plays, seemed to say enough.

Franny spent hours on the back porch pouring over Ivan's photo album. Lying face down on her stomach, her thin legs swaying knee-bent in the air, she turned inward with her obsession. The dark hours once spent wandering the sidewalks and inventing gossip about neighbors were now taken up by an exhaustive beauty routine. Each night she wound her hair over a set of plastic rollers she'd found at a garage sale, buffed her chewed off nails until they shone, and spent at least an hour posing in various outfits in front of the full-length mirror that hung on the back of the laundry room door. She spent her allowance on gossip magazines, put her cutoffs in the rag pile, and stole Mother's lipstick. She might have gone on like that all summer (Mother and I were used to Franny's obsessions and had long learned to ignore them) but she began to get on Father's nerves. At the dinner table, she affected an expression of annoyed nonchalance, as if every word in her direction made her weak with boredom.

One evening, when Father told her to sit up straight and pass the saltshaker, she looked at him through eyes messy with mascara and said, "I believe you can reach it yourself, David." We all fell silent, our forks suspended in mid air, our mouths full of food, and watched as in one swift motion, Father took Franny by the arm and directed her up the stairs to her bedroom.

"Wash off that makeup," he said, his voice carrying to the dining room. He slammed her bedroom door and came back to the table. No one had moved since he'd gone, but now Mother took the salt and set it in front of him. The rest of us went back to our meals but Mother continued to look at Father. She leaned back in her chair and drank slowly from her wine glass. "I'm tired of it Nora," Father said, feeling her gaze. Ivan looked at me. I waited for my mother's silence or anger, but instead she just sighed and stood.

"Where are you going?" Father asked, looking up.

"I think I'd rather eat on the sun porch," she said. We watched her cross through the living room and sit in one of the brown wicker chairs, the light of evening coming through the window panes in a dusty, blinding glare. Someone had left a package of cigarettes out there, and she picked it up, fingering the torn wrappings. She stayed on the sun porch until we had finished eating, until Father had closed himself in the den and Ivan and I had finished washing dishes. She sat still with her half-full plate forgotten on her lap. I watched her. She was narrowing her eyes and tilting her head in a certain way, a motion I knew because she had taught it to me; tilt your head and narrow your eyes and the glow of light through the windows will break and scatter, making the brightness bearable. She was doing this when Ivan went to her side, a matchbook in his hand. "You don't have a match," he said, taking the chair across from her. She took a cigarette from the forgotten package and placed it between her lips. The first flame that Ivan lit blew out before Mother was ready, but the second one caught, casting her profile in orange glow. As they sat together, the light went out of the room, hazy rings of smoke circling above their heads.

Later that night, I heard my mother outside Franny's door, knocking a soft rhythm into the wood, trying to get her to come out. This gesture surprised me; Mother didn't usually stand for back-talk, and at any other time would have spanked Franny herself for being rude at the dinner table. That summer, though, there was a new way of doing things; I could see that I had been wrapped into a trio with my sister and mother, the three of us in unspoken alliance against Ivan and Father. Up until that night it had been only a feeling; there had been no open recognition of these terms, and I did not want there to be one. Now the change seemed complete, Mother's attempt to bring Franny back from punishment a timid declaration of the new treaty.

It was Ivan who brought Franny back to normal. The next morning, after Father had left for work, I found Mother and Ivan talking in the kitchen. They stood at the counter, examining something before them. Mother still wore her dressing gown, and her hair was twisted from sleep. She reached out and touched something in front of her. "This," she said, and Ivan nodded. Hearing movement behind them, they turned in unison, and I saw Ivan's photo album spread open on the counter. Mother held a picture out for me to see; it was the snapshot of Ivan standing in front of the Hollywood sign. In the photo he was turning away, looking up at the white letters on the mountain. Ivan took the photo and wrote something on the back, then slid it inside an envelope and licked the flap closed. He turned to me.

"Take this up to Franny," he said. "Slip it under her door."

I took the envelope and left the kitchen. I could have opened it; they wouldn't have heard me on the stairs; they were busy opening cupboards and measuring coffee. Outside Franny's bedroom I paused with the letter between my palms, the flat paper cool and alive against my skin. A thin stream of sun was freeing itself under Franny's closed door, and the light blinded me a little as I bent and slid the envelope through the slat.

6.

Despite the distractions of Harvard Sharp and her alliance with Ivan, Franny's insomnia persisted, and she eventually went back to her nighttime wandering, dragging me along with her when I could be rousted from bed. I seemed to match Franny's insomnia with a new and overwhelming need for sleep; if no one woke me, I found that I could sleep for ten or more hours, even then having to force my limbs into movement. Mother blamed the exhaustion on puberty, and then said that it made her feel old, and asked me if I thought she looked as though she had a teenage daughter. About Franny's ailment, Mother was less sure. She took her to the doctor when the circles under her eyes took on a violet hue, returning only to tell Father that they must change physicians immediately, since the doctor had informed her that Franny's insomnia was most likely an effect of poor pre-natal care and current psychological deficits.

Franny wasn't bothered by the sleeplessness; at night she had a whole world in which she was free to spy or to sit up in bed reading tabloids. She would shake me awake after her prowling hours, offering the stories of what she' d seen and heard. There was the corner house that had been vacant for three weeks now, a strange smell beginning to develop in its surrounding bushes; Ellen Tray spent long hours in a dark car with her boyfriend; Mrs. Sparton had left town for another dog show, and the waitress from the Felix Diner seemed happy again. I listened with half an ear, mumbling responses until Franny finally quieted and fell asleep beside me.

I feared what Franny could so easily discern; it seemed that the neighborhood could hold nothing secret for long. If Franny could take a simple stroll and learn about affairs and strange visitors and sex in dark cars, how evident were our own secrets? I began closing windows and drawing shades when nighttime fell, but this only annoyed Father, who came out of the den with drink in hand to ask why the house felt so stuffy.

On the nights when I accompanied Franny on her nighttime trips, we would wait until Mother and Father were asleep, then let ourselves out the sliding glass doors to the backyard where the red current shrubs marked the boundary between our house and the next. The air would be cool, loose of the day's heat save for an inch or two above the broken pavement that radiated up still warmth. The dusty smell of Russian sage met us as we walked in nightgowns and bare feet, Franny's hair done up in her plastic curlers. In the night, we felt a courage that only dark and stillness could afford us.

Our neighbors were people who cared greatly about their

houses and lawns, caring seemed almost a prerequisite for living there, and every inch of grass that we passed was sheared evenly; in the dark the blades appeared almost black. There was contentment in walking past these houses, a feeling that if in ten years one were to revisit the street, everything would look very much the same. The cleanliness, too, gave an impression of simplicity; the problems, the arguments or deceits—these hid themselves stoically behind new paint and potted plants. In the river houses, where longing and heartache stood naked on sidewalk and front lawn, there was no hiding from travail. For the river houses, strife was ornament unabashed; where we lived with our mother and father, trouble kept itself out of sight. And yet there was no belief in this kind of shield, out of sight did not mean out of mind. If Franny's insomnia walks revealed anything, it was that secrets only became bigger, more interesting, the more tightly they were bound.

We were walking together like this one night when Franny decided to steal the poppies from Mrs. Tray's garden. Mrs. Tray was known for her flower gardens; they comprised at least two thirds of her lawn. She grew great bushes of roses, lilacs, and camellias; there were tulips in spring, daisies and iris and lupine in early summer, and tall stalks of sunflowers bending their heads in exhaustion when the strongest heat came. Nearly every inch of earth was carpeted by color. She grew no vegetables; her gardens were for the eyes. The poppies were our favorite because they grew randomly, brashly, scattered here and there in stands of twos or threes, as if Mrs. Tray had spilled a seed packet in her organized work and had neglected to sweep away the sin. That night, as we passed the garden that edged the sidewalk, Franny paused long enough to finger some petals. "I'll carry poppies in my bouquet when I get married," she said.

"Who will you marry?" I asked.

"Harvard, of course," said Franny. Of course. She eyed the Tray house, then looked at me, her face sly. "Let's take some," she said.

"Better not," I said, but Franny had already severed two stems with her thumbnail and forefinger. "That's enough," I hissed, daring to glance at the windows of the Tray house, one of which—upstairs, the bedroom—was still lighted. Franny ignored me, making her way up the curving border of the first flower bed like a crab, her nightgown hitched up between her legs exposing her thin, pale thighs. She had an armful by now: poppies and hyacinth and dry sprigs of lavender. I looked behind at the silent street to check for signs of movement; when I turned back, the front door of the Tray house had opened, a wide beam of light throwing itself across Franny's bent body.

Ellen Tray stood in the doorway. She wore a miniskirt and tall boots, her bright hair falling to her waist. In a panic, I realized the state of my own dress; my summer nightgown was sheer and a size too small, exposing nicked and stubbly shins not yet accustomed to shaving. I crossed my arms over my chest and tried to shrink back into shadow, the metal of my braces seeming to expand as my mouth dried with fear and embarrassment. But Ellen wasn't looking at me. She was studying Franny, who had frozen in her sudden exposure, grasping her ragged bundle of stems, one plastic curler falling loose against her cheekbone.

Ellen closed the door behind her and loped across the lawn. She stopped a few feet from Franny and pulled a pack of cigarettes from her purse. "Still can't sleep?" she said, tapping the pack against her palm.

Franny didn't move. She looked from the flowers to the

house and back again.

"Don't worry," said Ellen, bending to strike a match on the sidewalk. "She's sleeping." She gestured toward the lavender that Franny held. "That stuff," she said, pulling in on her cigarette, "that'll help you sleep. Put some in your pillowcase." She started for the sidewalk, Franny at her heels.

"Are you meeting Steve?" Franny asked.

Ellen nodded. "Walk with me to the corner," she said. It was a command more than an offering. She blew a long stream of smoke into the air. "I'm meeting him there."

We followed Ellen in silence, caught by the steady knocking rhythm of her boot heels on the pavement. "Who'd you see tonight?" she asked, looking down at Franny.

Franny shrugged, swinging her arms. "Everyone's asleep," she said. "Boring. But Mr. Sparton's wife is back. I saw her car in the driveway."

"Cool," Ellen said. She pulled in deeply on her cigarette and flicked the butt to the ground before speaking again. "Who's the new guy at your house?" she asked, looking at me this time.

"That's Ivan," Franny said before I could answer. "He's an actor. He's staying with us." She fingered at the loose curler by her cheek; beneath, her hair was still knotted and damp from her bath. "I'm going to be an actor, too," she said. "I'm going to marry an actor."

"That's cool," said Ellen.

"He's our mother's cousin," I said, my words coming as a rush. I could feel my heart beating heavily in my chest.

"Who?"

"Ivan. The actor."

"He's not either," said Franny. "He's our father's friend."

"Cool," said Ellen. Then she winked at me. We had

stopped at the corner. Across the street sat a shining black car; its engine was running but the headlights were dimmed. Through the open driver's side window we could see the lights of the dash and radio. "That's him," Ellen said. "Come say hi." She was staring at me with her steady, permeating gaze. I couldn't decide if Ellen was trying to understand or intimidate me, perhaps neither, but I felt the quick impulse to shrink back, and I snatched at Franny's hand.

"We have to head home now," I said.

"No we don't," said Franny, pulling her hand free.

Ellen smiled and shook her head. She seemed to be deciding whether or not she should say something. Finally she shrugged and pulled her purse higher on her shoulder. "See you girls around," she said. She gave a quick salute and sauntered across the street.

Franny glared at me. "What's wrong with you?" she said. "Why'd you say that about Ivan?"

I didn't answer her. "I'm going home," I said. "Do what you want." I crossed my arms and walked away, my bare heels thudding against the pavement.

Everything seemed amplified by the dark; there were eyes looking out from every window. Every eye, every manicured lawn, every perfect garden, every painted mailbox—I hated all these things. It was all just wasted time. They would all move away some day. They would all want different things. Everything would become interrupted.

I didn't hear Franny running up from behind; she must have been running through lawns; and I jumped when her hand caught my elbow. I shook her away, angry at being startled. "I just want to go home," I yelled in her face. My foot caught on a deep crack in the sidewalk as I turned, sending me face first to the ground. I lay still for what seemed a long while, my mouth filling with the surprising heat of blood, before I felt Franny beside me, pulling at my arm and plucking at the cloth of my nightgown, saying over and over in a voice like our mother's, "stand up now, stand up."

We went in through the front door, which was almost never locked, even at night. In the kitchen, Franny got a clean dishtowel and held it to my face. "I saw Ellen's boyfriend once," she said. "Steve. He's got big front teeth like a rabbit."

I nodded and tried to smile. Blood dribbled down my chin and dropped to the front of my nightgown. I had never been able to cry easily in front of Franny, a restraint that confused me.

"How could you kiss someone like that?"

We were laughing silently when the door to the den opened, and Ivan emerged, squinting. "Something the matter?" he asked.

"Grace fell."

He crossed to the kitchen and switched on the overhead light. He took my face in his hands, studying the swelling lip. "Can you open your mouth?" he asked, and I parted my lips. He lifted the upper lip a fraction, examining the cut. "Well," he said, moving away, "just a small cut I think. It didn't go all the way through the lip, which is lucky. You won't need stitches." He disappeared into the bathroom, coming back with a roll of cotton that would be tucked under the lip until the bleeding stopped. His motions were quiet and unhurried, and he didn't ask questions. When he was finished, he turned out the kitchen light and headed back towards the den. Through the open door, I saw the glow of lamplight and the couch where a blanket lay crumpled. It was the safety blanket that Father always used to pack in the car on road trips, a red, scratchy, woolen thing. A stack of books sat on top of the television set. "Make sure to change your nightgown, Grace," Ivan said before closing the door.

Franny got into my bed without asking. She lay on her back and chewed her nails, studying the plastic stars glued to the ceiling. "Why don't you like Ivan?" she asked.

I could offer no simple reason. I thought only of everything in between the walls of the house. Ivan. Here or gone. Our mother. Our father.

"He gave me that nice photo album," said Franny.

"Yes."

"He fixed your lip."

"Yes."

"I feel sorry for him," Franny said.

The memory of the two men behind the piano seemed ready to spill over into the small enclave of space between us. This picture had expanded in my head over time; it filled every corner of the house as I went through the motions of each ordinary day, yet it could remain secret, something between the two of us, turned free in a darkened room. I opened my mouth to speak, but Franny was sighing and turning away, pulling the sheet off her legs. Sleep was finally filling her up and I let it; I didn't try to wake her now. I hoped that it would fill her for a very long time.

I took the wad of cotton from my mouth and held it in front of me, turning it round. The dark parts were blood. The white parts were cotton. There was no in between.

7.

August was the month when Mother declared that she wouldn't be going back to her work until the school year began. She wouldn't work even if it killed her. We had all heard this refrain before, and knew that sooner or later she would be suffering from insomnia, worrying over her autumn class load, and would undoubtedly begin to shut herself in her office upstairs with her legal pads and typewriter. Until this worry set in though, we had our summer mother to enjoy.

She liked to preserve things in the summer, jellies and pickles and beets, all bought at the farm stands on the outskirts of town. She grew nothing but houseplants by hand, but she had romantic notions about agriculture, and marveled at what food could turn itself into if given some time and attention.

She would wrap herself in Father's oversized apron and turn the kitchen into a sauna of sterilized jars and boiling fruit, going about this hard work with content determination; she could be found in the kitchen as early as six, her dark hair plastered to her temples, her hands and forearms red from exertion and steam. She had been brought up in a house full of this kind of work—physical work—and though as a woman she made her living with her mind, she held tight to some vestiges of the house into which she had been born. Perhaps out of nostalgia for her own mother, always apron clad and frustrated with her flock of children, my mother took comfort in aching bare feet at the end of a day of preserving or cleaning, and felt pride at her blisters and burns.

We ate our meals on the sun porch during this time, since the dining and kitchen tables were covered with bright jars of preserved foods, foods that would keep all through the winter and remind my mother, when she came home on cold nights with legal pads to fill and papers to grade, that she was capable of many kinds of work, of many hopeful energies.

Ivan loved to work with her in the kitchen. He taught her about chutney, and together they made sixteen small jars of the stuff, from green tomatoes and dried fruits, traveling back and forth almost daily to the ethnic market to visit Mr. Selini, who found Mother charming, and gave her a free center cut of roast beef whenever she came to see him.

It was during an afternoon of preserving when Mother learned of Ivan's plan to go back to New York. He hadn't seen his mother, he told her, since he'd first left with the acting troupe that had led him west, over a year ago. Mother found that she had little to say about this plan; she was a bit shocked at his decision, though surely she had been on the lookout for this change, surely there had been more than a small part of her that had wished for it, willed it into being. But she had grown comfortable with Ivan. She was aware of a growing kinship. What void would be left in his wake? Standing beside him in the kitchen, stirring a pot of blood red jam into thickness, she could only say, "whatever you'd like, Ivan. Whatever seems best." She might have added, "we'll miss you", which would have been true, but she did not.

In truth, Ivan was a stranger to us. We knew little of his past save for vague stories of his mother on Long Island. He held a degree in English Literature from Brown, and had fallen into acting the summer after graduation, when a friend had suggested that he audition for a spot in a traveling troupe that would be going around the country. This friend knew of Ivan's desire to leave the east, and his often sorrowful relationship with his mother, who depended upon him greatly. On a whim, Ivan found himself in a New York nightclub on a Monday afternoon in early June. The director of the troupe knew the owner of the club, and had arranged to hold his auditions there. Ivan had been in the city, interviewing for a job at the public library. This interview had gone well, and he'd been offered the position; thirty hours a week at the reference desk, quiet times to be spent re-shelving books amid the endless sea

of dusty stacks. After the interview, he had gone to browse the
shelves. He wanted to take something home to his mother,
something that would be appropriate for summer on Long
Island. She liked family dramas. She liked gossip. "Has she
read *Sabrina Fair?*" the woman at the reference desk asked.
"She's from Long Island?"

Ivan nodded.

"It's a play," the woman said, leading him through the
shelves. "But I personally like to read plays in the summer.
A little bit lighter, no?" She looked over her shoulder at Ivan
and winked.

He took the slim copy out of the great stone front of the
library and onto the streets of Manhattan. On the subway, as
businessmen in suits and women with crying children and
shopping bags swayed around him, flushed and lost to their
thoughts, Ivan read the play and found himself laughing out
loud. He repeated lines of dialogue under his breath. He
paused to study the faces around him; he longed to tell them
something, but he did not know what. A pregnant woman
got on the train and took the seat next to Ivan. She asked him
what his book was, and what made him smile so. He told her.
He told her about his interview. He told her about his mother
on Long Island. He told her about his college friend who was
an actor. "He's my dearest friend," Ivan said, and the woman
nodded, smiled. Ivan knew she was only being patient with
him, he knew she was only being polite, but he found himself
overwhelmed by her acceptance, by her round face and red-
checked summer dress. She kept wiping away a line of sweat
from her upper lip with an embroidered handkerchief. When
he told her about the acting troupe she became excited. *He
must audition, he must!* She felt that somehow, his very life's
happiness depended upon his auditioning. She had once

had an uncle, she explained, who was a brilliant pianist. All through her childhood, when she had visited this uncle, he had played the piano for her, any tune she wanted. He could play Irish ballads, and waltzes, and serenades. He knew Mozart and Brahms. One weekend, on one of these visits, she discovered that her uncle's upright piano was no longer in the living room, where it had always stood. The piano, she was told, had been sold to pay off a debt. The instrument was never replaced, and her uncle was never the same man.

There was a silence after the woman told this story; the train stopped and several passengers went out, leaving Ivan and the woman relatively alone. The woman folded her handkerchief and tucked it inside her purse. She smoothed her hands over the mound of her pregnant stomach and laughed. "I was supposed to get off two stops ago," she said.

The memory of the woman's uncle, Ivan would mention when telling this story later in his life, had relatively little to do with his decision to go to the audition, but he liked to include it anyway; the woman had seemed such a thing of luck that day, one of those spontaneous connections one makes throughout life without warning or invitation.

What had drawn him to that nightclub, then? Franny and I would ask when Ivan told his story. *If it wasn't the woman, then what?* "I don't really know," Ivan would say. "Perhaps it was the heat of that train…all those men in suits with blank faces. What was underneath them? What hadn't they done? What had they let slip by?"

Before she had gotten off the train, the pregnant woman had turned in a fever to Ivan. She had clutched his hand in her own. For a moment he thought she may have gone into labor, but she met his gaze with ferocity and spoke. "How can I be myself?" she asked. Her voice was hoarse. She was trembling. It was not a question that you asked out loud. It was not a question to ask of strangers, yet she was here before him, speaking. "How?" she asked again. She was unattractive to him then, and slightly ridiculous, but he listened. "I must be who I am," she said. "What else can I be?" She was gripping his hand, staring at him. Ivan shook his head, at a loss. She let go of his hand then, and looked down at it, swiftly subdued and confused, as if she had just woken in an unfamiliar place. Ivan offered to help her up to the street, but she shook her head and said goodbye.

At the nightclub, Ivan said that he hadn't a monologue prepared, but that he had just read some pieces of a play that morning on the subway, and might he recite what he'd memorized? He held up *Sabrina Fair*. The director was tired of holding auditions; the afternoon was warm, and he wanted to be fishing upstate. He motioned for Ivan to begin.

With the acting troupe, Ivan had gone west. He had eventually landed in Los Angeles, and fallen in with a group of those of similar pursuits, as often happens. This was where his story fell off, and became vague and somehow frustrated, full of diversions and attempts at grandiose statements about success and money and human connection. It was clear, however, that in Los Angeles, something had gone awry. He'd shared an apartment with Harvard Sharp and two other actors, and there had been some competition and hurt pride. Harvard had landed the job on *Those Boys,* and not long after that Ivan had come north, staying with friends and taking odd jobs along the way, until he'd landed with us.

"But that's the way with everything," Ivan would say, finishing his story. "You never really know what makes you do something. You never really know where you'll end up." He did not believe in destiny, or a guiding force; he believed

that all success was random fortune or the product of hard
work. He was a mysterious and profound person—we let him
be, for we knew no other way to regard him, he had changed
the pattern of our lives so.

8.
The second week of August, we took the trip to Hollywood.
It happened this way: Franny's obsession with Harvard
Sharp took a strong turn. She had covered every inch of her
bedroom walls with photos of him, and when Mother told
her she wasn't going to give her any more allowance if she
was just going to spend it on *Teen Beat,* Franny got picked
up for shoplifting at the drugstore on the edge of campus. It
happened on a Monday afternoon. Ivan and I were at home
and in the kitchen, making a key lime pie. Mother was in
her office on campus, her canning endeavors forgotten for the
afternoon. Franny had gone out that morning, her skateboard
in hand, with the news that she was going down to the river to
hunt up snails. She hadn't come for lunch, and Ivan had only
just begun to wonder after her when the telephone rang. Ivan
answered the phone without thinking now, but he always
answered with *Birch residence,* careful not to become too casual.
That afternoon, he stood silent for some time after answering,
the receiver clutched between chin and shoulder. I watched
him, forgetting to grate the lime rind. "I see," he said at last.
"Someone will be down directly." When he hung up there was
the shadow of a grin on his face. From the drawer beneath the
telephone, he took a red leather book in which Mother had
printed necessary numbers and dates. At one time, it had been
common for Franny and me to spend whole days alone in the
house when our mother and father were both at work, and
the red book was stamped with a fat, white emergency cross,

as if paramedics and firemen would magically sprout from its interior. I was old enough and had spent enough time alone with Franny to know that the help we truly needed appeared only in the shape of our mother coming through the back door, her loafers already off and dangling from one hand, or in our father, coming in still later, smelling of cigarette smoke and sweet bourbon. I would forever be somehow comforted by that musky, bar smell.

Now, Ivan opened the book and turned the telephone dial with slow, almost forced precision. We both listened to the faint ringing on the other end of the line, the kitchen waiting with us, and then Mother's voice came through. "I've just had a call from campus security," Ivan told her. "They're holding Franny for shoplifting."

It wasn't that big of a deal. That's what Franny said when we arrived at the tiny campus security office, which wasn't much more than a screened-in porch off the side of the pharmaceutical building. The long room had a cement floor and was shielded from the afternoon sun so that the temperature inside was blissfully cool. Franny was lying at the end of the room on an army cot made up with a posy-patterned bedspread. Her sandals were off and on her stomach was curled a large orange cat. When she saw us, she turned on her side and hid her face in her hands.

Stuart, the student representative for campus security, who looked to be about nineteen years old, sidled up to Mother, explaining that they couldn't technically charge Franny because of her age, and because the drugstore had been on campus property, and because he was really only a volunteer, but he thought she ought to be picked up anyway. When they got her she'd been hiding a *Teen Beat* and a box of candied cigarettes under her blouse. "Next time you try something like that, kid, wear a thicker t-shirt," Stuart said, grinning. Mother watched him with a stony face and he turned away, clearing his throat.

Mother sat on the edge of the cot, her purse in her lap. "Franny girl," she said, "let's just go home, okay? I'll come home too. I won't go back to work anymore today."

Franny kept her back to us; her face was flushed and the hair along her temples was dark with sweat. "I love him," she said quietly.

"Oh Frances," Mother said, shaking her head. "He's an actor! He's playing a part."

"I love him."

"Who do you love, Franny?" asked Ivan.

Mother looked up at him.

"Do you love Harvard Sharp the man or the person he plays on television?"

Franny turned over and sat up, drawing her legs to her chest. One of her kneecaps was skinned and bleeding lightly. She rubbed a grimy thumb under her nose and considered Ivan's question. From his desk chair, Stuart had turned in our direction and was listening closely. "I love the man," Franny said finally. "I love him on T.V. too, but he isn't a cowboy in all the magazines. He's a real person. Like we are." She looked around at our faces, the challenging darkness in her eyes coming back slowly. "I love the man," she said, and nodded her head. Stuart the student representative for campus security nodded his head and turned back to his work. Ivan nodded his head and held out a hand to help Franny up off her cot. Mother sighed, but nodded too, and took my hand. Then the four of us went to the Felix for a malted.

It was Father's idea to take Franny to Hollywood. We had

eaten the key lime pie. I was in the den watching television with the door open, and Franny was upstairs taking a bath. The conversation happened in three bursts. Father suggested a dose of reality might be in store. "Hollywood," he said.

Mother laughed. "Don't be ridiculous," she said.

Ivan cleared his throat.

"If we take her to Hollywood so she can really meet this guy, maybe the phase will pass," said Father. He got up from the table and poured drinks for the three of them.

"Don't you think that's a little extreme?" asked Mother.

"It could be a vacation," said Father. "For all of us."

"What makes you think you can get him to meet her?"

"I've been in touch with him," said Ivan. He leaned back in his chair, arms crossed, eyes downcast. "I wrote him that David and I might be coming down sometime." This statement was met with a long silence. The words *David and I* seemed to reverberate throughout the kitchen. Through the open door to the den, I could see my mother's back, and I watched her, wondering where these words would hit the hardest, whether they were some final twist to the thread that connected her with Father, or the beginning of the end of the quiet alliance with Ivan that had been growing during the past few weeks. More than anything, I believe what she heard was an admission; in his quiet way Ivan had declared the indefinite thing that had been lurking about the house since June. In one swift moment my mother felt herself become unanchored. Powerless. No longer young. I thought of the poems she had written about the flowering trees in the back yard, words and longings that at once lifted and shamed her. She had given these to me, stowed them away in my lunch bags. If her poems were the secret she kept, were the glimpses of her more honest, hidden self, then what was the face of my father's secret life?

Somehow I knew that it involved the evening of the solstice party, and the moment—believed hidden—behind the piano; a memory grown so worn with use I was almost bored of it. What I had seen had not been a trick of the dark or of too much champagne. I had been unable to look it in the face then; I hadn't known how to name the thing I'd discovered. Sitting now on the rough carpet in the den, hidden by the shadow of the open door, listening to these three adults for whom I held a surprising amount of love, I sensed the problem of our home was actually quite simple, and that, after all, it wasn't even a problem. It was only what was true.

"Well then," I heard my mother say. "I guess it's decided." She took a last, audible swallow of her drink. "How about over Grace's birthday?" she said. "I won't be working anyway."

9.

The trip to Hollywood was a vagabond affair. We traveled the twelve hundred miles in a borrowed van. Mother made us a bed behind the last row of seats, just inside the rear door, where we felt encapsulated and a little like stowaways. Father and Ivan took turns driving, and Mother resigned herself to the back seat, where she read aloud to me and Franny, played hand after hand of gin rummy and go fish, and stretched out for long naps on the cracked leather of the seat cushions.

We stayed one night in a campground just off the highway. Across the road from the campground was an all-night diner, and we ate dinner there for my birthday, the fifteenth of July. Mother gave me a carved ring made of blonde wood, and Father gave me a copy of *Streetcar Named Desire*. Inside he had written: *You are a beautiful girl. Happy Birthday from Father.* I was fourteen years old.

That night, as we were lying tucked into our hidden bed, Franny practiced how she would greet Harvard Sharp. "What about this, Gracie," she said, facing me in the dark. I could feel the heat coming off of her and smell the butterscotch from the sundae she'd had for dessert. "Listen Gracie!" she whispered loudly. "Listen now."

"I'm listening."

"Mr. Sharp, my name is Frances," she said. "And as long as you live, you'll never meet anybody who'll love you as much as I do."

"Your breath stinks."

"What do you think he'll say?"

"Didn't you brush your teeth?"

"The bathroom is in the middle of the woods! Tell me. What will he do?"

"Run away."

"He'll stay."

We laughed silently, biting our blankets to keep from making noise. After a while, Franny began to snore. On the floor of the van in front of us, our mother and father lay side by side. They had whispered together before falling asleep.

"Wait until we get home," Mother had said. "Just wait till home, David." There had been the sound of skin touching, nothing more than palms, cheeks, perhaps the brush of someone's neck, and silence.

10.

Harvard Sharp was a very slight man. Perhaps behind the camera he had been standing on a box, or a filming technique had been used to give him the on-screen appearance of someone hulking and brave, because the man we encountered on the lot of Studio 29 the next morning could not have been more than five feet tall. Franny could almost look him straight in the eye. I felt a little sorry for him, watching him standing there all in white: white cowboy boots, white jeans, white sports jacket. Above his collar his face was a burnished copper. When he smiled, a bit of his character broke through; his teeth were startlingly white against his skin, and his eyes were every bit as blue as the television promised.

Even in the face of disappointment, Franny blushed crimson. Her long night of practiced speeches fell completely from memory, and it was all she could do to smile and nod politely while Harvard signed a headshot for her and shook her hand.

When we had entered the lot, Father had said, "Maybe we shouldn't all meet him, it might seem too much."

"Isn't that why we came?" asked Mother.

"Nora," Father said, putting a hand to her waist, "why don't Ivan and I go with Franny? You don't really care about meeting Harvard Sharp, do you?"

Mother began searching through her purse for something. "That's fine," she mumbled. She put her sunglasses on. "That's just fine."

I stood with her by the gates while Father and Ivan circled Harvard with handshakes. Father, becoming irritated with Franny's shyness, had pulled her a bit too roughly towards Harvard so that she might get an autograph, and now he stood with both hands on her thin shoulders; Franny studied the photograph in her hands, the breeze moving her fine white hair across the nape of her neck. I looked around the bright lot while they talked; the studios loomed like ships, sturdy and anonymous in the black asphalt, and everywhere women clicked by in high heels, every one of them slim and stylish and unafraid. Beside me, Mother smoked with shaking hands.

She kept lifting her head and turning slightly away from the scene surrounding Harvard, but under her sunglasses I could see her watching Father. She looked down at me once, smiled nervously, and dropped her cigarette to the ground. From the group there came the jolting bark of laughter; the sound echoed off the walls of the buildings around them, blooming in that space. Franny had been edged out of the circle, and she turned back to us, her face confused. In an instant, Mother came to attention, as if someone had flipped a switch inside of her. She reached a hand out and Franny came to her. "Let's see the picture," Mother said, and nodded her approval when Franny extended the photograph. "He's a real human," she said. "That's for sure."

The three of us went out of the studio gates and ordered ice cream from a man with a silver cart. As we walked back to meet Father and Ivan, Mother began to hum the opening theme from *Those Boys*. She licked her ice cream cone and dribbled chocolate on the front of her blouse.

"Oh dear," said Franny, pointing.

Mother looked down at her blouse and shrugged. She sauntered along, her hand tightly clasped with Franny's. "I hate actors," she said.

We stayed for one night in a hotel on Hollywood Boulevard. "One night without camping," Father said to Mother, patting her on the back.

"I like camping," she said.

Father's face fell momentarily before it brightened again, falsely, to greet an approaching valet.

"What do you think of the hotel?" I asked, taking Mother's hand. Her nails had grown a little long and ragged, and the pink paint was chipping at the edges. "Let's you, me and Franny all get our nails done," I said, though it was never something we'd done before.

"There's a salon in the hotel, Nora," said Father. He tipped the valet and together we emerged into the cool, dim interior of the hotel lobby.

"I think I'd just like a drink," said Mother as we filed into a waiting elevator. "Certainly I'll need a nap."

Ivan's room was the last on the hall. The others were two adjoining, the first off the elevator. Ivan said he'd be in the lobby for dinner at seven. We watched him recede slowly away, the thick carpet muffling his footsteps.

This is what happens next: Franny and I are sprawled on the king sized bed in one room. Mother is taking a bath, and Father has closed the drapes and called for cocktails from room service. This is entirely fancy, Franny has concluded. She props open the door that connects the two rooms and re-fills her glass with ice from the bucket on the dresser. She stands on the counter in the bathroom and poses up and down in the mirror. "Do I have nice legs, Grace?" she asks. I look at the scabs on her knees, at the cluster of veins she was born with at the top of her right ankle.

"You have beautiful legs."

"I wish Father would pour *me* a nice cold drink," says Franny. She seems to have forgotten all about Harvard Sharp and their awkward meeting.

We both want the bathroom to fix ourselves up for dinner, but I am the unlucky one to be in there when the light bulb flutters out. I have to wake Father up to tell him. He is lying on the bed, his shoes off and his shirt collar loosened. He is frowning in his sleep and when I poke him on the arm he squints up at me, his frown growing deeper.

"What is it?" he asks, his voice hoarse.

"The light bulb is out in our bathroom," I say.

"Use the bathroom in here."

"Mother's in there."

He has closed his eyes again.

"Couldn't you put in a new light bulb?"

"I'm trying to nap, Grace," he says. "You look fine to me."

"But I'm not finished getting ready!" I yell down at him, my heart pounding. I am filled with a strange kind of anger, detached and cold. I have never before yelled at my father.

He jerks himself up and moves lithely through the open door to the bathroom. I can hear him flinging open cupboards and unscrewing the old bulb from the sconce on the wall. Light beams out from the room, and I can see how red the back of his neck is. He comes back into the bedroom and takes me by the arm, pushing me back through the doorway.

"There you go, *woman*", he says, and his breath is warm on my face, smelling the same sweet way it always has, of mouthwash and cigarettes and bourbon.

Franny and I sleep with Mother in her room that night. Father stays down in the lounge after dinner, so that even in this strange place the night is familiar: the three of us abreast in an oversized bed, half-sleeping, half-wondering when Father might reappear. That night he does not. Under the covers, I feel that Mother's legs are soft with weeks of stubble. "Your legs are like peach fuzz," says Franny. She falls asleep first.

"Maybe if you shaved your legs?" I say into the dark, like it is the solution we have been searching for all summer long.

At dawn, I wake to the sound of the garbage truck. Outside the window, Hollywood Boulevard rises scrubbed and without angst. I get up from the bed and go in my nightgown to the hotel lobby. In the restaurant, Father is sitting at the counter, his hands in his head, a clean white coffee cup before him. A stack of newspapers sits by his elbow. I walk over and hoist myself up onto the stool next to him. "Coffee?" the waitress asks me.

"Please." The waitress rests a second white cup in a saucer and pours.

"Re-fill?" she asks Father.

My father lifts his head and looks over at me. His eyes are bloodshot and ringed with shadow. He nods. "Please," he says. He never stops looking at me.

When the waitress has gone, I try the coffee. It is hot and very bitter. "Do you like it?" Father asks, bringing his cup to his lips.

"I've never had coffee," I say.

Father calls the waitress back and asks for cream and sugar. "Try it this way," he says. "Better?"

I nod.

"I used to drink it that way," he says. "Now, just black."

"What's with all the newspapers?"

He pulls the stack towards him and hands me the top copy. "They found Harvard Sharp in his apartment last night," he says. "He killed himself." He pushes his coffee cup away and rests his head in his hands again. "I went around the whole neighborhood, trying to get the papers so Franny wouldn't see." When he looks up again, he is smiling in a defeated sort of way, the same way he smiled the night Mother smashed the gravy boat. "What do you think she'll do?" he asks. "What will she do?"

I do not answer. I look away from my father and into my coffee cup. He has poured the cream for me; he has stirred it in gently with the sugar, so that the bitter taste will no longer bother me. I drink it now, though it is cooling quickly. It is good.

11.

Harvard Sharp hanged himself with a white silk tie. *The L.A. Times* printed a picture of his body—taken down from his noose. The headline on the front page was small but near the top. It read: "Popular TV star dead at 37." In *Those Boys*, Harvard had played a nineteen-year-old cowboy. I was strangely comforted by the fact that he had waited to die until his late thirties, and I began imagining him at his actual nineteen, slender and full of fervor, seeking fame and feeling somehow that he was destined for greatness.

Franny saw the story, despite Father's best efforts. "But it must be someone else," she said. "He was only a teenager."

No, Father told her. He was the same man. He had only been playing a part.

"I see," said Franny. With a small hand she folded the front page of the newspaper and tucked it in the pocket of her skirt.

My father left home on the nineteenth of August. It was an ordinary day. Ivan had gone before him, in the week after we'd returned from California. He took the train back east where he'd visit his mother and make decisions about school, jobs, places to live. We'd driven him to the station and waved goodbye. He wore a navy blue sweater and his old pair of sneakers; he carried one duffel bag. He had been happy, that morning, as he secured his cap to his head and kissed Mother on the cheek and clasped Father's hand. "Goodbye, goodbye," he said, looking us each in the eye and touching the tip of Franny's nose. Just like that. And was gone.

The day that our father left, Franny and I were sunbathing in the back yard. It was the last week of summer vacation; Mother was at home, working in her upstairs office, her fingers keeping a steady rhythm on her typewriter. That morning, Father had risen early. He drank two cups of coffee and read the newspaper standing up, leaning against the counter. He washed his cup and placed it in the drainer to dry, all usual actions, though completed, perhaps, with a bit more determination that day, a touch more purpose. He packed one bag—an old tan suitcase that had been stored with all the other suitcases in the closet outside the first-floor bathroom. He did not take the station wagon. He walked to campus. In his office, he arranged the papers on his desk and left a note to his secretary.

Across the street from the entrance to the university there was a block of businesses: the Felix Diner, a barbershop owned by the man named Jack Leroy, a record store, and at the far corner, in a vacant lot big enough for its trade, a bus station. When I think about it, I am confused about this detail of his leaving; why not the train station, like Ivan? Why not the station wagon, after all? The bus station was perhaps the only signal of slight hesitation, of a plan not quite fully conceived. I like to imagine that he woke that morning without an agenda, with no scheme to his name. The suitcase, the arranging of papers—this might be explained away. Perhaps the suitcase contained a change of clothes for a dinner meeting or a squash game he would go to after his daily work. Perhaps, when he went out of the office at noon, headed for lunch at the Felix Diner, he had seen the bus station sitting where it had always been, and on a whim he'd gone to the ticket window and asked about the connections between coasts. *New York,* he told the agent. *Long Island.*

The trip to New York by bus would take him six complete days. He became grimy and exhausted on the ride. He washed his socks in gas-station bathrooms. He ate eggs benedict at two a.m. at a diner in St. Paul. From Detroit to Boston he sat next to a woman so pregnant she suffered excruciating back pain. He gave her the aisle seat so that she might stretch her legs and read aloud to her from scripts he had tucked into his suitcase. In Manhattan, he left the bus station and wandered about the city, listless; the morning was soft and bright. From a payphone inside the lobby of the public library, he called Ivan on Long Island, and Ivan answered his call. He took the train in to meet him, to embrace him and gather him up and take him to a new home.

BOOK TWO
Leroy

Nora is twenty years old. She is nine months pregnant. It is late July. She is asleep in the dressing room of the theater. David kneels beside her, pinches the taut skin of her stretched belly, tells her it is time to wake up. "I'm going to take Alice home," he says. Nora smiles her waking smile. She goes out of the theater still sleepy, her body always heavy and sleepy these days. The actors like her; she is an anchored woman, she loves her husband, and she is his friend. They buss her cheek and pat her stomach as she waves goodbye.

Alice Leroy has red hair flaming in ringlets from her head. Otherwise she is plain. She is married to Jack, David's childhood friend. Jack cuts hair at the barbershop by the Felix Diner. Nora likes Jack because he is patient with David, and because he watches her with deep, kind eyes. He seems to understand something important about her. Alice fits Nora into a hug. "Ten bucks says it happens tonight," she says, poking at the belly. Nora laughs and squeezes Alice's hand. *Goodnight,* she says. *Goodbye.*

Nora goes to the Felix Diner. She eats chili with vinegar. Soda crackers. One chocolate malt. She smokes half a cigarette on the street outside then throws the entire pack—almost full— into the trash. She knocks on the glass of the barbershop as she goes by; Jack looks up from sweeping and smiles out at her, his face tanned above his white smock. It has been a fierce, dry summer. She walks home, and as she walks she feels that nothing is strange about the night. Later, she will pretend that she did feel something. That in some way she predicted what was to come. She did not. She walks and thinks about what radio hour might be on when she gets home. She tries to decide if she has the energy for a bath. She thinks about how she sometimes worries that the baby will slip out while she is in the bath; just slide its quiet way into the water between her legs. She is a smart woman. She reads many books, but even smart women have silly fear when things are miraculous, when things are unknown. When this baby comes, after it has grown a while, she will go back to school. These are the thoughts she keeps hidden from David.

At the apartment building, she waves to the woman whose living room window is next to the front stoop. Her blinds are open, and through the screen Nora hears the sound of multiplied laughter. In a city somewhere, one thousand people wear diamonds and laugh in unison and their voices come through the night to Nora. She unlocks the front door. In the hallway she puts her shoes next to David's. She turns the radio dial and runs a hot bath even though it is July. She leaves the door to the bathroom open so she can hear the radio, and she plans that David will come home and find her like this.

Eleven or later, and he is still not home. The bathtub is drained, the radio off. She paces the floor barefoot, her white nightgown billowing around her. She goes to the telephone and tries the number at the Leroy place. Jack might be there with the baby, but the call doesn't go through and the operator's voice comes back at her metallically. *Sorry miss. This number is not connected. Shall I try another?* Nora can't think of any other number she knows by heart. Her own number. David's number. It is nice to think they are the same. She hangs up and goes to the living room, turns on Cole Porter for company. All the records are David's. Most of the books. She runs her fingers over their soft spines; some are so worn their titles have rubbed off. When she opens them they smell dusty and familiar; David has marked his name on the inside cover, and she runs her fingertip over the letters of his name, her own name. It is nice to think so.

When Nora met David, she was working at the Felix Diner. She was eighteen years old. He came through the door of the diner wearing a blue suit. His shoulders didn't quite fill the corners. "This is my father's suit," he told her as she poured him coffee. She leaned on the counter. A piece of her hair fell from its pin and hung heavily by her cheek.

"Are you going to an interview?" she asked him.

"An audition," he said. He was not afraid. He looked her in the eye.

"A play?" she asked. She pretended to be excited because he was handsome and she did not want him to go away just yet. She had seen one play in her life, when she was fourteen years old. One called *The Man Who Had All the Luck*. She had gone to visit Ivy, her oldest sister, who lived in Culver City and whom everyone said could have been in the movies if she hadn't gotten into trouble so young. In Culver City, Ivy lived in a boarding house. A couple from her church—who had money, she said—had taken in her baby. Nora had taken the train from the North, where she lived on a farm with her mother and father and five brothers and sisters. Nora was the second youngest, and the trip to see Ivy was supposed to look like a birthday present, but Nora understood that she was also there to check up on Ivy, and to bring her home without the baby. "We'll just tuck that trouble away," Nora had heard her mother saying to her father the night before she left. She used the same expression for spilt milk, for chores that had to be taken care of, for minor bumps and bruises that the children brought in.

Ivy was sixteen. Ivy was beautiful. Ivy would be brought home. There were simply too many children at home anyway. Nora would not end up like her sister. This was why she had taken the job at the Diner her first summer out of high school, even if it meant walking home in the dark after she had finished her shift, too late for the last bus out of town. In the dark, the world was Nora's to predict, and she walked the dirt road listening to the call of crickets, too many to count, and breathing in the smell of dried and hot pine left over from the day's sun. She planned to make money, to go to college; she planned on never, ever knowing a life like her mother's. Walking in the dark after a good day, she sometimes held a tight fist before her face and struck the air triumphantly, punching the space ahead of her, molding time with what she had planned.

She would have liked to tell David what she had planned for her life when he came in to the diner that night, but instead she let him do the talking, and as he talked she reminded herself that she had wide, dark eyes like her mother and that the pink of her uniform often matched the flush in her cheeks that came from working behind the hot counter all day. He told her that he was going to the college there, that he was an actor.

"Could I come see you in this play?" she asked. Her mother would have pinched her for being brazen.

He grinned at her, and she saw that he had two neat rows of wide, white teeth.

After that, he came into the diner every afternoon to study his lines. He read them out loud to her, and she listened while she served coffee up and down the row of red stools, while she whirred the shake mixer, while she rinsed the Coke glasses in the steaming water till they glinted back at her in the high, yellow lights.

There was a night, two or three weeks into their knowing of each other, when David waited for her in the alley behind the diner, and after everyone had left for the night, she unlocked the back door and led him through the dark kitchen. His hand gripped hers with a timidity that was surprising; he had never been afraid to meet her eyes, to lock his there. She felt that perhaps he had never before held a girl's hand.

At the counter, she set out ice cream and tins of syrup: chocolate, cherry, butterscotch. She went to a cupboard and pulled down jars of walnuts, pecans, slivers of almonds so fine you could etch your fingerprint into the waxy surface. They sat facing each other in a darkened booth, their sundaes between them. Nora ate every bite of hers, then reached to fish out the bits of fudge from David's bowl. He watched her eat, watched her wrap her tongue around the cold steel of the spoon. "You like ice cream," he said, grinning.

She nodded.

He moved around to her side of the booth, and with a soft hand traced a vein that ran steadily from her lower jaw to her collarbone. His mouth on her skin was cold from the ice cream and his lips shook. She guided his hand and pressed his palm against her covered breast, the fabric of her uniform worn and oily from the day's work.

It was after their marriage that he started disappearing. Plays took him on the road, and at first Nora tagged along. She got used to sleeping back stage in strange cities, the smell of thick makeup and musty costumes all around her. She knew how to sew; her mother taught her young, and she grew up mending holes and fastening buttons on her brothers' and sisters' clothing. She fixed costumes in between scenes; the actors came to her, bright or inconsolable. She knelt and moved around them, pins in her mouth.

David was lithe on the stage, his two perfect rows of teeth glinting at the audience, and for a while, David on stage was enough. Nora let herself forget about the plans she had made. She felt power in the way she could claim David as her own when the other actors hummed around him, watching him during a performance with wide, brimming eyes.

The first time he went away, he left her in a motel room by the side of a highway. The whole troupe was staying there, spending days at the theater in town a few miles down the road. Nora was bored and tired; she had seen the play so often she knew every line by heart. David stood at the dresser in their room, fastening his watch, looping his belt buckle tighter around his narrow waist. Nora sat up in bed, the sheets mangled around her. She watched David's face in the mirror above the dresser. There were blue shadows below his eyes.

"You need a haircut," she told him.

"I'll get one in town," David said. He took up his jacket and wallet. He tucked the little script into his back pocket and stood by the door, studying her for a moment before leaving; her shoulders were bare and freckled, and the hair under her arms had grown into a soft patch.

"Stay here," he said as she moved off the bed. She stood facing him in her slip. "I'll be home late though, you know how these things run." He left after kissing her brow, after she pressed herself to him for just a moment, standing with the sun filtering through the window, warming her calves and heavily veined feet.

In the morning he was still gone. All along the row of motel rooms, curtains were drawn and doors went unanswered. The actors came home late and slept late, weary after pretending to be someone they were not. Nora packed her bag and walked the three miles to the theater. The marquee over the main door was bare. In the dressing room she found the stage manager. He shrugged when she asked after David, and told her she could use the phone for free at the bar on the corner. There was no number she could think of to call, but she walked there anyway, her suitcase banging against her legs.

The bar was dark at eleven o'clock, and Nora had to blink away spots of sunlight as the door closed behind her. There were three people at the bar; a woman in a black dress, her legs bare and her heels kicked to the floor; a man in a suit beside her, his tie loosened. He kept a hand on the woman's knee at all times. Another man sat at the far end of the bar, his face buried in his arms. The bartender looked up and nodded in Nora's direction. She asked to use the phone, and at the sound of her voice the head at the end of the bar came up and David's eyes stared down at her.

They ordered coffee. Added sugar, cream. "Someday I'll drink it black," David said, wiping the back of his spoon against the thick china.

"Where did you go?" Nora asked. There were a dozen questions in her mind and every single one of them made her feel like a wife. She had heard her mother ask these questions of her father, mornings when he would come in from town, a night of no sleep and drink played out mournfully on his face. Her mother asked questions angrily, a baby on her jutting hip. "Where you been, Arthur? Where you been?" And although her father kept leaving, kept attempting that running start at disappearing completely, her mother's questions became weary as the years passed, and the babies left her hip, and moved themselves away, one by one, till Nora was the oldest one left, out of high school, working at the diner, running into her father coming out of the bar as she walked home from work, kissing his cheek; he was her father after all, when she saw him she loved him because never had he been unkind to her and always he had come back home.

Nora sat up straight on her stool and leaned towards David. "Where did you go?" she asked again.

The bartender was watching them as he polished glasses in the middle of the bar. David nodded at him. "Can I get a refill?" he asked, nudging his coffee cup. The bartender brought the coffee pot, poured out the steaming liquid, then left them again.

David shrugged. "We came here, had some drinks," he said. "I guess I had one too many." He watched the couple at the other end of the bar. Nora looked too. The woman had her arm draped around the man's shoulders; her mouth was pressed to his ear. Every now and then the man would tip back the dregs of his drink and crunch an ice cube between his teeth. When he saw David watching, his lips curved into an open mouth smile, and the gleam of ice could be seen on his tongue. David looked away, but Nora studied the man a moment longer, realizing that she knew him.

"Who is that?" she asked.

"Pete Kline," David said. "He's in the company."

From across the bar, Pete Kline winked at Nora, not unkindly, but Nora looked away and swirled the contents of her coffee, now cold.

David covered his face in his hands; he rubbed his skin and scalp roughly to wake himself up. "Now we go home," he said. "Show's over."

Nora watched him, waiting, but there was nothing more. Together they swung off their stools. David stacked some coins beside his coffee cup and pulled his jacket on. As they passed him, Pete Kline looked up and smiled, saluting David goodbye, but David kept his eyes lowered and only nodded slightly, the skin underneath his shirt collar turning red.

Outside, the sky had muted itself, and a slow drizzle was starting. David looked down at Nora. He took her suitcase. "You warm enough?" he asked.

She nodded, but he set her case down anyway and took his jacket off, draping it over her shoulders. Even against the scent of wet asphalt she could breath him in through the fibers around her; she could smell his aftershave and his one-too-many bourbons and his first night away from her.

He swung her case up under his arm and taking her hand, led her across the empty street.

"I'm not sure what to do with you," Nora said as they walked. Inside she had her mother's words. She let them sway in her mind, a singsong. *Just tuck that trouble away, Davie boy, just tuck that trouble away.*

After that they moved back home, found the apartment, and David got the job at the university. Five times he left in the evening and didn't come back. Three times she found him at the diner, his head beside a cold cup of black coffee. Once she got a call from Jack, who was married to Alice by then, and was working at the barbershop. She went to collect David from them. Alice's face was blank as she led Nora to the kitchen where David and Jack sat at the counter playing cards. David looked up when Nora came in. "My beautiful Nora!" he cried. He swayed in his chair. Jack held out a hand to steady him.

"He recited Shakespeare outside our window till we let him in," Jack said, his eyes on Nora in that same way, the way that made her want to shield herself and embrace him all at the same time. He set out three coffee cups.

"David likes his black," Nora said.

When she found out she was pregnant he stopped leaving. He brought his lines home again and read to her as she cooked. She went to the theater in the evenings to watch rehearsals. The summer came and they slept late into the heat of the day, the curtains shielding them from the sun, Nora's stomach rounding out and tightening beneath the bed sheet. They woke up to shower and eat, then walked the canopied streets to the theater. They were living like artists, David said one afternoon, waking sweaty from sleep; only they weren't starving. The best way to live, he said. *We are so lucky,* he said, and he was right. He found the vein in Nora's neck and ran the tip of his finger along the faint, blue line.

Now it is July, and Nora has paced the floor for an hour. She is in bed when David comes home sometime after three. She has been lying on her side, two pillows tucked between her knees to support her back. When she hears the turn of the lock, she heaves herself from bed and goes to the hallway. David is just closing the door behind him when her open palm strikes his chest. She shoves him twice. Once, as she is walking toward him, her nightgown sweaty and caught up between her legs. Twice, as she catches a glimpse of herself in the hall mirror, and sees that her nipples and the dark v of hair below her heavy stomach are visible through the thin fabric that covers her.

David does not speak. He falls back with the second blow, hitting the mirror and sending it off its weak nail. The glass does not break, and something about this angers Nora even more. She reaches a hand up again, but David makes a noise, a moan, a low, hollow calling from somewhere inside his mouth. Nora looks down to see the stains on his shirt, crimson and almost purple, like deep, sticky bruises. She presses her hands to his body in a panic, searching him, asking him 'is it you? Is it you?' until he takes her wrists and moves her away. He is safe, he says. He is in one piece.

The truck that hit the side of David's 1941 Packard was going forty-five miles an hour. Alice Leroy's body was sent sideways and up, her head breaking through the glass of the windshield. The car skidded off the road and came to rest in the wet ditch just before the turn off that led to the Leroys' new house.

The way David told it to Nora, Alice had been sleeping when the truck hit. Watching her body come toward him, it seemed to him that she never really woke up. She opened her eyes just once before her head met the glass of the windshield, and looked over at David with complacency as if to say, 'Of course.' Her red hair got caught up with her red blood and when the ambulance arrived her head was like a dark, slick thing emerging from a shower.

David walked home from the hospital on two strong legs. He had been protected by the wheel, protected by position, by heavier build, even by Alice herself. He walked home after Jack arrived at the hospital, after sitting with him on the curb of the emergency entrance, Jack with his head in his hands, refusing to go in to claim Alice's body. Claiming her meant claiming her things. Earrings, wedding band, leather purse with lipstick and wadded up tissue. She had left one shoe in the car; David picked it up and carried it with him all the way to the hospital so that he might have something to offer Jack.

You can't go home with one shoe was what he had planned to say, a joke as Alice came out of the hospital, bandaged but breathing.

Alice's brother arrived at two and took over, demanding information from anyone in charge, ignoring David so David went home. There was nothing else to do. Before he left he reached a hand out to Jack, sitting on the curb. "Let me help you up," he said.

Jack, who had always been too gentle to ever show any real anger, looked up at David's outstretched hand and there was darkness in his gaze, a steady conviction of blame that made David pull back. David turned to go then, feeling foolish, feeling young, feeling horribly, sickeningly sorry for himself. He limped the nighttime streets home to Nora, Alice's lost shoe still swinging idly in his fingers by one thin, leather strap.

Nora attends the funeral alone, her belly camouflaged in black wool, sweat rolling between her shoulder blades as she stands at attention in the church pew, her pantyhose rubbing between her thighs. After the service, she goes to pay her respects to Jack. He is sitting alone at the reception in the church basement, hands dangling between his knees. He raises them and examines them, as if he's forgotten what use they have. Beside him, his mother stands holding the baby—Susan—her red curls creeping out from under a white cap. Nora offers to hold Susan; she reaches out her arms, but Jack's mother demurs, studying Nora's figure, searching her hand for the wedding ring that was tugged from her swollen finger weeks ago. Nora drops her arms, nods. She has not been able to cry; her own sorrow feels like a selfish thing. "I'm so sorry," she says, the only words she can manage. She watches Jack, but he won't meet her gaze so she turns to go, fitting her thick way awkwardly through the crowd.

Outside, the heat and the light of the day hit her with full force and she yanks her sweater away from her arms. Bits of black wool stick to her damp, bare skin. A man coming across the parking lot looks at her strangely and she stares him down, kicks off her shoes, and reaches up under her dress to peel away her panty hose. The man skirts around her and lets the heavy oak door of the church slam behind him. Gathering her shoes and stockings, she walks barefoot to the bus stop on the corner of the hill just above the church. Halfway up the sidewalk, she hears someone calling her name. Turning, she sees Jack coming after her, his tie loosened, his hands thrust deep into his pockets. Nora watches him approach; he is a handsome man. He seems incapable of judgment. This is how she knows him. He is infinitely kind. She finds herself relaxing as he draws near; finds herself opening up unhurriedly above the sidewalk, as if something has finally lost its grip on her. "Thank you for coming," he says, covering the last few feet with slow, laborious steps. He looks down at her feet; they are veined and heavy.

She holds a hand up to shield her eyes from the sun. "David wanted to come," she says. She does not look away from him. "He did want to."

"He couldn't."

"No."

They watch each other until the sound of the bus arriving makes them turn and look up the hill. The doors swing open, and they can see the driver looking down at them; the other passengers peer down through tinted windows. Nora turns away from the driver, she does not wave him on, though he's watching her still, waiting for her, just in case. An entire minute passes before he pulls away. She is suddenly overwhelmed with contentedness, it fills her from breast to toe, and her belly seems to loosen its nine-month fist. She feels that she could stand in the sun, on the side of the hill, forever. "I know you know about David," she says over the retreating exhaust of the bus. "You know about the way he is." She squints in the sun. She has never before said these things out loud. Why now? She doesn't know, except the day seems to demand it; everything is raw and stripped away and it feels heavenly to her. "It's okay," she says. "I know too." She feels the corners of her mouth twitch, wanting to smile, even laugh.

Jack takes a step closer to her. "What way is that?" he says patiently, his head tilted, not really asking. She can smell his soap and she can see that he did not shave that morning. She imagines that he lathered his jaw, studied his sleepless face in the mirror and washed the lather away. She imagines him fingering the fine blade of his razor, prodding a thick bulb of blood from his thumb, watching it fall into the sink and splay outward with the water. "What way is that?" he asks again. He has hold of her hand now. He urges her to go on. But she cannot think of the right way to say it. No one has ever told her how. She furrows her brow. "David loves you," Jack says. Nora doesn't argue. To argue would seem like fishing, and she isn't that sort of woman.

"Still," she says.

Jack nods, and it is this small gesture that finally buckles her heart, a familiar bending in half that makes her sway and blink, and Jack puts a hand to her shoulder to steady her. He is very close now, and in a quick, fervent motion he presses his forehead to hers. "Listen to me," he says, "it doesn't matter. David loves you." Nora moves her hands to grip the nape of his neck. His hands are on the small of her back, the pressure of his fingertips reminding her that she is still young, still a woman. "You must see that it doesn't really matter," he says, and his voice catches then, breaks, and she brings her lips to his forehead, to the thin tissue over each eye, to the hollowed out curve of his cheek, his rough jaw. Just before finding his mouth, he tightens his grip on her and moves his head away from her touch. "Nora," he says, his eyes lowered, "my wife is dead." He takes a step away from her, her hand still in his grip. Before he turns to go he bends and kisses the tender part at the underside of her wrist where all the fine, blue veins run together. He brushes her swollen stomach with his fingertips. "Go home now," he says.

She watches him lope down the sidewalk, his head bent, his hands in his pockets. As she turns to go up the hill, to sit on the green bench to wait for the next bus, she feels the wetness between her bare thighs swell for an instant, a quick, bursting tide, and she looks down to see liquid running down her legs, trickling along her ankles, and staining the grey cement with slow moisture.

When the bus arrives, the driver helps her up the steps and into a seat. The passengers crowd around her asking, 'Is it your first?' 'Where is your husband?' and telling her all sorts of things. 'Breathe shallow, breathe deep, don't crouch over, don't bear down.' A black woman in a red dress puts her shoes back on her swollen feet and wipes her brow with an embroidered handkerchief. A man in a bowler hat gives her a mint to suck on. At the hospital, Nora gives a nurse the number to the apartment and the nurse telephones David. He will wait in the waiting room for fifteen hours; pacing, muttering to himself, sitting up and dozing, dozing on his feet, smoking cigarette after cigarette, going out to watch the encroaching dusk, then the encroaching light of morning.

Less than a week ago he sat blood stained on the curb of the emergency entrance beside Jack and waited in vain for Alice to stride out, alive.

Around five a.m. he goes in for coffee; he asks the receptionist for some milk, maybe some sugar? There is none, she tells him, so he drinks it black, and the bitterness jolts him awake pleasantly; from now on he'll drink it just like this. The thought pleases him. He is imagining morning after morning of waking from deep sleep to sun lined walls, Nora's curved body in bed beside him, the first taste of coffee biting him into consciousness.

In a room down a bright, silent hallway, Nora raises her sweat soaked head, bears down once more, feeling that her whole body is splitting in two, and I am born.

BOOK THREE

Colt's Neck

1.

Across the road from the Leroy house on Colt's Neck Road was an old farmhouse, a place owned by a doctor in town and rented out to families who made a living from the land, when there was more of that sort of living going around. Lately, the doctor had been having trouble finding renters for the place, so he'd put the house up for sale. This was the house my mother went to see the first day Franny and I were back to school after Father left. She took the key from the rental agency and drove out to take a look. The field was overgrown and rocky. Several fence posts lay split and rotting on the ground. The barn needed painting and there was a smell of age about the place, a settling of foundation to earth that my mother loved. Here, in her confusion of loss and liberation, was a kind of permanence. She had known about this house because of Jack and Alice. On visits to their place when it was still being built, she had often seen the 'For Rent' sign; she had often listened as Jack had explained the doctor's story, talked about empty horse pastures and the massive vegetable garden the previous tenants had abandoned when they decided to move away. The place made her recall her childhood, and she had kept the memory of this house with her for years after the accident that had caused Alice's death. She had considered, more than once, taking a trip to Colt's Neck to see if it might still be rented, and then to square her shoulders, knock on the Leroy door, and say hello, *how are you.*

On the day she went to view the property, Jack Leroy was at home with a migraine. He watched from his window as she walked the perimeter of the house, the uneven terrain of the field, the length of fence posts running north to south, east to west and back again. He watched her stoop in her skirt and summer blouse and finger the earth. A thick lock of hair came loose from her bun and flew up with a hot and sudden wind. She stood, crossed to her car, and drove away.

She put in an offer with what little money she had left from her mother and with a portion of a fund Father had left for her in an account he'd opened six months before he'd left. Later I learned this money was quite considerable; it paid for my college and Franny's too. We did not have to move to Colt's Neck; we could have stayed in town, but I think my mother was desperate for escape and permanence, all at the same time. She sent a telegram to New York, Franny and I at her elbows at a desk in the post office, one day after school. *I've bought the doctor's house on Colt's Neck,* she wrote. *Needs work but good. Girls send their love. N.*

"Ask, 'what is New York like?'" Franny said, scrambling for the pen.

"This is enough," Mother said, standing and snapping her purse shut. She took us to see the house that evening. We sat in the tall grass in the front yard and ate hamburgers from wax paper. "I like it here," was what my mother said, and indeed, she looked a new kind of happy.

We nodded yes, us too, because we felt there was nothing else to say. We had few friends in town, and we'd always been good at finding ways to entertain ourselves. The wide space excited us; the vast field at the base of the mountain, the tall, stretching planks of the barn. We peered in smudged windows and claimed rooms as our own. Mother showed us the garden plot, where weeds clutched the dark earth like fingers; she pointed out places where flowers might be planted, where gnarled apple trees grew and gave shade. It was nothing like the nice house we were leaving, but we made no argument. We let the possibility of the space engulf us, and stayed long after the food was gone, watching the night come heavy until the tops of the mountains were as black as the sky.

The nice house was easy to dispose. Mother got rid of most of her plants, too hard to move, she said, looking out the windows of the sunroom that seemed blurred and dirty, though the late summer weather was typical, steady with clean heat and sun. She smoked in the sunroom, smoked as the moving men took boxes away, smoked as she sat on sheet-covered couches. Her ashtrays on the piano overflowed unless I emptied them. The plants gave up and let go of their leaves. We shared an upstairs bedroom together, sleeping on mattresses on the floor and dressing out of suitcases. Franny and I could hear our mother walking slowly around the house at night, and once I watched her from the staircase; she was in her long nightgown, the skirt billowing and catching around her bare ankles as she moved. I had expected to see her crying, to see her angrily wrapping plates in newspaper, but she walked languidly, sleepily, as if taking stock of what was around her. The house was nothing then, and she moved through hollowed, vacant rooms; her nighttime inventories lasted hours, until she would finally crawl onto her mattress next to us. Before she fell asleep, she would run a hand from her stomach to her forehead, slowly, palm down like a lover, like she was reminding herself of the person that was there.

On a bright, still Sunday, we drove away from the nice house for good.

2.

Jack Leroy raised his daughter in the house on Colt's Neck Road. Her name was Susan. She looked like her mother but she did not have her temperament; she was angry most of the time, and went about life with a furrowed brow. She was born in the spring of 1954. I was born in the summer of the same year. We became friends because it was what my father wanted. There had not been a first day of school in my life when I'd come home without hearing Susan's name. My father asked after her routinely, wanting stories of her friends, her studies, her routines. I kept track because I wanted to please him, but I did not truly befriend Susan Leroy until after my father had left.

Susan lived not four blocks from us now, if they could be called blocks. The houses in the new neighborhood were spread out along a single dirt road, three miles long, and Susan's house was the black and tan one at the corner of the road, where the sidelong ditch had been trampled so much that the irrigation pipes below were exposed like bones of the earth. I could see Susan's house from my bedroom window. Sometimes in the afternoons, Susan would dress in a red tutu and practice her baton twirling on her front lawn; she had a silver baton with tassels attached to each end. It was Susan's secret desire to be head cheerleader at our high school.

Franny and I ignored her at first. At fourteen, Susan was a tall, thick girl with a massive head of red hair. She sat alone on the school bus, and she had a nervous habit of chewing on a front lock of her hair. She hurried on and off at stops, arms crossed, face furrowed, her legs moving in a stiff, anxious way. I felt sorry for her, but was unsure how to approach her; making new friends seemed somehow dangerous; there would be so much to explain, so many uncomfortable questions.

In preparation for these anticipated questions, Franny and I invented a new game: The Best Lie. We were a curious family now, and we knew it. Our neighbors had watched us leave frankly; peering out of windows and stopping by uninvited, looking for information under the guise of offering help. Mrs. Tray had been the worst. She had come by everyday, following Mother about the house as she packed, dropping questions about Father's whereabouts with a sympathetic smile. *A new job?* She asked. *A family emergency? He was so good at his plays, he was a talented man, of course he would want to look for more. These things,* she said softly, *were never anyone's fault.*

One afternoon, being followed by Mrs. Tray like this, Franny and I had heard our mother tell a lie. *My husband,* Mother said to Mrs. Tray, her voice sharp, *is directing a play in the east. It was a job he simply couldn't turn down.* She slammed cupboards and crumpled newspaper. *We may all move out there, if the job goes well,* she said. The house was simply too big for three people, and besides, we couldn't rent from the university forever. *We've got to grow up sometime,* she finished with a laugh, the most honest thing in her whole speech. After that, Mrs. Tray didn't come around so much, and when she did, it was with an express errand: food, extra boxes, her son's strength for lifting furniture.

Franny was best at the lying game, and in the space of three weeks, between the time we returned from Hollywood, the time it took Ivan to move out and Father to follow him, and the days spent moving out of town and into the country, our Father's public face in our college town changed drastically.

He had always been an unusual man; an artist, a passionate man, a husband with a working wife, but now he lived a life abroad. Greek Isles, Franny told Mr. Crux, her fourth grade teacher. Pamplona, she told the moving men who came to the new house in August, even though they hadn't asked. The best one was the CIA story. Franny thought that one up when we ran into Paul Tierney, the man who had been Father's accountant, one day on the street. "That's all I can tell you, Paul," Franny said, shaking her fair head. "They wouldn't call it the CIA if I could give you every little detail." Paul looked skeptical, but he shook Franny's offered hand. He shook my hand too.

"The best to you both," he said, walking away. Before he was too far down the block, he turned back and with his pointer finger lifted his hat up an inch on his forehead. "How is your mother?" he called back. I looked at Franny, who shrugged.

"Okay, I guess," I said. Paul nodded and settled his hat back into place.

"My best to her, as well," he said, and ambled away, hands thrust deep in his pockets.

"He's weird," Franny said. Then she said, "I bet he loved him too." Without thinking, I reached out and pulled Franny's hair hard enough to separate a few strands from her scalp. We stood looking down at the hair in my fist before anything else happened, at the tiny white roots at each tip glinting in the sun like dandelion spawn. Then Franny reached out and slapped me across the face in a hooking motion, as if she'd meant to make a fist and punch but had changed her mind mid-air. A car drove by and honked at us, the man at the steering wheel leaning out and yelling something that got lost in his momentum. A woman coming down the sidewalk with a sheaf of papers under her arm veered around us. A few of the papers came loose and tossed themselves in the breeze, but she did not stop to gather them, only looked back and hurried away. Franny and I stood on the street corner, bullied up in broad daylight and refusing to meet one another's gaze. Though it was not our first true fight, it startled us more than any quarrel before. Franny's hand was pressed tight against her head, her small knuckles turning white. I could feel the heat on my cheek where Franny's palm had landed, but I didn't feel mad anymore. Instead I felt sleepy, and strangely hollowed out. I opened my palm and let Franny's hair float away.

"Fran," I started, but Franny shook her head, her eyes filling with tears and her whole body trembling.

"We're the weird ones, Grace," she yelled. "We're the weirdoes here and you know it." She walked away; her back and head bent low, her hand still on her head. I followed a few feet behind until we came to the bus stop. On the bus, Franny sat right behind the driver until we were almost out of town, where the bus stopped and a load of paper-mill workers climbed on. They all wore the same outfit; navy pants and shirt, black belt, brown work boots. Sweat stains lined their underarms like thin, damp pockets. Franny turned to the man who had taken the seat next to her and said, "Excuse me, sir, I'll have to sit by my sister now."

"Of course," the man said, standing and gesturing her past him, out into the aisle. Franny scanned the faces around her, shiny and besieged with exhaustion from the day, until she found me a few seats down.

"Thank you," Franny said quietly to the man, nodding in her remote, decisive way.

The man gave a little bow to her, as if she were all grown up and a lady.

3.

My mother grew up on a farm. She had seven brothers and sisters. Her own mother, a hard-lined woman who never smiled in photographs, woke and lived in the same manner almost every day of her adult life. She had married at seventeen and had given birth to her last baby by twenty-eight. The evening after the final baby was born, she stood up and changed the sheets on the bed where she had labored and went out to take the laundry off the line.

This was a story that my mother began telling Franny and me whenever she had finished hanging our own laundry on the side lawn of the farmhouse. That last baby would have been Aunt Lisa, who had died of breast cancer when she was thirty-two. I was not sure why the story had never been told before, but something in it felt revealing, like learning a secret. I often think about how my mother came to be the way she was, an odd mixture of discipline and steady, determined happiness. She worked harder than most women I knew but she was not a cynic; she did not complain. She believed in letting go and giving up every once in a while. Until the summer that Father left though, her giving up had been resigned to papers she couldn't stand to grade any longer, or to diets she couldn't sustain when Franny brought home potato chips from the drug store. When Father went away, when my mother was suddenly faced with this kind of letting go, she must have needed to turn to some strain of herself that was a pure passing down of her own mother's resolve. On the first weekend in the new house, she dressed fully before going out to collect the paper; she did not linger in her nightgown and robe the way she had done every Saturday before. In her bedroom, the bed was tightly made, and the singular mound that was her pillow sat at the headboard, hidden beneath the embroidered pattern of the bedspread that had been a wedding gift from her mother.

To get a better sense of what the farmhouse was like, first imagine yourself somewhere with a great deal of sky overhead. Stand in one spot and look around. To the north, to the south, the west, the east, to all corners there is open sky. There is a mountain abutting the back of the barn. This mountain is small, but it is only a beginning mountain. It begins more and more mountains, a whole living range of them that go far back into the horizon. We think of this small mountain as ours. Here there are ponderosa and tamarack and Russian sage growing wild. The house sits on five acres of pasture. To the north, the neighbors are the Mullans, a very blond, married couple with a son, Charlie, who is deaf in one ear. He is one year older than me, and is home-schooled. After his lessons, he spends his afternoons perched on the corner fencepost of his parent's property, looking at things through a telescope pressed to his eye. To the south is Sedina Harris, farmer by day, painter and blues singer by night. Sedina is a widow; she lost her husband in a strange way about ten years ago, when there was a rash of random murders in and around the town. Mr. Harris, the deceased, was found slumped over the wheel of his Buick on a Sunday morning, three bullets in his stomach.

This is a piece of information that has stuck with me, though like many of Colt's Neck's stories, I know very little about it. I still have a dream about Mr. Harris sometimes, a dream that I used to have nearly every night when we'd first moved to the farmhouse. The dream is quick. There is a Buick, a Sunday morning, and a man whose face I cannot see. Across this picture comes a sound I've heard before—bang, bang,

bang!—three shots, just like that. I watch Mr. Harris being shot; I stand across the road from his car, halfway hidden in a gathering of trees. The man doing the killing turns and smiles at me, and I see that it is Harvard Sharp, dressed in cowboy boots and blue jeans, a white silk tie around his neck.

The house directly across the road from us belongs to Jack Leroy. We sometimes watch this house the way we'd watch a play from the balcony; peering out, straining for a glimpse backstage where the real story lived.

The house where we live stands closest to the road. This road is grooved deeply with ruts from years of use. Each car that passes leaves a great cloud of dust in its wake, and if you happen to be outside working, the dust will get mixed up with your sweat and suntan lotion, making you feel worse if you are hating your work, or perhaps better, if you find working with the earth a satisfying thing, which my mother does. She is trying to teach us the same.

In the section of field closest to our house grows a row of apple trees. There are ten in all. Six give decent fruit. Go through the trees. Go over or under the planks of the wooden fence. Here is the side yard, wide and long and shaded. At one end, behind the garage, are the clotheslines and a picnic table with two overflowing baskets of wet or dry laundry, depending on the hour and Mother's mood. Step off the grass into the breezeway that is connected overhead by a slanted roof and underfoot by cobblestone. To your right is the garage. Inside is the green station wagon—nearly new, Father's gift for Mother the year she turned thirty. Ahead, through the breezeway and beyond the driveway, is the barn. The barn is a narrow structure, filled with rusted metal and mouse droppings. Pigeons nest in the rafters. To the left off the breezeway is the backdoor to the house. Inside, there is the immediate impression of being very low to the ground. The ceilings are not abnormally low but the rooms are small and close quartered, with walls made out of bookcases and brick. Through the narrow, brown-tiled kitchen there is the dining square, a right turn off the living room, which has a fireplace at one end. There is a picture window that faces the road and the Leroy house. Down the only hallway there are three bedrooms and one bath. Mother's room is small and painted white. Franny's wide and wood-paneled. I keep the room at the end of the hallway that looks out into the field. There is an unfinished basement beneath all this, a surprisingly airy, cool space with two more bedrooms, another bathroom, and a laundry room in which a painting remains from the previous tenants. In the painting, a man rides a horse through a wind-blown night. The glint from the horse's hooves is the only bright spot in the picture. Franny is frightened of this picture. Mother says that one day we will finish the basement and Franny and I will move downstairs. She assures us that one day we'll want this seclusion. Probably she envisioned this when she was renting the place—her daughters, towheaded and dark-headed and tired of her.

I try to imagine a day so far ahead and cannot. In the early time of Colt's Neck, we live in a state of slow and insistent distancing, every day taking us further from what was before. The nice house. Cocktail parties. Insomnia walks through darkened streets. Ellen Tray gliding towards a waiting car. A stumble on broken cement. A cut lip. A savior in disguise. David's hand gripping the steering wheel. The swell of Nora's hip beneath a bed sheet. Texas cowboys. Boulevards. Coffee cups. Actors.

4.

Susan, Franny, and I were the only students to get on and off the bus at Colt's Neck. The bus was not a school bus, but a town bus that made two runs daily up the main road that eventually found Colt's Neck and the other dirt roads that ran close to the county limits. This bus mostly transported a group of paper mill workers who lived in a trailer park two or three miles north of Colt's Neck. We got on the bus where Colt's Neck met the main road, at the same spot where fourteen years prior, a truck had taken a curve too carelessly and barreled into the side of my father's car, killing Susan Leroy's mother.

Susan and I had vague memories of one another from the years in our childhoods when our parents still visited each other, and for the first three weeks of school, waiting for the bus to arrive, we watched each other tactfully but did not speak. Then one day in late September, I found myself alone at the bus stop with Susan. Franny was forever running late in the mornings, and I usually waited for her, but that morning, for some reason, I had not. I'd left her at the house, still in her nightgown and stirring a spoonful of sugar into a cup of coffee. Mother hadn't come out of her room yet, and Franny had been clanging pots and pans too loudly, opening and closing cupboards, in an attempt at rousing her.

Outside, the morning was very still and cool; there was a low hovering of fog at the base of the mountain, and besides the occasional cloud of smoke emerging from a chimney, the houses stood blank and quiet. I thought of my mother in her little bedroom, the smell of new paint still lingering. After Franny left she would sleep until noon.

When I approached, Susan was squatting at the side of the road, her hair in her mouth. She was studying something.

She looked up when she heard me coming. "Snake skin," she said, her hair dropping. She stood up and pointed. "Shed it right there."

I stood next to her and looked.

"We know each other," said Susan. "My dad knows your dad."

I nodded.

Susan began pacing the width of the road, her arms tucked over her chest. She stopped at the snakeskin and put her hands on her hips. "Is Franny your real sister?" she asked.

I looked up at her. "Of course she is."

"She looks like your dad?"

"I guess she does."

Susan cocked her head. "And what's he like?"

I thought for a moment. "He's an actor," I said finally.

"And where is he now?"

I shook my head and took a step away; Susan was coarser than I had guessed.

"I mean, he's obviously not living with you." Susan looked up the road as she spoke, her gaze intent on our two houses that faced each other as if in stand off. I looked too; the lawns needed mowing. We did not own a lawn mower.

Then Susan sighed, and looked away. She seemed to deflate, her attempt at bullying having failed her. "It's no big thing, you know," she said. "My mother doesn't live with us, either."

"Your mother is dead," I said, startling myself.

Susan did not reply. She studied my face, then walked out to the main road. "Where is that damn bus," she said. She was standing in the middle of the pavement and her long legs, where they emerged from the tops of her knee socks, were freckled and pale.

"I'm sorry," I said, and stepped closer. "I'm sorry Susan," I said again, calling to her.

Susan looked up and shrugged. "No big thing," she said.

We turned at the sound of thudding footsteps. Franny rushed to a halt beside us, her shoes untied, her book bag flapping open and sending loose papers into the air. "Mama said she wasn't going to give me rides anymore," she panted.

We had to scramble to gather up all her papers as the bus pulled in to view, Susan in the ditch gathering muddied spelling lists and math tests, her shoes and socks wet with dew, a slow smile on her face.

I did not hate high school, but I did not embrace it. If Susan and I weren't exactly best friends, we somehow grew into a comfortable routine of keeping each other company, and every day I was more grateful that I wasn't alone when I stepped off the bus and walked through the crowded hallways to my locker. Susan stayed close by, chattering about the cheerleaders and the snakeskin that she'd taken home and preserved in a glass jar and what had happened on her favorite television programs the night before.

At Susan's house there also lived a woman named Joni, who had been dating Jack Leroy for more than a year now. She had moved in that summer when she'd lost her job at the cosmetics counter at Woolworths and could no longer afford to pay her own way. Susan hated Joni, and after explaining the situation as factually as possible one afternoon on the bus, asked that the subject be dropped for good. Clearly, Joni's presence was something that must be silently and stoically endured until it went away, which would surely happen sometime soon, Susan said. A man like her father never got on very long with women like Joni. About Jack, Susan was fiercely protective, even while she seemed to recognize his less than powerful status about town, his quality of inconspicuous humility. He owned the barbershop next to the Felix Diner and carried his lunch in a wrinkled paper bag. On Friday evenings, after closing his shop, he took a glass of scotch at the corner bar, but he did not belong to the men's club near the university; he did not attend concerts or play poker on Saturday nights with a group. In winter he drove a faded brown pickup into work. In warm weather he rode his bicycle.

Out of politeness, I refrained from asking after Joni, though I found her to be intensely curious. Once or twice I had seen her—her curlers wrapped carefully under a purple silk scarf—walking back up Colt's Neck from the corner store. She was always friendly but her expression was somewhat distracted, as if she couldn't quite focus her eyes. Something in the way she walked suggested that she cared little about what the days ahead might bring to her, and perhaps, as Susan said, suggested that she cared little about Jack. Franny and I would return her passing wave, then turn and watch her all the way out of sight.

The heat of summer that year that had held such a tight and earnest fist for so long seemed to dissipate almost overnight, and one morning we woke to a fine frost, a whiteness that coated the tips of the long grasses in the field. By mid-morning, the sun had melted everything away and windows were opened again, but the season had turned without warning, and in the house on Colt's Neck there was a sensation of something loosening, a crossing over into less precarious territory. My mother woke that morning and said she felt her feet more firmly planted.

At school, Susan and I continued to be respectfully ignored. We had come in on a wave of new students from the two junior high schools in town. There were people our age whom we had never set eyes upon, and it began to dawn on us that the small corners of the world we had inhabited up until that point were quite unimportant, and that there were a dozen other girls our age whose mothers were gone away, or sad and angry, whose fathers had given up and disappeared. There were girls from the river houses who washed their hair with lye soap and owned only one pair of tights. There were boys who came to school with black eyes and ripped t-shirts. Some people didn't own winter jackets. Some dressed in angora and pearls but walked home to empty houses. Two girls I had known in junior high concealed pregnancies beneath mounded sweaters. Ellen Tray still slinked about the halls in her boots and mini-skirts, but her brother had been drafted along with a dozen other boys who had once been the backbone of the social structure, and there was palpable rebellion in the crowd. People cried in bathroom stalls and fought in hallways. Everyone was tired, or hungry, or sad, or lonely, or excited, or hopeful, or muted to a kind of inescapable dullness. Susan and I fell in among them, knowing we were nothing new.

5.

On a Friday in early October, Susan invited us over for dinner. "Your mother too," she said as we walked home from the bus stop. We parted at Susan's gate, promising to meet later. At home, we found Mother in the barn, digging through stacks of rotting hay with a pitchfork. She was dressed in jeans and an old shirt of Father's, the tails hanging down to her thighs, her pant legs rolled up above her dusty work boots. Her white shirt was the brightest spot in the dim cave, and slats of afternoon sunlight etched the depth of the barn like gleaming prison bars, their straight beams moving with loose dust and pollen. She was sweating and swearing, and when she saw us standing in the door of the barn she threw the pitchfork away, her body twisting awkwardly with the effort, and came towards us.

"How was the day?" she asked.

"Shitty," Franny said. She gnawed on a piece of straw.

Mother frowned and took the straw from Franny's mouth. "Anything new and exciting happen?" This was her stock question. We had been at school for two months, and everyday she asked this question with decreasing interest. We were somewhere sheltered during the day; we may or may not have been educated. For Mother, at that time, it didn't make much of a difference so long as we came home at a reasonable hour and spoke correctly. My mother believed that the greatest education came after high school, came away from school walls, came in freely chosen books and conversation and the right sort of company. This was a belief she and Father had shared adamantly.

"Susan asked us to dinner tonight," I said.

"All of us?" Mother asked, looking suddenly frightened.

"We want to know about the woman living in her house," Franny said.

"The woman?"

"The woman with purple curlers in her hair," Franny said.

"Jack's girlfriend," I said.

"I see." Mother looked in the direction of the Leroy house, one hand shielding her face from the sun.

We arrived at half past seven. Mother had spent the afternoon throwing things out of the barn into a great heap; rusted hubcaps, split and molding saddles, empty gas tins, blankets humming with moths, and stack after stack of rotting hay. At six, she'd finally come inside, her shirt stuck to her back with sweat, her face streaked with lines of dust and grit. I followed her to the bathroom, where she washed her bare feet in the sink, the water running in black rivets down the drain.

"Are you going to dinner like that?" I asked.

Mother looked down at her shirt; rust colored sweat stains had gathered under her breasts.

"Couldn't you change first?"

"Yes, of course," she said. She was quiet for a moment, the lather foaming between her fingers and toes as she scrubbed, the fresh, sharp scent of soap filtering through the bathroom. "I'll be right along," she said as I went out.

Now we stood three abreast at the Leroy's front door, Franny in a purple dress that Susan had donated to her, me still in my school clothes, Mother in a sweater and summer skirt, slightly wrinkled. Susan answered the door. "Hello there!" she cried. She beamed at Mother. "I'm Susan," she said, extending her hand.

"I remember," Mother said. Susan stood back and let us enter. The front hallway was dark. We followed Susan's shape into a wide room with a wall of windows that gave a view of the back yard, a space hedged neatly in flaming red bushes. At a wooden table in the yard sat a woman talking on the telephone. She was wrapped in a thick grey sweater. Through a sliding glass door in the wall the phone cord was stretched taut, and every now and then the woman brought a cigarette to her red lips. Her legs were pulled up, crisscrossed in her chair. Her hair hung in waves down her back, free of curlers, and the sun caught the glint of it as it came through the bushes. Susan went to the door.

"Joan!" she cried. The woman looked up. "My guests are here."

Joan murmured something into the telephone and stood up. She came towards us in one smooth, continuous motion: the phone moving away from her ear, the cigarette being tossed to the ground and stubbed out, the arm extending itself and sliding open the door, letting in a soft gust of cooling evening air.

"I'm Joni," the woman said to Mother.

"Nora."

There was silence for a moment and then, as if nudged by some invisible cue, Joni came to life. She beamed and clapped her hands together. She swung her sweater from her shoulders, revealing a green turtleneck that strained over her breasts, and put an arm around Susan, who grimaced visibly under her touch. "What fun!" Joni cried. "Susie's been wanting you all over for weeks." She gestured for us all to sit down and moved towards the kitchen, which was divided from the rest of the room by a tall counter lined on the front edge with a row of porcelain elephants, varying in color and size. Franny watched these with intent eyes. Jack Leroy had still not appeared, and his absence was a felt thing; from the corner of my eye I could see Mother looking about the room, as if she expected Jack to appear from behind the bookcase or grandfather clock.

"What would everyone like to drink?" Susan asked. She went to the cupboard and began taking glasses down. Franny had perched herself on a stool in front of the elephants, and she was gingerly running her finger along a milky blue figure, its trunk flung high in the air.

"Do you like them?" Joni asked.

Franny quickly pulled her hand away.

"I've got one from every city I've lived in."

"You've lived this many places?"

"Oh God, probably more than you see there, but I broke a few in all the moves," said Joni. She knelt and opened the oven; a smell of curry filtered through the living room. When she stood up, she leaned across the counter and pointed out a black elephant. "This one does a trick," she said. They all watched as she lifted the elephant's trunk and removed a cigarette from his mouth. Immediately another white stub appeared there. "See?" she said. From her pocket she pulled a slender white lighter. "Now," she said, exhaling a long stream of smoke, "we have shrimp for appetizers if anyone's hungry, it is a little late, but Jack called and said he'd be along soon. He had business in town today, right, Susie?"

"I guess," Susan said sullenly. She was glaring at Joni. In the light that filled the room her hair stood up like an unruly halo.

"Well anyway," said Joni, seemingly unbothered by Susan's tone, "why don't you bring in something to drink? There's ginger ale, but I don't suppose anyone would mind if we ladies had a cocktail or two?" She looked at Mother.

"Ginger ale is fine," said Mother.

Joni shrugged and came around to the living room where she perched on a stool next to the elephants. "Now," said Joni, "how old are you, Franny?"

"Twelve, this month," said Franny.

"Twelve," said Joni, nodding slowly. She leaned back against the counter, her eyes studying the ceiling, as if her entire twelfth year were painted in detail on the white plaster.

"That's quite a year. Quite a year." She began humming softly to herself, then turned abruptly to Susan, who had delivered the ginger ale and taken a seat on the arm of my chair. "Could you bring me a gimlet, Susie?"

Mother cleared her throat.

"Are you sure you won't have one, Nora?" asked Joni.

"Oh, no thank you."

Susan let out a ragged sigh and went back to the kitchen.

Joni turned to me. "Now," she said. "Grace. Susan tells me that you two ride the same bus."

"We're in the same class," said Susan from the kitchen.

"And how do like high school?"

"It's alright."

"Freshman year is hard, don't you think Nora?"

Mother nodded. "I suppose," she said.

"I got into all sorts of trouble that year," Joni laughed, her long neck thrown back. She took the drink that Susan handed her. "All sorts of trouble," she said again.

"I'll bet," Susan mumbled.

"Pardon?" asked Joni. For an instant her face became wary, and she looked around the living room at each of us in turn, as if she had missed the punch line to some communal joke.

"I ate my lunch in the girls' bathroom when I was a freshman in high school," Mother interjected loudly. We all turned to look at her. "Every single day until almost the end of the year, when I met a girl whose name I don't even remember now. But she ate with me then. In the band room." She took a small sip of her ginger ale and brushed some dust from her skirt.

"In the bathroom?" asked Franny.

"In the bathroom."

"Poor Mother."

Mother laughed. "I'm fine now. Now I like to eat alone, don't you?" She looked at Joni, who seemed to be trying to remember a time when she'd eaten any meal without company. Before Joni could speak, there was the sound of the front door opening, and Susan jumped up and ran to the front hall. Mother stared after her, her body erect.

"Guest, guests!" we heard Susan whispering loudly, and then they appeared together in the living room, Jack's tie loosened, his thick hair standing up raggedly on his head, Susan holding tightly to his elbow.

He saw Mother first, or perhaps, his eyes searched for her first, and when they found her he nodded, clearing his throat. "Nora, hello," he said. He reached to grip the hand that she offered. She seemed breathless at the sight of him, having stepped too close in her greeting, as if expecting an embrace.

Susan tugged at his arm. "This is Grace and Franny," she said. "Grace is in my class."

Jack nodded again. He seemed ill at ease even in his own living room, his smile half-drawn and uncertain, his jacket clutched and strangled in his left hand.

"And I'm Joni!" Joni laughed boisterously, breaking the thick silence that had fallen. She stubbed out her cigarette and blew a kiss in Jack's direction. "We're all starving, Mr. Leroy," she said, going around to the kitchen, "so hurry up and wash."

Though it wasn't really quite warm enough for it, we ate in the Leroy's meticulous back lawn, our fingers growing cold around our silverware, the wicker furniture creaking under our every movement. "I love the fall out here," Joni said, licking her fingers clean. "The colors are so beautiful." She sighed and leaned back in her chair, drawing her thin legs up to her chest. "I could eat every meal out of doors."

"I thought you hated the out of doors," said Susan.

"The house is still lovely," said Mother.

"Alice loved it," Jack said. He looked straight at Mother when he spoke.

"Alice was Jack's first wife," said Joni. Her face had paled slightly.

"Yes, I knew her."

"How did you know her?" Franny asked. Mother looked at her and waited before answering, as if trying to find something familiar in her face.

"Your father and I knew her," she said. She looked at Jack. "David's back East now," she said.

Jack only nodded.

"He's back East," Mother repeated, not really addressing anyone anymore.

"Oh, honey," said Joni, giving Mother a knowing look. "It's an impossible thing, keeping a man."

"Excuse me?"

I hid my face in my hands.

Joni seemed confused. "I didn't mean anything by it," she said. "I've lost my share of men too." She gazed at Jack. "You've just got to wait for the right one to come along. That's all there is to it."

Jack was studying his dinner plate, his face red.

"I'll have to remember that," Mother said. She took her empty glass and tilted it far back, searching for any remaining drop.

6.

In October we burned brush. We helped Mother haul cartloads of dead or dying branches and leaves to a heap in the center of the field, a good distance beyond the grove of apple trees, where we lit the whole thing and let it burn down, watching it with buckets of water in hand until it made a great black circle in the earth. The smell was the best smell I could imagine. In the old neighborhood people would occasionally burn their leaves in October, sending small funnels of smoke rising off their manicured lawns, but the smell was a sharp and rotting one, not at all comparable to the scent of dead pine and field fire. Late in the evening, when the pile had burned far down and nearly all the light had gone from the sky, we re-filled the buckets and placed them around the periphery of the smoking circle and went into the house, our faces and eyes stinging from exposure, our hands lined with ash, the tips of Franny's blonde hair singed in places from times she had gone too close to the fire. I felt that I had never known such perfect exhaustion; everything felt clean and good after that day. The water from the shower ran in dirty rivets from my feet to the drain. That night we boiled tamales on the stove and ate them with ketchup and peas in front of the television. Around ten, Mother went out to put a final bucket over the fire. Franny and I were in bed together, and under the sheet our skin still smelled like the woody smoke. Out in the field, there was the swoosh and slow hiss of water seeping into the hot spaces buried deep in the pile and the clank of the bucket handle falling down. Mother went to the side of the house, and the squeak of the faucet letting open and the hose filling the bucket again could be heard through the open window above the bed where we lay together. There was silence then for a time and only the occasional movement far out in the field that was our mother, still at work.

"Someone's out there with her," said Franny, breaking the silence. She stood up on the bed so that she could see out the window. "I hear him."

"Who?"

"Mr. Leroy," she said. I knelt beside her. Outside, leaning

against the top rail of the fence halfway down the field, stood Jack Leroy. He was barely visible in the dark, but his height and the way he would occasionally run a hand backwards over his head, nape to brow, gave him away. Mother stood on the other side of the fence, a full bucket in each hand. They were talking; I couldn't make out their words but their mouths moved and their bodies responded, yes, no, a laugh or two. Mother turned to look back at the burn pile, and while she was looking away, Jack knelt swiftly and ducked through the wide slats of the railings, rising up beside her and taking a bucket, following her when she started across the field. They threw the water over the pile, two arcs and splashes, two plumes of smoke rising in the air. We watched them speak a few minutes longer until Jack gave a final nod of his head and strode away, ducking again through the fence and swinging his way across the dirt road toward home. He was whistling. Mother stood still in the field. Watching her, I had a sudden and full longing to be out there too, to be older, a part of a story, like my mother was, to trade everything with her, whatever she had been dealt.

Franny and I made careful watch of Jack Leroy after that night. We were becoming aware of our mother in a new way, as a person separate from her duties as guardian and provider, as comforter in rough times. In this place, where the house and the land that surrounded her were her own, bought and paid for slowly, in monthly chunks, she held a greater authority than she had in the town house with Father. With Jack, she perfected an air of solemn confidence; she listened intently while he advised her about winter insulation, leaky roofs, broken fence posts. Watching her, I put it down in my mind that close listening, and perhaps even a carefully feigned naivety, were qualities a woman should perfect.

Jack was a tall man, becoming slightly stooped as he grew older, but he was graceful all the same, and kept a head of thick, neat hair. He never spoke very loudly; he was perhaps incapable of visibly strong emotion, and he gave his advice to Mother in a deferring manner, waiting for the moment she might stop and correct or doubt him. He liked to feel helpful; Joni, it seemed, did not require a great deal of assistance in her daily makings. He carried over his ladder one afternoon and cleared the rain gutters, Mother watching him from the barn where she was struggling with a pitchfork and a great mound of hay—she had purchased a milk cow and a confused, squawking brood of hens. All together, along with Susan, we went on excursions into the woods behind the house where Jack cut trees and split the wood, neatly lining the cords in the bed of his truck. Susan and Franny and I ran wild on these trips; hatless, unhinged, and hoping for snow. There seemed no danger of becoming lost; through any stand of swaying pines we could pause and listen, waiting for the sharp sound of Jack's ax, reverberating through the still, cold forest.

The sky had been a stubborn grey for weeks. Joni stayed at home, doing her nails or watching soap operas, Susan reported. Despite her prior claim, Joni was generally fearful of the out of doors. Susan herself was fearful of woodcutting, though she was loathe to admit as much. The chainsaw, the ax, the splitting maul back in the field, where one could cleave the larger pieces into burnable chunks—these implements were loud and capable of destruction, if one were to become careless, and Susan kept a good distance while Jack and Mother felled trees, coming close only when the cry of the saw had stopped for good. She came along to escape the house, to escape Joni. *God forbid*, she had a habit of saying, when Jack was just out of earshot, *she turn out like her.*

For all his assistance to her, Jack rarely showed much more than a friendly interest in Mother. Every conversation concluded with a nod of his head, a definitive goodbye and a resolute stride away, his head bent against the cold. Mother would watch him go; she followed his form across the field, the road, down the path to his own property where his own daily work must be done. She required a good deal of help that fall; though she was ashamed of her ineptness, her incomplete knowledge of the place. Jack never seemed to weary of her though; he had a knack for knowing the right moment to appear—as the bailing twine could not be cinched tightly enough around the bales; as the well seemed in danger of freezing over; as the hens got loose on the mountain—there Jack would be, wool jacket on, cracked palms open and ready, face calm and careful. He was a sure and steadying presence, and we quickly became accustomed to him.

The cold weather came on early that year, and with its encroach Mother's work took on a new ferocity; she was finished with the barn by mid-October, the milk cow and chickens snuggly settled, the winter supply of hay neatly stacked. Once the fence posts had been mended, the rain gutters cleared, and the storm windows cracked sharply into place between aged and swollen frames, she moved to the garage and the house, where unpacked boxes still remained.

In the garage, she dug through dozens of boxes, all of them containing books, and most of them Father's. These would eventually end up in one of the spare bedrooms in the basement. She would work feverishly on this small space for the next week, filling it with a single bed and side table, bookcases, and a small desk with a long, shallow, and empty drawer. It was a room for him, I realized; the deep ochre on the walls had seemed strange at first but was fitting; it was easy to imagine my father in that room, if he were to come back for a weekend, a month, a season. The light from the lamp would make the whole room glow softly, and he would lie in that single bed, one leg thrown on top of the blankets, and leaf through the pages of the books he'd read as a student, in the days and months when he was first loving my mother. This was what she must have envisioned, those afternoons spent dusting and painting in the basement; she must have been remembering an earlier time, years of which Franny and I were ignorant. It was true that we could not fathom the pattern of our parents' lives then; we could not understand why our mother would keep such books, such seemingly boring and forgotten things. "Why are we keeping them?" Franny asked as we arranged the bookshelves with tattered jackets and spines, her arms smeared with traces of drying ochre paint.

Mother shrugged in answer. "They're not all mine," she said, running a finger swiftly over the bumpy trail of bindings. "Not all mine to give away." After the work in the room was complete, she shut off the light, closed the door, and left the space to stand quiet and waiting, never saying another word about it. For some time after, we were acutely aware of the room's presence beneath us when we were in the upper part of the house. Sometimes, when folding laundry or searching for a board game, Franny and I would dare each other to open the door to the room and sit on the bed with the light turned off. We could not quite understand the somewhat dangerous thrill of this game; he was not dead, but his absence, in the first months after his leaving, held an impression of permanence, and though no one ever said it, it was his ghost that lingered soundlessly behind the closed door in that small, cleanly swept space.

Actual contact with our father was delegated to brief, somewhat scripted exchanges that took place over the phone every Sunday afternoon. His conversations with Mother were less formal; they ranged wildly in emotion, on her side at least, swinging from feverish and stubborn accusations, to calm and businesslike debates; occasionally there would be kindness, perhaps a brief moment of laughter. Franny and I were adept at deducing each phone call's mood from a distance, since the conversations between our parents were kept cloistered, tucked away from us and mostly conducted in the early morning, before we'd risen, or late at night when we were supposed to be sleeping. But there was a pattern in the aftermath of these exchanges; if they spoke in the morning, we would come home to an empty house. Mother would have gathered enough energy to go to campus, leaving a note behind that read either *Your Father says he loves you* or *Call your Father to say hello.* These were the happier talks, the adult steadiness of the exchange momentarily buoying Mother's spirits, returning her to greater confidence or autonomy, a place where she was capable of driving herself into town to the streets and the office that retained so much of an earlier life.

A late night conversation, though, produced a much darker tenor. There would be no note for us, no quick relay of our father's continued existence. The morning after would be strained; Mother would not have slept, and would walk around aimlessly, drinking cup after cup of coffee and picking up objects that had yet to find a place in the new home, examining their contours as if mystified; *who bought these things?* She'd ask us as we readied ourselves for school, trying to avoid looking at our mother. *Where the hell do we put all these things?* She would stay in her robe until noon or later, eventually setting upon a project around the house that required a great deal of physical labor, and late in the day we would find her, flushed and wild-eyed, her hands raw and her hair knotted.

When Franny and I spoke with our father, the conversations never lasted more than ten or fifteen minutes. A conversation with him on the telephone, we discovered, was really no different than a conversation with him in person. When he was still living with us, he would direct dinner table conversation like a board member keeping minutes: *You— Franny, Grace—what did you do today in school? Did you enjoy yourself? What homework do you have?* These were the same questions that now came through the telephone, our father keeping up with us from two thousand miles as he had kept up with us from the head of the dinner table.

There came a point, in each phone call, when his voice changed for a moment, and the distance to him, the fact of his going away, would find its way into the wire. He would grow silent, and there would sometimes be the murmur of another voice behind him. Then he would come back asking, inevitably, *Everything is fine?* Not a question at all, really, but a moment of doubt, a desire for one of us to calm or secure him. *Oh yes,* we would reply in unison, our faces pressed together over the mouthpiece, our voices going up in octave, so alike it was funny. Oh yes, everything is fine.

It got to be a joke between us: *and is everything fine with you, Franny? And you, Grace?* we would ask each other in mock, singsong voices around the house, when we crossed paths after school, when we woke in the morning. *Oh yes, everything is just fine,* we'd answer, laughing, but feeling all the while, underneath our humor, the tinge of dangerous sadness that had the capacity to grow and lodge itself permanently inside.

This was a grown up sort of sadness, something we'd never felt before but had surely seen in our mother, clinging to her like a desperate animal. *Something with claws,* Franny once said, trying to describe the sensation. *Something you've got to shake off and scare away.* The feeling would linger for an hour or two after every phone call, then would dissipate with Mother's arrival home from campus, or the finishing of outside work for the day, and we would all begin to look forward to dinner and what was playing on the television that evening. All these distractions—everyday junctures of coming in from the cold, the release of feet from walk-worn shoes, the promise of food and the final settling into evening routine—all of this could make us forget the slow seeping feeling of sorrow that was like a drip, a broken faucet hidden somewhere we could not find. Only late at night would the feeling surface again, in the minutes between turning off the bedside lamp and waiting for sleep to come. There were no distractions from it then; the only trick was to close one's eyes and let it be. We became accustomed to it, all three of us, though we did not discuss it at length. How did one own up to a thing like that, anyway? Sadness became like a shameful secret that could come out and rub at us until we were resigned and raw. Openly admitting to sorrow would seem like a final surrender, and even worse, a selfish weakness. Here was a good day or a bad day, but a day just like the one before, like the one to come; we woke under warm blankets; we stepped into slippers that knew the contours of our feet; we opened cupboards to food, walked the path to school, to work, came home again. Above all, we had each other. Someone had gone missing, but what else could we do? Who were we to say we were unique? Who were we to assume we were the only ones who had ever known a sadness.

7.

On the afternoon of Halloween—Franny's birthday—we returned home from school to find Mother kneeling in the basement beside a mound of clean laundry. "Something came for you," she said to Franny, easing off the cold cement, the knees of her pant legs dusty. "Look in the kitchen."

On the kitchen table sat a flat box with a New York postmark. Franny found a pair of scissors and sliced through the cardboard. Father had sent a box of drawing pencils, a sheaf of cardstock in a muted yellow, candied cigarettes, and a small, thick book called *Birds of North America.* On the inside flap he had written, *My favorite is the Yellow Warbler. They are tricky little devils. A very happy birthday to my small girl.* We thumbed through the book to find the Yellow Warbler, a small, bright bird. "Pretty pencils," I said, running a finger over the sharpened colors.

"I guess I'll be an artist," Franny said, taking out a candied cigarette and practicing her fake inhale. It seemed just like our father to send a present like that, another attempt at trying to make artists out of us in some way, and I missed him fully then, fully and in a way I had not yet known, a yearning that made my head ache. I was beginning to learn that missing was an emotion of varying colors; it was possible to miss the idea of someone, the knowledge of them, without really longing after their true person. In another way—this being the tougher of the two—it was possible to miss someone's full body, their actual presence, and then you got to thinking that you'd like them there beside you, simply so you might smell them and hear the tenor of their voice.

I left Franny to her cigarettes and birds and went back downstairs, feeling that it was foolish to miss anyone over a box of drawing pencils. Mother looked up when I came in.

"He sent nice things?" she asked. I looked at my mother; on her face was poorly concealed curiosity, and I knew that she had been eyeing the box since it had arrived, willing herself not to care about its contents. But she did care. She had been desperate to open the box, to test the smell of the wrappings, for she'd surely find the same familiar scent that made her heart come loose from its hold; she'd surely touch objects that he had touched—an instant of distant, fragmented union— and sent her way.

"Nice things, yes," I said, kneeling to help her with the laundry.

Mother made hot shrimp for Franny's birthday dinner, and we sat around the kitchen table with paper napkins tucked into our collars, dipping the shrimp and bread in the big pan of oily sauce. "If you don't eat too much candy, there'll be cake when you get home," Mother said.

Franny hollered and leapt from her seat, throwing her napkin aside. "Put your costume on, Gracie," she yelled as she raced down the hallway.

Mother was in good spirits that evening; she seemed to have forgotten about the package from Father, and she hummed as she cleared the table. She turned on the radio in the kitchen, and every now and then while we were dressing we could hear her singing a low note or two.

Franny's bedroom was awash with pieces of clothing she had collected from every closet in the house—she had even unearthed old suits of Father's. She had decided to dress as Charlie Chaplin. I was to be Cleopatra. From a pile on her desk, Franny took an old sheet and a frayed gold belt and draped these about me with flare. "We'll have to iron your hair," she said, studying me. "Cleopatra had straight hair."

So we set up the ironing board in the living room and had Mother do the straightening. Lots of girls at the high school straightened their hair, securing it in place with gobs of Dippity Do, but I had yet to perfect the art of ironing my own hair; the first time I'd tried I'd singed off a two-inch section in back.

When Mother had finished, Franny ran her palms over my head. "You're like a lady in a movie," she said. Mother took our picture before we left, our long underwear poking out in odd places from beneath our costumes, Franny's bowler hat not quite fitting over her winter cap. We waved to Mother, leaving her dark figure moving about the warm, well-lit rooms of the house, and wheeled our bicycles out into the cold darkness to meet Susan at her front gate.

Susan was waiting for us; we could make out the halo of her blond wig and white dress across the road. Her long underwear was nude colored, bought special for the occasion by Joni, Susan explained in her best Joni imitation. "She said, Marilyn showed skin, and you've got to also if you're going to be her." She rolled her eyes. Franny plucked at a corner of the long-sleeved silk shirt, testing its elasticity.

Susan had been instructed to stop at Sedina Harris's house, which stood at the very end of Colt's Neck, closest to the main road, before heading for town. Sedina threw a Halloween party every year, Susan explained, but this year Jack had too much work to finish in town, so Susan should stop by for a moment to at least say hello. This explanation carefully covered up the deeper reason for Susan's desire to stop by the party: Susan was infinitely fascinated by Sedina Harris.

Around Sedina there existed a quiet rumor of promiscuity, a certain nonchalance when it came to the number of gentleman friends she entertained in a month. She seemed to draw people to her, and there were always strange cars parked in her driveway, always different men and women stopping by and leaving late in the night or not even until morning. These comings and goings could be easily observed from the windows of the other houses on Colt's Neck; Sedina's house was set up higher on the hillside, and held a vantage of the small, smooth valley through which the dirt road ran. She must have had a beautiful view, but everyone else had a view of her—Franny kept count of the figures leaving at dawn in a single week; one week counting ten silhouetted bodies in all, stumbling into the cold morning and struggling to get their engines running again. We longed to see the inside of that house.

"Joni was dying to go, of course," Susan reported. We wheeled our bikes slowly in the direction of Sedina's house.

"Why didn't she?" Franny asked.

Susan scratched angrily at her scalp where her wig was pinned too tightly. "My dad keeps the shop open late Fridays," she said.

"So go alone."

"Doubtful." Susan gave a barking laugh. "Sedina only included her to be polite. Besides, she had some other party in town, at the hotel." We'd reached the foot of the wooden staircase that wound up the hill to Sedina's front door.

"The Franklin Hotel?" asked Franny, but Susan was no longer paying attention. Her gaze was locked on the house.

"I've been in before," she said. "At some party when I was little. She had one bathroom all painted purple, even the floor was purple."

"Then let's go in," Franny said, impatient. She skipped around Susan and took the steps two at a time, her oversized men's shoes, held in place by layers of thick socks underneath, slapping against the cold wood. Susan and I followed.

We waited in silence after Franny rang the bell, listening to the low vibrations of conversation and cracking bursts of laughter that filtered through the door. The door itself was framed by a border of multi-colored panes of glass, and after a while, we began to make out a contorted shape of a figure approaching from the other side, a woman's figure, tall but well-rounded. The knob turned, and Sedina stood before us in a long white dress. Her feet were bare, and her graying hair was loose down her back. Her face remained blank for just an instant too long, long enough to make all three of us shrink back, but then she smiled, and we saw how white her teeth were, and how the bones of her face were still strong under the aging skin of her face. "You've come," she said, standing aside and gesturing to us with a long, tanned arm. We passed through the door with the colored glass. Inside, there was the strong scent of cooking oil and a sweet spice, hard to identify. "We're all in the living room," Sedina said over her shoulder as we followed her down a dimly lit hallway. Then she winked, catching Franny's eye. "The candy's in there, too." The hallway, made up floor to ceiling of dark, polished wood, ended in the living room, a bright, circular room with two walls of windows that looked out onto the dark Colt's Neck valley. The room was full of people in various states of bizarre dress; there was a priest and a nun, a man in a grey robe and a headdress, a woman with all exposed skin painted sky blue. Franny found the candy bowl, and Sedina searched for someone in the crowd; in the room there was the pleasant sound of low voices working together, the hum broken occasionally by a high pitch of laughter or the knocking of ice against crystal.

Sedina found the person she'd been looking for, and

she waved us to follow her across the room. She guided us towards the wall of windows where there stood a thin boy, hunched in a corner and glaring out at the room of painted faces. This was Charlie Mullan. He was about fifteen, with a head of hair so thick it had a beaten look; no doubt his mother would have attacked it with a wet boar bristle brush before pushing him out the door with his father. Mrs. Mullan did not attend parties, but was the kind of woman who felt it her duty to interact socially in some ways, to keep face. She did not know that the face she'd cultivated over the years was that of a frightened, awkward woman married to an angry man and mother to a watchful, silent, half-deaf teenage boy.

But Charlie Mullan, silent as he may be under the protective palm of his mother and the frustrated fist of his father, was not frightened. He was just too busy watching other people to say much about himself. He'd watched us since we'd moved into the old farm house. He'd watched us and no doubt he'd learned some things from listening, when he could, to the stories his father brought home from The Roosevelt, which was the bar where his friends gathered for beers each night before heading home. It was easy to watch and see that there was no father in our house, but there was no mother in the Leroy house, either, also easy to see, and this wasn't such a strange thing. Charlie had known Susan all his life, and so knew about the death of her mother, and about the way Jack Leroy carried on afterwards. Jack wasn't a happy man, but he wasn't a grief-dweller—he'd moved on and found another woman. These were Charlie's father's words—another woman—and they held in them a note of respect, even though Charlie knew his father thought Jack Leroy to be arrogant, or a little strange, since he didn't go drinking with the other men or come to talk about the weather or the way the price of gasoline was going up. Charlie liked Jack Leroy because Jack Leroy was quiet and watchful, like he was, and he liked him because he was nothing like his own father.

At Sedina's party, Charlie watched his father stumbling around the room after drinking too much whiskey. He'd refused to wear a costume, but at the last minute had let his wife thrust a mask into his hand. Now the mask was flattened and cracked from where he'd been sitting on it all evening.

Charlie had been staring at his father, watching for the reddened neck that would signal an end to the night and a silent walk home, when Sedina appeared with the three of us in tow. Charlie shrank back when he saw us, but Sedina reached out and drew him forward with one of her long arms. "Where did your father get to?" she asked, though Charlie knew she'd seen him at the bar, for where else would he be. She didn't wait for Charlie to answer, but turned him, her arm holding him firmly, to face us. "You all know Charlie Mullan?" she asked.

We nodded in unison. Certainly we knew Charlie Mullan, though 'knowing' was a loose term, as to know any of the Mullans was mostly to watch them from a distance, as Charlie watched all of us, and to form slightly darkened opinions of them, however untrue. Susan was the only one who knew the inside of the Mullan house; before Jack had trusted her home alone after school, she'd gone to the Mullans' for dreary afternoons spent doing homework at the kitchen table, drinking carrot juice, and listening to Mrs. Mullan's radio, which was always tuned to the religious station. When she'd turned ten, Susan had refused to keep going, and since Charlie was being homeschooled by then, she saw little more of him.

Franny and I knew Charlie from the distance that

divided our homes, a wide pasture of sweet grass that Charlie navigated every afternoon when his mother set him free from his lessons. Afternoons, Charlie made rounds of his parents' property, walking the perimeter of the fences and watching for any human activity at the neighboring houses. And so we watched Charlie Mullan watching us, when we were out in the barn or the garage or the side-lawn. We watched him watch and began watching him right back, and in this way we came to an understanding with him that was something like friendship. At school, Charlie Mullan was a source of some gossip because of his handicap, and his homeschooling, and his often drunk father at the corner bar, and his crazy mother. He was also interesting because Charlie Mullan was considered handsome. At fifteen, he was already nearly six-feet tall, and his skin had a ruddy, wind-blown look from all his time out of doors. Only the somewhat timid expression on his face made him look his true age.

This was the expression on his face as he let Sedina hold him in place before us. "You're not dressed up," said Franny, surveying Charlie's clothing. She spoke through a mouthful of sticky candy.

Charlie looked at her blankly, then bent forward with surprising gentlemanlike precision, one hand behind his back, the other cupped to his ear. "Pardon?" he said.

Franny took a step back, landing on Susan's toe.

"You'll have to speak up," said Sedina. She turned to Charlie. "Left ear, is it?"

Susan looked shocked, but Charlie only nodded, pointing to his right year. "Ask me on this side," he said.

Franny giggled and ducked behind me.

"I thought Charlie might make the rounds with you," said Sedina.

"Has he got a bike?" Susan asked, crossing her arms.

"I have," said Charlie, and Susan turned crimson.

This satisfied Sedina, who left as quickly and ethereally as she'd appeared, saying that she'd fix things up for Charlie's father, which meant that she'd get him along home somehow, probably walking him herself, so he wouldn't end up asleep in the ditch but in his bed with his nervous wife.

At the Mullan place Charlie ran ahead into the barn and came back wheeling his bicycle, a flashlight tucked through a belt loop of his jeans. He took this and held it out to Susan. "Balance this in your basket?" he asked.

Susan watched him a moment before taking the flashlight and switching it on, its quick yellow beam lighting up the weeds and water pipes in the ditch beside us. With the light balanced forward in her basket she led the way down the road. At the head of Colt's Neck, where the paved road began, one of Susan's heels flew off and she caught her ankle on the ridge of her pedal, ripping a hole in her tights. Charlie was off his bicycle in an instant, searching for the shoe in the wet grasses. He found it and came running back, kneeling to cup the heel back against Susan's foot, then re-mounting his bicycle and turning onto the paved road that led us towards the lights of town.

We left our bikes in the alley behind the Felix Diner and headed for the houses of the university neighborhoods, where the best candy was found. There were throngs of kids out, darting over lawns and flowerbeds, running in groups down the streets. Windows threw long arms of light from their frames, and in a few yards, fathers had lit fires, tossing in armloads of the dead leaves they'd raked up earlier that day. Franny ran ahead, ringing doorbells and calling out for us to keep up, but Susan and I found ourselves suddenly self-conscious, embarrassed at what now seemed a childish activity. Charlie didn't seem to think anything of being out without a costume, of being out trick or treating at fifteen; he followed Franny politely, his hands tucked in the pockets of his jacket, listening with his cocked head while she described the intricacies of candy; what was good, what was bad, what was considered random good luck or a sign of household wealth.

Susan was constantly stopping to adjust her stockings, which rode up underneath her dress, or her wig, which itched behind the ears. "Probably we're a little too old for this," she said to me at one point, watching Franny run screaming across the street with a group of boys from her class at the elementary school. "I heard there were some parties going on," she said. "Not that we'd get invited."

I glanced at Susan, limping along beside me; there were blue shadows beneath her eyes, and the skin at the edge of her face was red and irritated from itching at her wig. I thought about her going home to Jack and Joni; Joni already a few gimlets in and asking Susan to fix her another; Jack silent and withdrawn in his arm chair, smiling wanly at his daughter when she came in the door dragging her sack of candy; Jack watching his daughter, caught in his daily surprise over how much she resembled the long-dead woman he had once loved. I reached out for my friend and linked an arm through hers. "Franny's birthday cake is at home," I said. Then, "and maybe you could spend the night." This seemed to cheer Susan slightly, and together we ran a few yards to catch up with Charlie and Franny.

Franny was stopped still on the sidewalk, looking up at the house in front of her; her bulging pillowcase slumped at her feet. We had come, without noticing, to the block where the old house sat, taking up the corner lot. Even in the shadows I could detect a fresh coat of paint around the windows, and the way the half-moon flowerbeds by the front stoop now had a cleaned out, cared for look; little gates stood around them marking their shape and the earth was black and waiting for spring planting. We had heard that a retired couple now lived in the house; the man used to teach political science at the university and his wife gave piano lessons from their living room. There were three sons, all grown and gone from home, and the husband sometimes wrote editorials for the newspaper that Mother read simply so she could say out loud that she'd read something written by the man who now lived in the house, a lifeline she must have felt was important and somehow healthy to maintain.

Inside the house there was a party underway; through the thin fabric of the curtains I could see figures moving about, a great number of them. There was the sound of someone at the piano, thundering out a waltz, then an abrupt stop to the music and a shout of laughter. "Are we going up?" Charlie asked, shaking Franny from her reverie. But Franny looked to me and I shook my head no. We moved on, Susan and Charlie following without question.

It was Charlie who spotted Mother and Jack. We had collected our bicycles and were wheeling them out of the alley when Charlie stopped and touched my shoulder, nodding towards the wide front window of the diner. Mother and Jack were sitting at the counter, halfway down the long row of stools, their heads bent together, talking in earnest. At that hour the diner was almost full; groups of students filled the side booths, their voices a rising and falling din as the front door was swung open, people leaving and arriving, the bell over the entryway a steady ringing. Mother was still in her working clothes from the day; her boots and jeans were dusty but she'd brushed her hair smooth and it glinted in the high, yellow lights. Now and then she would twist it in a long rope and settle it along her back. Jack was watching her over his coffee cup. When she reached for her hair again, he said something, a grin on his face, and she began laughing, letting her hair fall loose around her back and shoulders. Jack reached out and gathered the hair, holding it back loosely in his fist. When he let go, his hand lingered on her body without shyness, his fingers spread wide between her shoulder blades.

"Your mother?" Charlie said, and I looked away to find that Susan, too, was staring through the window, her face quite still and empty. She looked away and met my gaze, but I could not read what was there; the paleness of her face seemed to overtake her whole being. Franny had not seen; she was kneeling on the concrete, digging through her bag of candy. I stared at her, her thin limbs crouching crab-like on a sidewalk on an October night. Time seemed to stretch around me, making any swift movement or clear thought difficult. There was that odd sensation one has when any definite emotion seems elusive; it did not seem particularly right that Mother and Jack should be sitting and touching as they were; nor did it seem quite wrong.

I kept watch of Susan's face, hoping for some guidance, but Susan had turned resolutely away and was positioning herself on her bicycle. "Home?" she said, then reached down and snatched off both of her high heels, tossing them into the basket a bit too forcefully, so that they bounced together and almost fell out.

The road was darker riding home, and the beam from Charlie's flashlight wavered and sputtered, finally giving out as we made the turn onto Colt's Neck. Behind us came the crunching sound of car tires on gravel, and we turned blinking into the burst of Mother's headlights as she swung the station wagon onto the road. She was rolling the window down as she slowed beside us, and she was smiling, her face flushed and bright. "Good loot?" she called out, resting her forearm on the open window. Franny let her bicycle fall and rushed forward, opening her bag for Mother to see.

Susan watched Mother, studying her face and hands, both of which were young but weathered, the work on Colt's Neck already having changed her since our arrival not three months ago. The long rope of hair was now hanging down her breast. Susan absently scratched at her own damp and matted hair, finally freed from the blond wig. "See my dad in town?" she asked.

Mother looked up. She took a moment before answering, turning back to Franny and smiling carefully. "I did," she finally said, not looking at Susan when she spoke. There was cake at home, she said, and we all should come along, Susan and Charlie too. We slowly followed her taillights up the road, but at the driveway Susan stopped and went no further, considering the dark windows of her house across the way.

"I'd better go in," she said.

"Don't you want cake?" I asked.

"I think I'll go in."

"You could come over with Jack."

Susan looked at me and gave a snort of laughter. "He'll be at the hotel," she said, "gathering Joni." She wheeled away without saying goodnight, and I watched her white dress bobbing away.

Charlie said he'd better leave too, fearing the state of his father after Sedina's party. He said goodbye with a lopsided salute, walking his bicycle in perfect balance with one steady hand and whistling as he went, the sound of it cutting clear across the dark fields.

In the house, I found Mother alone in the kitchen.

"No Susan?" she asked, poking candles into the cake.

I shook my head. I felt a strange timidity, so that I kept to the edges of the room.

"You have a fight?" Mother asked. She took a stack of plates from the cupboard and struck a match, calling for Franny.

"Something like that."

"About?"

"You and Jack."

Mother looked up. "Don't you like Jack?" she asked, and I could see the familiar desire for confession swell up in her, a look I had seen a dozen times or so in the wake of Father's leaving. Then, each time the urge had come upon her, she'd stopped herself, caught by fear, mine or her own.

She stopped herself again now, and I shrugged. I was not so young anymore that I couldn't look my mother in the eye, and from my shadowed place at the edge of the kitchen I said, "There's Joni to consider." The words felt awkward leaving my mouth, too adult and too practical. *What about Father?* was what I wanted to say.

Mother nodded. There were, indeed, many others to consider. She could have said, *and Alice, too. We must consider Alice,* but then that was ancient history, and the one to blame for all that old news, my mother thought—she got to thinking in her wicked moments (this she had confessed to me)—had disappeared, had left in August for an Eastern town. What she said instead was, "It's nice to have someone who knows."

"And who won't tell."

Mother furrowed her brow. "I don't care about that," she

said. She looked at me, confused. "We won't bother with what other people say, Grace."

Franny came careening into the kitchen then, sliding on her stocking feet. I came out from the shadows and switched off the overhead light and together my mother and I began to sing. Franny blew out the candles in one huge, gasping breath.

We slept together in my room that night, Franny and me, after we had organized our candy into piles on the floor, after Franny had crouched beside me in bed and counted out her collection with upraised hands; fifteen chocolate, twelve coconut, nine cherry. Five boxes of candied cigarettes that she'd stow in her dress pockets and pretend to smoke or barter for better stuff from other kids at school on Monday. This plan outlined, she climbed under the blanket and tucked herself into a ball. Just before my breath deepened, I felt a small hand against my shoulder. "It's nice she has a friend," said Franny.

I lay watching the movement of Franny's thin shoulders for a long time and listening to the sounds of the house. Down the hall, my mother was still awake. I could hear her as she moved around her bedroom, as she adjusted the blind over the window that faced the road. From that window, she would look out upon blue darkness interrupted by silent masses—dark fields marked by bleached fence posts, curved mountains cutting into sky, the contours of horses, barns, rusting plows in the distance. She would look out and see Jack Leroy's house. Inside he would sleep sheltered by walls he had built the summer of his daughter's birth and his wife's death. In her own bedroom, my mother wore a pair of heavy blue pajamas. She shuffled on bare feet over the floorboards. Sometimes in the night I could hear her moving like this, slowly, as if injured, as if she'd woken up aged fifty years or more.

My mother liked to sleep with a window open an inch or two, even in winter. She would wake with cold cheeks and burrow further beneath her blankets like some kind of small, hibernating animal. I cannot remember if my father liked to sleep that way, or if he slept that way simply because Mother wanted it so. Early on, when they first slept together, I imagine he would have wanted to please her, to fit himself into the patterns of her life or to prove that he was like her in small, elemental ways so that she would believe she had chosen the right person to join with for what might be a lifetime. After a number of years, in cold weather, he might have gone from the bed and closed the window after she had fallen asleep, and then even later he would stand to close the window while she was reading, telling her it was a waste of good heat. Or not. Or he would burrow next to her, loving being in the cocoon of her body, her body and his body giving off so much heat that sometimes when their skin touched—stomach to hip, breast to back—they would startle for a moment, nearly burned, and wonder at the way a body could generate something like safety, like home, after a while of knowing it there beside you every single night.

8.

Time began to flow together, the days and weeks, and for a while there was nothing very large to mark our passing. Susan and I went through the first winter of high school together, friendship intact, though there was a certain tremor now that was between us, a threatening—greater than any adolescent jealousy or change of heart—that promised quiet disintegration.

We spent nearly all of our time together. Susan took to the farm house as a refuge; after Halloween, Joni had come down with a bout of unexplained depression, and was now constantly at home, cooking strange things and drinking and filling the house with the ash from her cigarettes, all of this done in her dressing gown and purple curlers. We listened to Susan's troubles with serious, sympathetic faces, but secretly we doubted her. We would sometimes see Joni come out of the house done up in pencil skirts and blouses with collars and cuffs that blossomed at her throat and wrists. She would walk down Colt's Neck to the main road in her winter boots, then exchange her boots for the high heels carried in her purse and catch the bus to town. We debated what she did once she was there, whether she visited Jack, or went shopping or took lunch at the Franklin Hotel, just to have something to do, someplace to dress for.

Joni was a young woman, too young, really, to be living with a man of Jack's age, though he wasn't old himself. He was nearly forty, she was but twenty-two. The problem, if one was to be identified, was her lack of people, of a family who might claim her and calm her, but Joni had none—none that Susan or Jack knew of at least. She'd come to our town after she'd finished high school, thinking at first that she might take some classes at the university, but Joni was not the kind of woman who could stand doing one thing for too long; an hour in a musty, echoing lecture hall was enough to make her eyes water and her feet jump nervously. She spent two weeks studying "The Evolution of Thought" and "Basic Home Economics" (courses for which she'd bought and then kept the required texts, so that any visitor to her home could see these books displayed on the coffee table, though only the first twenty pages of each showed any signs of use) before giving up and searching for full-time jobs and interviewing for a room at a ladies' boarding house on the outskirts of town, near the river and its crumbling houses. The lack of desirable men in the town disappointed her (they were all rowdy college boys, or bearded professors, or mill workers, or church-going family men) but this was during the short period of time after leaving her home when she'd tried to do things she felt her mother—who had died of tuberculosis two months before Joni's high school graduation—would approve of, and her mother would not have approved of Joni looking for a man with a bit of money to share. Joni had no siblings, and she did not know her father. She'd been raised poor; the river houses and the thin, barefoot children who darted down alleyways and into back doors were comforting to her because they seemed a known world.

She found a job as a maid at The Franklin Hotel. Maid work—she was good at this; she'd been housekeeper and cook while she'd lived with her mother, especially toward the end, when her mother rarely left her bed. And she met people at the hotel. She'd always made it a point to know people, and to be someone that people knew. She met people but she did not tell them about the way she'd lived when she'd lived in the tiny town where she'd been raised by a single and sickly mother. She knew that they would have recognized the name of the place; many had probably visited there, or at least stopped as they drove between the larger towns. Montana was a state with a great deal of open space and not many towns, so any place that had a few houses, a school or a gas station or a post office, was on the map. Joni knew that no one would think less of her, but when her mother had died, and when she'd finished high school, she'd taken it upon herself to become someone new. It was a romantic notion at first, but the further away from that small town she got, in time and space, and the easier her grief over the death became, the more the idea of reinvention took hold. One day it was suddenly no longer a plan that lived in the dreaming mind, but a series of tasks that would and could be accomplished in the waking hours, with a little footwork and a few earnest words and dollars.

It was at the Franklin Hotel where she first met Sedina Harris, who would occasionally take a suite there when she was singing a few nights in a row at the piano bar and didn't care to make the drive back to Colt's Neck at three when things finally closed down. Sedina was kind to anyone who waited on her because for so long she'd known the hard work of being in service. So she didn't fault Joni when, one morning, she'd come in to clean and had discovered Sedina in bed, the mayor's eighteen-year-old son face down beside her.

Sedina had looked up, caught Joni's eye, and smiled. "Maybe a little later," she'd said. Then, "What's your name?" She spoke in a normal voice, and Joni feared that the boy would wake up. She stared at his bare back on the bed; his shoulders were wide and freckled and narrowed down to a neat waist where the white sheet just covered him.

"I'm Joni," she breathed, wondering what her mother would have thought of such a scene.

"Thank you, Joni," said Sedina.

Joni had left red-faced, feeling at once a pressure of dread—Sedina might tell the manager, and that would be the end of the reinvented life—but there was also the feeling of her new life becoming bigger, blossoming open in a quiet but certain flush of possibility. The emptiness of the life—the walk to work from the boarding house where the other girls didn't like her because she was pretty; the cleaning out of rooms where people had used up the beds—seemed to become more distant when she walked away from Sedina's room that morning. For Joni was an orphan. She knew no one well in the town; she had friends but they did not know her the way they might have, had she let them see her truly.

They met again, one evening when Joni was leaving and Sedina was coming into the hotel, this time with an older man on her arm. He was a tall man and had a slight slope in his spine, so that when walking or standing still he gave an impression of great timidity. Yet Joni saw that the muscles in his neck and forearms were strong. He nodded to greet her. This was Jack Leroy. He owned the barbershop by the Felix Diner, Sedina told Joni. Joni was introduced as though she were an old acquaintance of Sedina's, then bid goodnight with the promise of another meeting soon.

These days, living on Colt's Neck, Joni would tell anyone, were they to ask her, that this was the moment she had fallen in love with Jack Leroy. That night, she'd walked home feeling the weight of her braid down her back as a suddenly cumbersome beauty. At the boarding house she'd borrowed a magazine from another girl and thumbed through the pages, studying the new styles that were becoming so popular.

His was really a men's shop, Jack explained the next day when she showed up with a picture and her pocketbook. The place was quiet on a Tuesday morning though, and he said that he'd always cut his mother's hair, and his wife's too, when she'd been living. He would do his best, he said. While he cut he told her about his daughter, who was twelve and mostly unhappy, and he did not know what to do about this. Joni said that not having a mother must be difficult for the girl. Then she told Jack that she'd only had a mother growing up, and that she'd often felt the absence of a father the way one must feel the absence of a limb after it's been taken away, for one reason or another.

"A phantom," Jack had said, nodding, brushing against her shoulders as he moved around her.

"Yes, like a ghost," Joni said. The scissors slid through her hair with surprising ease and she thought how quickly a long-held thing could be simply snipped away in the space of a summer morning.

They kept the affair a secret for nearly eight months before they were found out. Jack had wanted it kept secret—he said that he couldn't stand the scrutiny of the town. He'd already been pegged as the widower with the strange daughter. Joni wanted to know why he'd stayed in the town then, if he felt as though he was the brunt of gossip. Jack looked her square in the face and said, "everybody's somebody here." He did not mean it in a good way. Then he said something about doing it for Susan, for the business he'd built up. They were valid reasons, of course, but by then Joni knew him well enough from watching (her mother had talked to her once about the art of reading the truth beneath a man's silence) to guess that his staying had a lot more to do with fear, and the ghost of the dead wife on his shoulder. She made it a point not to ask too many questions. This was also something her mother had advised when it came to men. She gave this advice from the bed where she died, having only had—to Joni's knowledge—one important lover in her life. This was Joni's father, and he had left before the birth. Perhaps due to her illness, or in spite of it (many would have chosen cynicism), Joni's mother looked upon the world with an almost ingratiating optimism. The man she had loved truly had left her behind but this did not sour her on the opposite sex as a whole. One had only to seek the good ones, she'd told Joni, and to know a few tricks to accomplish the long-term keeping.

Jack was older, and he had a daughter who didn't like her. Joni knew this well; she wasn't naïve. She wasn't the type of woman who would try to get someone to like her who clearly did not. Yet Joni knew that Jack Leroy was what her mother would have called a 'good one'. He was, perhaps, too good, and so she did her best to keep their relationship quiet because he wanted it so. She did her best; she stayed on at the boarding house and at her work at the Franklin Hotel. She visited Jack at the shop when it had closed and sometimes out at his house on Colt's Neck when Susan was at school.

Sedina was the first to figure them out; her birds-eye view of the comings and goings of Colt's Neck was practically inescapable. Joni feared her at first; she'd never been entirely sure how well Sedina knew Jack, whether they'd visited the hotel together for time at the bar or time in one of the bedrooms. But Sedina was not angry; instead, she seemed amused, and she began watching Joni in a different way. The old understanding—the feeling that Sedina knew her simply by looking at her—had gone away. Now there was curiosity, not always kind. Sedina wanted to know how it was going. "How's your new man?" she would ask.

Joni did not care for the implications of this question, but told her that it was going well.

"It's fun to have a secret," Sedina said. It was the only cutting thing she would ever say to Joni, though she certainly could have said more. They continued to be friendly to one another when their paths crossed, but Joni understood that she was now different in the eyes of the town and as was her way, she didn't do much to dispel this perception. She had never spent much time worrying what others might think of her; she had found that it was much easier simply to become the person others saw, another scheme, as she discovered, of the reinvented life.

On a day in springtime, the road melting and muddy under the tires, Jack took Joni to Colt's Neck, her few belongings boxed and lined neatly in the truck's bed. She had met Susan only once before this arrival; Jack had taken them for supper at the Felix, and Susan had not said one word the entire meal. Now the girl with the flaming hair watched her from a bedroom window. She thought this woman must be in some sort of trouble, maybe pregnant; why else would her father bring her here? But there was no trouble, not yet. There was only loneliness, and an attempt, however futile, to answer it.

9.

Christmas that year was a quiet affair. Susan went with Jack and Joni to Oregon where Jack's parents were still living. "I can't stand her," Susan said, her face bright red, when I went to visit her the first afternoon of Christmas vacation. "Want to know what she's getting my dad?" Susan asked. "A membership to one of the goddamn tennis clubs. Would you believe it?"

I tried to picture Jack Leroy in tennis whites. There were three tennis clubs in town, an abundance of riches if you loved tennis and of absurdity if you did not. In addition to the clubs, there were public courts in every park, and hundreds, certainly, of building sides and empty lots where one could hit a ball around for an hour or two. These were not my observations; I had heard my mother and father laughing about the issue of tennis on several occasions. They had been friends once with a couple called Boganvie, a childless pair who attended a few of the parties at the nice house and drank too much and stayed too long. They were devout tennis players and at every party would try to convert Mother and Father with words like match point and aerobic and love. "Does your dad play tennis?" I asked Susan.

Susan shook her head and shoved her suitcase off the bed. "I doubt if he's ever played a day in his life," she said. "But he'll do it for her, he will. He'd do anything for her."

We said our goodbyes then, and I left thinking of tennis, and Christmas gifts, and love; I thought that perhaps love was really a simple thing, one that was just a matter of willingness to do, to try, anything and everything.

We cut a tree from the base of the mountain that bordered our property. "Is this legal?" Franny asked, standing back as Mother chinked the trunk with an axe. Mother paused to catch her breath and looked left and right; the neighboring fields stood bare and grey in the falling light. It was the twenty-second of December; Jack and Joni and Susan had left two days earlier, Susan sulking in the back of the car. Without them, Colt's Neck had become strangely bleak and silent; however random her moods, at least Susan provided us with distraction. The holiday made Father's absence return in sharp relief, and for the past two days Mother had gone overboard trying to entertain us, this latest tree-cutting excursion her favorite idea. The notion of driving to town and picking up a tree at the Boy Scout sale was out of the question. In the country, Mother declared, one cut one's own Christmas tree. The legality of the act had clearly not entered her mind, but so far, our outing seemed to have gone unnoticed. The Mullans had departed the day before to visit family in Seattle, and though Sedina's windows were lit, she was not one to promote rule following.

Mother breathed out, her breath turning white in the cold air. "Of course it's legal," she said, setting back to work. "Besides," she said breathlessly between swings, "it's our property, practically, this space here." So we continued on, Franny and I taking turns with the axe, and pulled the tree over the field towards home. The ground seemed to freeze beneath our feet as we walked, the cold falling down like a cupped palm from the sky, closing in and making us giddy, almost frightened, aware of some large change in weather coming.

It came. The next day we awoke to a fog so thick we couldn't see past the side lawn, where the posts of the laundry line stood like cleaned bones shunted into the hardened ground. There were forgotten sheets still hanging from the line, and Franny and I ran out to gather them in our nightgowns and boots. They were solid as anything; we knocked them with our fists and listened to the hollow tone they made, then left them in the garage, standing against each other like slabs of drywall. "What dummy hung sheets in the middle of winter?" Franny demanded as we ran back to the house.

"It was sunny a few days ago," I said, not wanting to admit that I'd been the one to do it. I'd been alone at the house and hadn't wanted to linger in the basement to hang the clothes on the inside line. In the basement the pipes were exposed and made odd creaks and moans as they sent heat and water up into the rooms above. It was easy to get to believing that they were alive, or that something alive had come into the house without you knowing, and was waiting for you to come up the stairs. It had been a warm day, with a chinook blowing up from the south, so I had taken the sheets to hang on the side lawn, and while I'd been hanging them Charlie Mullan had come along, offering to help. I couldn't quite admit to the forgetting of the sheets, for I'd have to tell Franny about being afraid of the basement and about Charlie, and how he'd made me so nervous I'd come into the house after he'd left, unable to remember why I'd gone outside in the first place.

Charlie had been coming around too often anyway, and Mother and Franny had taken to giving each other knowing looks, teasing me about his attention. The day before Thanksgiving that year, we'd looked out the window to see him cutting across the field towards our back door, a dark, limp thing swinging from his hand. It was one of the turkeys that he and his mother had raised and fattened, and he held it out to Mother without a word.

Mother stared down at the bird. "Will you clean it?" she asked.

Charlie cupped his ear.

"I don't know how," Mother said, pulling a few dark feathers loose and letting them fall.

Charlie nodded then and took the bird from her. She followed him to the garage, where he plucked and cleaned the bird, filling a paper sack with the tough, silky feathers.

After the turkey there was the turning up with a snow shovel in hand at the base of the driveway, and later, at the back door again, looking for Franny and me, asking us down to the river to give his shotgun a try. We began going with him into the woods, hiking behind him while he looked for rabbits or grouse, stopping at the little shack he had built one summer with his father when his father had been a different sort of man, and eating the apples and boiled eggs carried in our coat pockets.

Charlie didn't speak much, but when he did he asked hard questions, and asked them unabashedly. He wanted to know about Father and where he'd gone, and about Jack and

Joni. He was curious about Mother, and said he thought she'd come to Colt's Neck to find something she'd lost. *New York, with a friend called Ivan,* Franny said, offering everything up. I pinched her but she pretended not to notice. She told Joni's story and Mother's too. *Joni was terrible. She drank gimlets at ten in the morning. Mother taught classes. Made wonderful Yorkshire pudding. Didn't sleep well. Yes, was probably lonely.*

Hikes with Charlie meant staying out until our toes were numb in our winter boots, meant crashing home through twilight in the hard, crusted snow of the mountainside, then waving goodbye at the corner posts that joined the fields. Goodbyes with Charlie meant his gentlemanly half-bend, his salute, his eyes catching on mine a moment too long.

Susan did not accompany us on these trips. She pretended not to be interested when Franny told her about Charlie's secret shack or the white rabbit he'd let go even though the shot had been clear; she pretended not to care that Charlie believed white to be a sign of God, or that his father had once been a pastor in a Lutheran church over near Seattle, but was now retired and a more than part-time drunk. "I already knew that," Susan told Franny.

"Why didn't you play together when you were little?" Franny asked. "You grew up across the road."

Susan only shrugged, her face turning crimson.

Later Franny told me that I'd better do something or I'd have trouble on my hands. That was the way it worked in the soap operas we watched after school on the television. "What way?" I asked.

"This way," Franny said, squaring her shoulders. "Susan likes Charlie but Charlie likes you and you'd better do something."

I laughed, though later I began to fear for the first time

the possibility of losing my friendship with Susan. I felt that perhaps I didn't know Susan as well as I had believed, that perhaps Susan's quick temper masked a great deal more sorrow than was visible to the naked eye.

In the coming cold, we spent the next day feeding and bedding down the milk cow, chasing the chickens into their coop inside the barn, and bringing in wood for the stove. With an old cart we moved half the wood that Jack had stacked alongside the barn to the breezeway between garage and house, close enough so that if it did storm—as Sedina was promising it would— we could reach it without much trouble. It was dark by the time we finished working, and there was a kind of steady, climbing down cold that settled itself around the house as we placed the last pieces of wood in the breezeway. We could feel the frame of the house locking itself up against the change in weather. Mother sent Franny and me inside to find something for dinner, then pulled off her gloves and wandered to the end of the drive; we watched her looking to the south, where the sky was a resolute white, full of waiting snow. If an ice storm came, or a blizzard, like those of her youth, we'd be stuck, Mother had said, her voice almost hopeful, but Franny was frightened. "We don't have Father here," Franny said to me inside. "We don't have enough wood."

"We don't need Father here," I said, full of a kind of feminine ardor. "We can make it on our own."

Inside the house the rooms were dark with only the dim light of dusk coming through where the curtains were still open. I didn't close them right away, and even kept the lights off, trying to hold on to the sensation of the outside labor in my limbs, the feeling of heat slowly returning to my numbed fingers and face. The pattern of this kind of living—the forgetting of the inside life, or the inequality between indoors and outdoors—had become an accustomed thing since we'd moved to Colt's Neck. Mother had changed the pattern of the days; there was no pattern anymore, or little semblance of one, anyway. There were days when she would stay in the basement, working at her desk, the sound of her fingers at the typewriter coming up through the kitchen floor. There would be days when she would wake early and stay outside until long after sundown. Early on, I had looked at the outside days as the hard ones; I had assumed that Mother's escape to physical work was an escape from the worries she could not hide from inside the house, where Father's absence was like a living pocket of air—a ghost to avoid looking at, but I slowly realized that my mother enjoyed being outside more than any other thing. It was easy to forget the type of living my mother had known as a child, one that was certainly the kind of keeping up with the earth and its seasons, the weather of every violent or gentle Montana day.

We drew the curtains and switched on the lamps and sliced bread for dinner. Outside, her breath coming in puffs and her boots thudding dully on the freezing ground, Mother continued to work. When she came inside at last, the cold air trapped in her clothes and hair, she brought with her a box of kindling for the kitchen. Then there was a great deal of dusting and clanging as she examined the chimney that rose to the ceiling. Jack had assured her of the stove's ability, but the thing was like a strange animal to her, one that had a potential for violence. Up to this point, the weather had remained mild, and we'd been happy to rely on the old gas furnace that lived—itself an ungainly creature—in the bowels of the house. Mother did not like to own things she did not use, however, and so the cold snap was as word from above that the time for the woodstove had arrived. She finally got a small fire going with the kindling and the funny pages from that morning's paper and three pieces of Jack's neatly split wood and stood back from the stove proudly, her gloved hands on her hips, her face and shirt-front covered with soot. She looked around at Franny and me and smiled, her eyes bright above her dirtied cheeks, and we saw plainly that she was happy.

So it was that we spent the days before Christmas doing nothing but eating and napping inside the house; Mother moved the dining room table close to the woodstove, and there we established a monopoly game that could be played in bored fits. We were not in danger of keeping warm, of course, but we all pretended, for those first few days of feeding the stove, that we had escaped a fate of frozen death. Franny and I shared a bed for extra warmth on the first night of the freeze; on the second night, we discovered that Mother had pulled her mattress into the living room and was sleeping where she could see the stove. So another mattress was moved, and the living room became crowded with pillows and blankets and the sharp-smelling Douglas fir that we'd cut illegally and placed in one corner. Franny played a game where she pretended that the living room floor was a deep ocean, and the mattresses lifeboats, and would try to walk the circumference of the room from armchair to couch to mattress without falling into dark water. At night the little golden bulbs on the tree glinted in the occasional flicker of dying fire that could be seen through a slim gap on one side of the stove hatch, or in the light coming through cracks in the curtains, that light a blue, seeping light that had everything to do with cold so sharp that even the fog that had stilled itself over the ground could find no reason to move. We felt, all in all, the kind of fleeting compassion for one another that only extreme circumstances can bring. Perhaps it was strange that we should not have been offering this care all along, in the wake of the storm that had brought us to Colt's Neck in the first place, but we were all alike in that proud sensibility that allowed little room for open admission of loneliness or need. We moved about each other politely, but there was the notion of being moored together, in Franny's dark sea, and the feeling too that were this to be an end of sorts, we should want for no other company.

Mother had decided that she wanted to go to the late Christmas Eve service in town. We had never been particularly devout; Mother had been raised Episcopalian, Father strictly Catholic, and he was wont to subdue the facts of his upbringing—his mother and father, his childhood home, his school years at the Catholic High School in the town where he'd grown, and especially his religion. He refused to go to church. Mother had learned early on not to press him for stories, and Franny and I learned this behavior from our mother and did the same unquestioningly. Mother, however, went to church often, every other week or so, and more often in the spring when the weather turned fine and she could walk—when we'd lived in the nice house—the ten blocks to the cleanly bricked Episcopal church. Sometimes Franny went with her because she liked the sweet wine at communion. Near the end of that life, when Ivan had come to us, Franny told me that secretly, on the warmest mornings, she and Mother didn't go to the church at all, but instead wandered around the neighborhoods with their shoes off, studying tree-buds and looking for the fattest robins, then sitting on a bench downtown guessing at the moods of the couples who walked by; sleepy eyes meant

there was a lot of passion in a house, Franny told me. A rested
face predicted boredom.

Mother had not been to church since the move to Colt's
Neck, but on Christmas Eve, after spending half the morning
shut into one of the back bedrooms wrapping presents, she
emerged and announced that we would all be going to the ten
o'clock service that night.

"I thought we couldn't go outside," said Franny. She
kneeled on the back of the couch and pressed her nose against
the frosted glass of the big picture window. "Everything's
frozen."

"Of course we can go outside," Mother said, but her face
fell a little when she joined Franny at the window and studied
the landscape. Everything was encapsulated in white; even the
vertical surfaces were plastered in snow and ice. There were
lights on at Sedina's place, but to the north and west of us
the houses stood stark and empty. When she'd gone out for
more firewood that morning, Mother had found that the
thermometer on the outside of the garage had broken, its
needle stuck solidly at negative twenty.

"I don't want to go out," Franny said.

Mother looked down at her. "We're going," she said.
She went to the kitchen and we heard her opening the stove,
pushing new wood into the fire. "It's not like we're living in
the dark ages," she called back to the living room, but there
was silence for a long moment after that and we knew she was
studying the broken thermometer.

She cleaned up the living room in the afternoon, pushing
the mattresses into a more organized fashion, pulling the sheets
taut and locating forgotten tea mugs and toast crusts behind
the couch and television. For about an hour at dusk there
came a clearing in the flat white sky, just a layer or two, and

the fog lifted from the ground and the grey light was replaced by a faded yellow glow, like aged paper, so that there was an impression of warmth as we stood watching the change from the living room window. Mother had always been optimistic about weather, summer and winter; *surely we'll have snow this Christmas,* she'd say hopefully, face pressed against the cold panes of the nice house. *I don't think there will be fires this year,* she said each summer, when in June, snow could still be seen on mountaintops and the morning grass was frosted over. Inevitably she would be wrong; the ground would freeze hard and we'd have a winter of nothing but angry wind; June would pass and by ten each morning the air would be humming with the sound of grasshoppers down deep in the tall weeds by the dried riverbanks, weeds so dry they seemed to spark when you brushed through with bare legs.

When the fog lifted and the color warmed that afternoon on Colt's Neck, Mother put a coat over her apron and went out to the road. She'd been cooking Christmas dinner. She looked up from mixing the stuffing, her hands slick with the butter and onion, and saw the change as it was happening. Franny and I watched her from the living room; she crossed her arms tightly to keep her coat closed and walked up and down the road, stumbling every now and then over the frozen ruts, her face turned towards the sky. "I'm not going out," Franny told me in a low voice. "I'm not going."

Mother came in through the back door and we went to meet her. "I don't think I've seen a thing like it," she said. Her face was pink with cold and she cupped her hands over her ears to warm them. "It's so locked in. We'll have snow tonight for sure, that'll break it." She went back to the stove. "Want to do the cranberries, Franny?" she asked.

Franny crossed her arms and glared at her. She was

still in her robe and nightgown and her hair stood out in a halo of knotted static. "I don't think it's very funny," she said. "You making us go out in weather like this. It could be dangerous."

"Don't you feel safe, Franny?" Mother asked.

"I'm not going," Franny said. She drew her body up straight. "I won't be going to church."

Mother scooped the extra stuffing into a casserole dish then turned back to study her daughter. "Okay Fran," she said. "If you don't want to."

Mother took a bath while the turkey cooked its final hour, and Franny pulled her bedding and mattress back to her bedroom. "You'll be cold back there," I called after her.

"I'm tired of being ridiculous," Franny said, huffing her way along the hallway, her mattress flopping heavily against the wall. She closed her door and I heard the click of her bedside radio come on, then the drone of the weather report.

One winter day when Franny and I were very young, our father took us sledding. We weren't living in the nice house then; we were all together in the back half of a small orange house a few streets over from the town's public library. Behind the library was a hill that sloped down into an old creek bed. The creek had dried up some years before, and now the bottom of the hill, which stretched beyond into an empty field and beyond that to the highway, was used as a dumping ground for large pieces of household trash. The creek bed framed the base of the hill in an arc of forgotten oil drums, bald tires, and gutted armchairs and mattresses, objects that could get the mind working if it was allowed; it was curious to imagine how someone's mattress ever made its way to an emptied creek bed. That the furniture now resided outside, subject to the elements, signaled a violence of some kind, a desperation or banishment or sudden move in the middle of the night. On summer days, without the snow covering them, you might take a book from the library and turn right one of the chairs, inspecting it first for signs of blood or spiders or mouse nests, then settle there and read away the afternoon as the former owner of the chair might have done in a living room somewhere. A chair was a chair. As children, Franny and I gave souls to the things we found in the creek bed, as we gave lives to many objects and places, and felt actual sorrow over their abandonment.

The day that Father took us sledding there had been a large snowfall. The hill behind the library was a sea of children. The sun was bleak that day, and with every head covered by a cap, it became difficult to keep track of one another as we took turns on the sled. I did not like to sled alone; I would sit with Father on the sled, insisting that he be at the front so I could shield my face against his back as we flew down the hill. Father's jacket was checked in black and white and made of sturdy wool. As the afternoon passed, the fabric became wet and when I pressed my cheek to my father's back, holding tight to his sides, I would catch my breath against the sharp, sodden smell there. By the end of the day my cheek was red from pressing it against the wool.

Father loved to sled, and we stayed on the hill well into the dusk. The day had warmed at its half mark, and the new snow of the morning was now frozen and beaten down by the sleds. There were still a dozen or so children on the hill and Franny, recognizing two girls from her class at the elementary school, asked Father if she might take her final runs with them. She raced away and Father looked to me, his face glowing with cold, the front of his jacket and cap thick with wet snow. "You sit in front now," he said. "I can help you steer."

Our sled was old and cumbersome; it had been Father's when he was a boy, and the runners were now rusted in places and the rope handle worn through so many times that it had been replaced with a long switch of leather. I sat in front and Father arranged the leather strap in my hands, and with his feet alongside mine showed me how to move the front of the sled left and right. "Ready?" he asked.

I pulled the leather taut and Father pushed us off, the runners catching a little in the freezing snow. Once we hit the crest of the hill the sled gained speed and we rushed, wind stinging our faces, farther than we'd gone yet that day, into the snow that was still thick and new until the runners slowed and we came to a stop.

Father rolled off the sled laughing and I stood over him unsteadily, smiling and shaking, not sure what to say. "Perfect," Father said to me as he stood up, brushing himself off. He placed a gloved palm roughly atop my head. "Perfect." Together we made our way back up the hill, scanning the remaining black dots that were children, looking for Franny's pale head. The sky was deep blue now, only the outlines of the far off mountains were darker than the sky, and the lights from the tall library windows, the panes colored red and gold, were being dimmed inside by someone warm and deft, moving silently along the shelves.

We couldn't find Franny. "Do you suppose she went home?" Father asked. We considered it. She knew the way; the library was not far from the small orange house, and Franny and I were trusted, as all children were, to walk to and from school, to walk anywhere in town, as a matter of fact, so long as we were together. Now, though, Franny would be alone, and I imagined her forgetting to turn off the side street into the narrow alley that led to the back door of the orange house, the front entrance to our hidden apartment. I imagined her turning down slightly familiar alleyways, thinking she had found the way, feeling sure that she had glimpsed the light above the door, the glow it set on the peeling orange paint, the shadow of Mother moving behind the curtain, only to discover that she'd been mistaken.

There was a group of children milling about the back steps of the library, four or five of them, and Father, his walk hastening into a lope every step or two, made his way to them. *Did they know her? Had they seen a girl in a purple coat?* They shook their heads and called him sir. Franny's friend with the blond curls had disappeared. "Do you suppose she went home?" Father asked me again.

"We could go and see," I said, but this plan wasn't good, and we both knew it. If Franny was home she would be safe, but Mother would be angry we'd left her. If she wasn't at home, then she was still missing, and we'd only worry Mother, who had a great capacity for worry. Father spent a good deal of time trying to assuage or avoid Mother's worry.

Father faced me, his mouth open. He was breathing hard. "Maybe she went in the library?"

I looked at him with a blank face. The library was closed, of course; it closed early on the weekends, but the situation called for me to be doubtful, I felt, for me to let my father take the lead. He rushed past me, taking the stairs two at a time to the library door. The librarian was just coming out as he raised a hand to knock, but the librarian, a woman in overalls and a plaid scarf, couldn't account for Franny either. She'd been working in the back all day anyway, she said, had let the high school girl handle the checkout desk so she could sort through the rare books collection. "So much dust you wouldn't believe!" she said, looking Father up and down with an uneasy face as she chattered on and pulled the heavy oak door closed behind her. "A girl about six?" she asked.

"Exactly six," Father said.

"In a purple coat."

Father nodded.

"Maybe she just went home," the librarian said. Father followed her down the steps and watched her take the path that curved around to the street. "Goodnight now," she called, but at the corner of the building she turned back to us. "Sometimes these kids, they just get to playing," she called. She was silent a moment. "I live just two blocks from here. I'll keep an eye open." She turned and disappeared around the side of the library.

Father stood still for a moment before he went to the top of the hill, and cupping his gloved hands around his mouth, began to call Franny's name. The sound echoed against the brick of the library and then dropped off down the hill and into the snow mounded creek bed and the vast field beyond. A single pair of headlights crawled the highway in the distance.

Father called out again and again and I covered my ears. His voice was hard and cracking in a way I hadn't heard before; he yelled as if punching through something, as if trying to break something in two. It must have only been a minute or two before we saw the movement in the creek bed, but it felt much longer. It was only a slight shifting of white shape, so subtle we couldn't be sure, and we stood rigid, scanning the curve of snow-covered oil drums and tires. There was one armchair in the creek bed, nestled almost at the place where the curve of the creek left off and disappeared into a tunnel that ran underneath the highway. As we watched, the chair shifted and a bit of snow fell away to reveal something dark

against the white. Father began to run. He slipped once on
the hard-packed snow, but was up again before I could reach
him. At the bottom of the hill I let myself fall and slide the
rest of the way down on the seat of my snow pants. Father
was already with Franny. She was half covered in snow and
half asleep, her small body curled into the sagging confines
of the chair. She looked up when Father began brushing the
snow from her face. "Hello," she said, reaching out for him
with both arms.

We walked home through the dark, Franny on Father's
back, me pulling the sled. Every block Father would swing
Franny down and rub his bare palms against her cheeks and
ears until she complained that he was hurting her. In the
alley we saw the yellow light and Mother's shape behind the
curtain. She was opening the door to let the cat out as we
came through the back yard. "Are you just getting back?" she
asked, laughing, and kissed each of us as we passed by.

I do not know if Father told Mother what had happened.
I remember that Franny and I took a bath together and ate
our dinner in our pajamas, listening to the radio in the living
room while Mother and Father talked in the kitchen; there
was only a curtain in the doorway between them, so we could
listen to their conversation. They laughed and Father uncorked
a bottle of wine. Mother read a story from the newspaper out
loud. The radiator hissed with heat and outside the new snow
from that morning froze over again. At ten, Franny and I got
into the bed in the back room we shared, and Mother came
in to read a chapter from Laura Ingalls. "Warm enough?"
she said before turning off the light, and Franny asked for
her baby blanket to be tied like a shawl over her head. We
burrowed together and listened to the muffled voices still in
the kitchen, Mother's occasional laughter breaking out like a

warm flame.

In the morning, the cat was missing, and the day became a sporadic search for her in between homework and piano practice and the setting of the table for dinner. I can remember waking in the middle of the next night and hearing my mother, standing on the back porch in her bathrobe, calling for the cat again and again until my father went out to bring her in. And so the time that Franny got lost in the snow became easily mixed and confused with the time the cat ran away, and I was never sure if Mother knew the truth. It became a forgotten thing over time; nothing bad had come of it, unless we could somehow connect Franny's momentary disappearance with the cat's permanent one.

For a time after the incident, Father changed in his concern towards Franny and me. For weeks we would find him waiting outside the school to walk us home at lunch, then again when the final bell rang. The snow dripped away by the middle of March, and Father went back to his usual self, present but preoccupied, and he hung up the sled by its runners in the shed out back. With the spring, Franny and I began dawdling on our way home from school, safe because we were together, stopping in at the library and checking out books, but never again settling ourselves to read on the armchairs in the creek bed at the bottom of the hill.

So when Franny refused to go to church that first Christmas on Colt's Neck, I could only remember her small body, lost and buried in snow in the creek bed behind the library. She might not have remembered it; she had only been six at the time, and I could not recall her being afraid when we'd found her, cold but not frozen. Still, the shadow of it might have been there, some unfamiliar nagging at the back of her mind when she looked out the window at the frosted landscape. If Father had been there, he would have gone down the hallway while he dressed for church, his face foamed with shaving soap, his suspenders hanging at his sides; he would have knocked periodically at Franny's door and told her jokes and stories about families who traveled whole continents on sleighs in snow so deep a buffalo could get swallowed up. "Those families survived, Franny!" he'd say, knotting his tie outside her locked door. "Why can't we?" Eventually she'd come out, bleary eyed, her green velvet dress a button off and too short above the knees, and we'd cheer for her. "Just the person I was looking for," Father would say, and let her sit between him and Mother as we drove down Colt's Neck and onto the main road.

But Father wasn't there and Franny didn't come out. I took a bath after Mother, the bathroom still steamy and smelling like the sweet goat's milk soap that Sedina made in her kitchen. Afterwards I sat on a hard-backed chair in front of the stove and Mother pulled my hair into a French braid. "What should I do?" Mother asked. "Just let her stay?"

I shrugged. "She'll probably be fine."

The radio kept us company for dinner. I helped Mother clean up and we made a plate for Franny to keep warm in the oven. At a quarter after nine, Mother went out to warm up the station wagon. She came in red-faced and rigid. "Wear your warm coat," she said, and I could tell by the strain in her voice, a note of command, that she was beginning to doubt her decision. We'd continue on though, we'd come this far; we were dressed and the car was running. Mother went to the stove and stirred the embers to make room for new pieces of wood. I put on my coat and winter boots and knelt on the couch in the living room, moving aside the heavy curtain so I could see through the window. My breath fogged the glass and the lights from within made it almost impossible to see what was outside; the window showed only a reflection of my face and the warm glow of the living room. A heavy stroke of wind moved across the front yard and the house creaked.

"You're not to bother with the stove," Mother was calling out. I went to look down the hallway. Mother was at Franny's door, pulling on her gloves. The camel hair coat that Father had given her for Christmas two years ago was draped over her shoulders. "Do you hear me Franny?" she asked.

Franny stayed silent. We could still hear the tinny refrain of the weather report, coming from her portable radio, repeating over and over. "We'll be back before midnight," Mother said, and waited, just one second more, to see if a reply might come. When it didn't, she sighed heavily and came back down the hallway. "I guess we'll go," she said.

The night was like ink and we had to grope our way to the garage and into the big, churning station wagon. It was still cold after thirty minutes of idling. "Here we go," Mother said, as if we were embarking on some long awaited journey, and guided the car out onto the road. We met no one on the main road off of Colt's Neck, and even in town the streets were silent, overtaken by the cold. We passed the Felix Diner and Jack's emptied barbershop, and I thought about Joni presenting Jack with the tennis club membership the next morning, Susan looking on furiously.

The church parking lot was half full, and Mother seemed to relax slightly as we parked and made our way up the stone steps. Inside, beyond the heavy oak doors, the radiators sent out waves of heat and a woman was at the piano, jubilant, as if none of the cold outside existed. We were halfway up the aisle when someone pulled on Mother's sleeve, making us stop and turn. It was Ellen Tray. She was dressed all in red and her hair was plaited neatly. "Sit here," she said, moving down the pew to make room. Mr. and Mrs. Tray peered around in unison and Mother smiled nervously.

Mrs. Tray, just as short and round as she had been the last I'd seen her, gave her husband a laden look before leaning around her daughter to speak. "So good to see you out and about," she hissed, her voice a half whisper. "We've all been wondering."

"Oh I've been around," Mother said. She peeled off her gloves one finger at a time and put them in her purse.

"Of course!" Mrs. Tray said. "Of course you have. Just not in the old neighborhood, is all."

"We live on Colt's Neck," I said, catching Ellen grinning from the corner of my eye.

"What's that?" Mrs. Tray asked, her face aghast.

"A road, Mother," Ellen said. "It's the name of a road."

"Out of town," Mother said.

"How lovely," Mrs. Tray said, and settled back in beside her husband.

"Where's Franny?" Ellen asked.

"She didn't want to come."

"Cool."

"Where's your brother?"

"Drafted," Ellen said matter-of-factly.

"Oh," I said, catching myself just before saying 'Cool'. "I'm sorry," I said instead. Ellen only took up her prayer book. The lights began to dim. "He'll come back," she said. Up front a signal was given and everyone began to stand.

My mother knew the prayers by heart. She showed me the pages so I could follow along, but she kept her face forward the whole service, even when we were asked to kneel and pray.

My mother prayed with her head up and her eyes open. I thought about the Sundays she'd gone alone to church when Franny and I were little. Sometimes, those mornings, Father would make Franny and me omelets or crepes. He flipped the frying pan with a practiced and contented hand. Mother came home from church in her dress clothes, smelling like candle wax and ate the breakfast Father had kept warm for her in the oven. We sat at the table with her in the sun while she ate and she took off her dress shoes—sturdy, square heels, always, and always a little scuffed from walking—and told us about the gossip at the church. The minister had a funny new haircut and blew his nose in the middle of the sermon; the lady sitting in front of her had a grandson with an acne problem visiting that weekend; the new couple to the church with two babies had argued during communion. Through all of this I imagined my mother sitting, solitary and calm, her soft hair done up in waves against her cheeks, her sturdy high heels secretly kicked off under the pew if the weather was warm and she'd worn pantyhose. She said the prayers she knew by heart and studied the picture of Jesus when she went up for communion, hoping that no one could hear her thoughts, could hear her thinking that Jesus had been a handsome man and wondering what it might have been like to kiss him, if his mouth would have been tender or full. She took her small sip of wine—what vintage? She wondered. She planned to have a glass of wine that night as she cooked dinner. She planned to laugh with David over the goings-on of the church; David was good with impersonations, with summing people up into neat pictures; old women with hair like snow and hats shaped like peacocks; the husbands of young wives snoring during the reading of the gospel; the minister's ongoing attempt to grow a healthy mustache. Even ministers have vanity, my

father would say, making my mother laugh, and Franny and I
would laugh too just because it was nice to hear the sound of
so much laughter, and later look up the meaning of 'vanity' in
Mother's dictionary.

Mother hadn't been to church since Father had gone,
and I wondered if she would call him later that night and
laugh with him as she used to, asking him to laugh with her
about Mrs. Tray, listening while he told her things she hadn't
known; *Mrs. Tray was drunk that New Year's Eve party last year
at the nice house, don't you remember? She'd sat down where there
was no chair.*

*And you were a perfect gentleman. You made sure no one
laughed at her.*

The last hymn was "Silent Night", and the lights were
turned down all the way while we were singing, only the red
pillar candles lighting the room. I only knew the first verse so
I hummed the tune when I ran out of words and stole glances
up and down the pews. Ellen sang with her eyes closed. She
wasn't wearing any makeup and up close her face looked very
young. Mrs. Tray caught me looking at Ellen and frowned,
her face pudgy and creased. I wondered how old she'd been
when she'd had Ellen. The end of the service came with a great
clanging of bells and organ drones. Mother looked down at
me and smiled. "We did it," she said.

"I'm glad."

Mrs. Tray pushed past us in a cloud of perfume. She
placed both her hands over Mother's outstretched one. "We
all have to keep going," she said, her face drawn. "We just
have to keep going."

The corners of Mother's mouth twitched. "Yes," she said,
nodding. "Thank you Faye. And Merry Christmas."

Ellen took a scrap of paper and handed it to me. "My

number," she said, shrugging on a long plaid coat. "We're friends, huh?"

I nodded.

"Cool," she said, following her parents down the aisle.

Mother pulled on her gloves and we went out into the night. "Look at that," she said. There was fresh snow on the ground. During the service the sky had broken as Mother had predicted, and we could see stars overhead. We huddled in the car while the engine warmed up.

"That was fun," I said.

Mother nodded, her face burrowed into the collar of her jacket. "Your father always liked the Christmas service."

"Maybe they went tonight. In the East, I mean."

"Maybe."

We listened to the engine struggling in front of us and watched the parking lot slowly empty, fat plumes of exhaust fading in the cold.

"Ellen's mother's name is Faye Tray?" I asked after a moment of silence, and Mother's laughter filled the car.

The house was bright when we pulled into the garage; Franny must have gone around switching on every lamp in every room. "At least she didn't burn the house down," Mother said as she unlocked the back door. A steady snow was falling and the fence posts were fat with white. "Come see the snow, Fran," Mother called through the house. She hung her coat in the closet by the basement stair and put the teakettle on. The big stove filled the kitchen with close heat. I went through the living room, past the little stolen tree that made the house smell of pitch, and down the hallway to Franny's room. Her door was open and beside her bed her radio was still on, tuned to nothing but static now. "Franny?" I said, looking around the empty room. I opened the sliding door of her closet; sometimes at night, if she was afraid, or during the day, if she simply wanted to be alone, she would hide in there, sitting on a pile of dirty laundry that Mother hadn't found. The closet was dark and empty. "Are you in here, Fran?" I asked. I stood waiting for her to emerge from some new hiding place. Franny's room was a mess of discarded clothes and books. Her candy stash from Halloween was still half full and resting in an open dresser drawer. She'd tacked up pictures of actors and cityscapes around the mirror that hung on one closet door; with one finger I pressed a peeling edge of Harvard Sharp's wrinkled picture back into place. Next to the picture was a yellowed scrap of newspaper print; Harvard Sharp's hometown obituary, not the one that had fanned the headlines of the L.A. newspapers, that long ago morning when I'd woken to a scrubbed and still Hollywood and found my father, alone in the hotel café after a night spent with Ivan, after a morning spent scouring the streets for every newspaper he could find, trying to protect Franny against something inevitable. Instead, Franny had tacked up the five inches of smudged print from a paper somewhere in Iowa. He had been born Franklin S. Murmin. He was thirty-four on the day of his death.

I stood a minute longer in Franny's room, not worried yet at her absence because I was so used to her presence that I couldn't find it in me to worry; she would turn up, eventually, unhurt and sleepy from some tucked away corner, some armchair covered in snow. 'Hello,' she would say, as if nothing had gone missing, ever.

Mother didn't panic right away, as Father had done on the sledding hill. I walked behind her through the house, peering into closets and even the washing machine, calling Franny's name. Her steps quickened as we searched the basement, a place Franny wouldn't even venture accompanied, let alone by herself on a dark night. Mother's capacity for worry was so engrained, so expert, that it revealed itself in slow, permanent waves. Mother didn't wring her hands or begin weeping; her face took on the distant, stony look she got when she was in the middle of grading final exams, or after she'd had a difficult conversation with Father on the telephone. Finally, after we'd searched the entirety of the house, she went resolutely to the coat closet and pulled on her snow boots and work jacket. I followed suit and we went out into the night, the snow coming down so hard now that our tracks were erased in seconds. The light in the barn was burnt out, and we fumbled for a minute or two before finding the big flashlights that stood side by side on the workbench. "Francis Rose!" Mother called into the high contours of the barn, her voice muffled and shortened by the stacks of frozen hay and the dark mound of the riding mower. "Don't hide!" Mother called, rapidly throwing her flashlight beam.

"Franny?" I called.

"She isn't here," Mother said, stepping deeper into the barn so that I lost her shape for a moment. I listened to her groping through a stack of rakes and shovels that leaned against a platform at the furthest reach of the barn. There was a space under the platform, I knew, where Franny and I would go on wet days and play cards, listening to the drumming of rain on the metal roof and watching the little brown mice burrow holes in the hay bales that surrounded us. I swung my flashlight until I found the dirty orange of Mother's jacket. She turned and shielded her face in the light. "What do I do?" she asked, her voice breaking quickly, and I felt my stomach turning, more out of fear over Mother's worry than Franny's disappearance. I was ill equipped to deal with a panicked, broken parent. In the past, Father had always been there to put things at ease; a hot bath, a glass of bourbon, a well-timed joke—I doubted any of it would work now. Mother ran from the barn and stood in the drive. She yelled Franny's name, just once, and we stood looking, waiting.

"Would Sedina know she was alone?" I asked after a moment, and Mother whipped around and stared at me.

"Sedina!" she cried, and began to run as best she could through the deep snow. We stumbled on the road, the frozen ruts, hidden from us now, catching our ankles every few seconds. The snow had changed the light on the fields. Now everything was bright, a knowable blue, and the shapes of houses and mailboxes stood black and stark and scarred into the white landscape. If Franny were outside, we would have caught her shape and movement easily, but only the falling snow moved around us, and every house save for Sedina's, set up on its low hill, was dark. The running seemed to take forever.

At Sedina's front door Mother paused to wipe her nose and smooth her hair. She swallowed and rang the bell. A long moment passed before we heard footsteps inside and I watched Mother's face begin to crumble again, the slope of her eyes widening and her full mouth sealing itself into a tight line. Sedina answered the door in a red bathrobe, her long hair swung in braids over her chest. "She's here," she said when she saw Mother's face, and held the door open for us.

Franny was sitting on the kitchen floor beside a box of kittens. She was in her nightgown and socks. "They were born this evening," she said when she saw us. Mother went through the kitchen without taking her snow-caked boots off, without saying a word, and picked Franny up off the floor. It was a rushed and awkward embrace; Franny's long, skinny legs dangled down from her nightgown as Mother gripped her, her feet almost touching the floor. "Can we take one home?" Franny asked, her face crushed against Mother's wet, woolen shoulder.

10.

That cat was called Tom, and by spring he was a sturdy, wild thing. He got into the barn and killed the little brown mice, bringing their curled corpses indoors if we didn't catch him first. On sunny days he perched on the top of the bird feeder that was nailed to a fence post and watched the sky for prey. (You're being too obvious, Tom! Franny would call out to him.) He came and went through an open window in Mother's bedroom, climbing up the steps of a splintered ladder she had wrestled out of the barn and leaping from the window ledge to the desk in her room where she'd left out a saucer of chicken scraps. On mild afternoons, the air outside lined through with a sure, heartening warmth, Franny and I walked home from the bus stop and sprawled in the sun that filled the living room, letting Tom come to us, kneading and purring in the folds of our hair.

Franny had changed over the winter. She rearranged her bedroom, taking down the pictures of the Hollywood stars and replacing them with the strange, swirling abstracts that she painted in art class. She asked Mother for dark blue curtains and made me help her dismantle her bed frame, setting her mattress flush with the floor. At a second-hand store, she found a tall pair of pale suede boots with tassels around the folded tops. She wore these every day, tucked over her jeans on weekends and with her skirts or dresses during the school week. She put a center part in her hair and it hung in satiny sheets against her cheeks at any time of day; morning and night she was fashionable while I stood in the living room, bent double over the ironing board, the hiss of the iron pressing my hair into submission.

She was forever trying to get me to talk about Ellen Tray. "What was she wearing today?" she would ask as we walked home from the bus stop after school. *What was she wearing? What did she bring for lunch? What crowd does she go around with?* Franny would pelt out, breathless as she rushed home, still playful in her walking, despite the cool new demeanor. There were some afternoons when I would make up answers just to quiet her, but having any answer made me feel important, truthful or not. I knew a few things, but not much; my Christmas service conversation with Ellen had granted me her smile when we passed in the hallway, and the occasional lunch time visit, but whatever her secret kindness, Ellen Tray was no more immune to the pressures of high school than I was; she knew where she fit in the game, and she knew how to play to keep her spot. What did I know about Ellen Tray? I knew that she went with the same boy as last summer, the one who'd wait for her at the end of the darkened street, in the neighborhood where Franny and I had once wandered, only the lit end of a cigarette giving him away. Once I'd seen her eating a carton of Milk Duds. Once the county granted girls the right to wear pants to school, she wore them every day. I knew that she had a pair of dark wash jeans that cupped her body like paint. I knew that eyes followed her through the halls, followed her jeans and her heeled boots and her long, swinging hair. She was queen, and I felt lucky, of course, to know her in any way, but more than that I felt a silent sense of communion with Ellen Tray. Somewhere within me I knew she knew the truth about us, the truth from which I tried so hard to hide; not that he'd gone away, that couldn't really be kept secret, and not even why he'd gone, but instead this: that he had gone, that others knew exactly why, and that they didn't really think a thing of it. I wanted my father's story to be important to other people, because it was important to me. I missed my father. I was confused and angry at his going. But I still loved him and, what's more, I defended him heartily in my mind. I could pick up the telephone and find his voice; I could think of him healthy and safe. And happier. Happier than he'd once been.

Were we happier? Perhaps. There was a sense of freedom to the place, the expansiveness of the fields and the mountains behind them; we were country living, Franny liked to say in a cowboy lilt when we'd first arrived, but it wasn't really country, not as it had surely once been. Even in those years the town had spread its fingers, marking territory and planting houses where true country had once been. Our neighbors kept horses and a few simple sheep; Mother planted herself a garden, but the hay trucks still rattled in from further north where a house was just an interruption in a sea of land. I believe we liked the sense that we had somehow escaped—the nice house, the manicured lawns, the watching faces. There was more room here and the calming sense of living closer to the earth. It is possible that we were happier there, once we had grown accustomed to the force that had driven us into the new life. Or perhaps it was plainer than that; perhaps the calm came from the decision finally made. Whatever its sorrow, when the break came, it came complete. The other side was a blinded, lush country, and a house that did not demand our history. When we got there, we were there fully.

Some afternoons that spring, walking home from the bus stop, we'd come to the edge of our property and see Mother raking dead grass and leaves from the thawed ground, and the sight of her could be happiness itself. Franny would take off running, her book bag slamming against her legs, returning for a moment to her old self. Once, early on during that first year on Colt's Neck, Susan had asked about Franny. "You don't look very much alike," she'd said. "Is she your real sister?" And I'd thought it such a strange question. Of course. Of course my real sister. I'd thought of the way Franny carried herself when she first woke in the morning, cautiously and quietly, as if she had emerged from a great interrogation and must take care to cover herself again. *This is how I know her,* I'd wanted to tell Susan, but you couldn't exactly divulge how you knew a sibling to another person, not in any way that they'd fully grasp. Every single intact memory I had from my life up until that moment contained something of Franny, either her presence or her opinion or the promise of her. It took Franny a good hour to shake her sleeping self, this I knew. When we were children she'd spent this hour pattering the hallways, a worn yellow blanket clutched in her fist and dragging out behind her. Now when she woke it was to slump into the kitchen in her bathrobe, to hunch at the table over the comics, measuring spoonfuls of sugar into the cup of coffee she'd snuck while Mother was dressing for work.

Spring was the season when people began to go a little crazy; everything would thaw, we'd spot a robin in the limbs of an apple tree, then we'd wake up to two inches of wet snow the next morning. The land was teasing us and we were growing restless, ready for permanent change. Sedina packed her bags, left her animals and the key to her windowed house in Mother's hands, and got on a plane for California where she'd visit the mother she hadn't seen in over twenty years. Franny got caught smoking behind the school one day and was suspended from school for a week. Susan decided she would try out for the cheerleading squad and spent every afternoon practicing jumps and cheers in her melting, muddy backyard. Charlie, in his austere, slightly ambivalent way, began dropping hints about the spring dance at the high school, and Joni, who for weeks had been carrying on with mysterious appointments in town, got caught having an affair with another man.

It was Franny who discovered her as she was walking across the Main Street Bridge one afternoon in early April. There had been a heavy snow in March, and then a great warming, so the river became swollen and brown, churning at the banks and carrying fallen trees downstream. It was a sight to stand on the bridge and look down over the water; the gravel path that ran alongside the river was swamped and mucky, making it impossible to walk without taking random detours across the lawns of houses and businesses that lined the water. During her suspension from school, Franny had been spending her days in Mother's office, doing the schoolwork that I'd collect and bring home for her. At two o'clock, when Mother had to teach (and when she couldn't stand Franny's boredom any longer), Franny was set loose, allowed to roam the streets near the university for an hour or two or buy an ice cream at the diner, before going back to campus to drive home with Mother.

With the melting, the place to be in those hours of freedom was the riverbank, especially the stretch of water that ran from campus to the Main Street Bridge. When the schools let out at three, this space would fill with Franny's classmates, all of them squishing along the muddy bank, sometimes taking off their shoes to feel the warmth of the spring earth, to test the temperature of the water, getting a little too close now and then to feel the power of the running

water that carried winter inside of it, to catch for an instant
the feeling of being pulled out, under, taken downstream so
quickly no one would even notice your going. Then there
would be a wild gathering of sticks, leaves, sheets of poorly
graded school papers—anything that would float would do—
and a designated starting line. The game: Drop in your object
when the others did, then race against the water, against the
scrap of your paper, brilliant white atop the boiling dirty flow,
the rush of kids at your elbows and ankles, your newly bare
shins and forearms spackled with muddy spray, race up the
rusting steps to the top of the bridge, to the edge, to look
over the railing to see who will win, who's made it up in time
to see their object passing by far below. They rarely win; the
river either cheats them, traps their sticks in swirling eddies,
or drowns their papers, or rushes them by with a ferocity that
only eggs the racers on, making them try again and again,
until the race isn't against the river anymore, only between
them, their kicking feet and pumping fists, their ragged breath
as they careen across the bridge and swing to a stop, staring
down at the water that could kill them if they got just a little
too careless, that could snatch them up and disappear with
them forever.

But it is not yet three. It is two o'clock on a Friday
afternoon, and Franny is suspended from school, so she walks
from Mother's office to the riverbank and plays the game
alone, rooting out chunks of wood and maple leaves twice the
size of her palm, letting them drop, racing to the top of the
bridge, looking down. What she sees on the opposite bank,
standing just outside the shadow of the bridge, is a man and
a woman holding onto one another; the woman's got her
hands in the man's hair; the man holds the small circle of
the woman's waist. It is a brilliant day, and Franny squints

against the sun, moving further along the bridge and peering over, feeling suddenly fearful, like she ought to run away. At any moment the woman will look up and catch her eye, and the woman will be Joni, dressed in her pencil skirt and ruffled blouse, her handbag dangling from the crook of her elbow, her high heels on and giving her trouble on the gravel. She'll look up and see Franny's bright head on the bridge, and snatch the hand of the man beside her, pulling him out of the sun, into the shadow, pulling him down the path, the river there beside them, an angry, churning threat. She'll stumble in the mud, thinking of her rubber boots hiding in the ditch along Colt's Neck. She'll wish for Colt's Neck now. And she'll think, as she secretly often does, that she has become wedded to a situation too large for her; she'll remember that she is still a young woman; she'll feel very young, indeed.

Franny told me, and I told Mother, but it was Joni who told Jack and Susan, in an act of aberrant sincerity, two days after Franny had spotted her beneath the bridge. The man's name was Pete Schiffer, and he was the concierge of the Franklin Hotel. The affair, Joni revealed, had been going on for nearly six months. She was in love with him. Susan told us the story of Joni's confession, sitting next to Mother on the couch and drinking honeyed tea. She'd escaped the house when Joni had begun to pack her things and Jack had taken pruning shears to the overgrown hedges in the back yard, a job he'd never bothered with until now, his face stony, his mouth a tight unyielding line. "He didn't say a thing to her," Susan told us. She was strangely subdued; we had assumed that the final leaving of Joni would be cause for deep relief, even celebration, but Susan sat slumped and grey-faced, her knees tight together, her feet flat on the floor. At four o'clock we saw the front door of the Leroy house open, and Joni came out wearing boots and jeans, a suitcase in each hand. Jack followed her, unlocked the car door, and together they made three trips in and out of the house, bringing boxes and dress bags, an overfed potted palm, and a portable phonograph. They got into the car and drove away. "He's taking her to the hotel," Susan said. We kneeled four abreast on the couch, Susan and Franny and Mother and me, looking out the picture window, following the car until it disappeared around the bend.

Jack returned an hour later and went into the house. Without a word, Mother took a sweater off the hook by the backdoor and went across the road, pulling the sweater tightly over her breast, and opened the front door of the Leroy house. She didn't even knock. The door closed behind her, and all I could do was squint outward through the living room window, trying to figure movement in the falling dusk. "I don't want to go over there," Susan said, looking up from the floor where she and Franny were flipping the pages of a dog-eared magazine.

I turned to look at her.

"He'll just sit there silent," she said. "He'll just sit there."

I looked back to the house, trying to see what Susan saw in her head, through the walls to Jack inside, mute and frozen, Mother beside him. Mother beside him. Talking? What about? Would she have taken his hand or embraced him? I couldn't imagine anyone embracing Jack Leroy; to me his very presence bespoke an unquestionable etiquette, kindly though it was, but one that did not make much room for demonstrative affection. Only with Susan. With Susan I had once or twice seen the kind of deep love her father held for her, a reverence that probably had a lot to do with sorrow, with the memory of a long-ago death. I was jealous of this love, though only vaguely aware of that fact. It was why though, I am sure, I loved Susan myself with a similar devotion.

After what seemed a very long time the door opened and we looked up, having to fight past our own reflections now to see. Mother came first, pulling her sweater on again, and Jack followed. She looked back now and then to see that he was still with her; he walked as Jack has always walked: hands in pocket, head slightly stooped, loping gait. They came into the kitchen and we heard the screen door slam, and then Mother's voice calling out dinner suggestions. "Tacos?" she called. "Spaghetti?"

"Pancakes," said Franny.

The memory of Jack and Susan leaving our house that night is one that I've long returned to; it has remained clear, though I cannot exactly say why. There is nothing complicated about it, no word or motion that betrayed a hidden anger or sadness, there is simply the feel of the night as I stand with Franny at the fence, watching our guests walk home. There is Franny swinging from the wooden posts, round and round, over and up; she fits herself through the gaps. In a year she'll be too tall to do this easily. There is Mother behind us in the lighted barn; what is she looking for? Something remembered at dinner. A picture frame, a can of paint, something. In a year there will be a fire in this barn, and Mother will lose the white hen she loves. There is Sedina's big horse, her sides beginning to swell with colt; she comes to the fence and heaves her flank against the rough wood. Her movement leaves last tufts of winter coat behind. We will help her birth this colt. Franny will call him Rusty. And there is Susan and her father. They walk a few steps apart before Jack stops, looks back, and holds out his arm to her. She goes to him and loops her elbow through his. They are standing like this in the middle of the road when Jack begins to whistle a three-note tune that means something to Susan. She laughs and looks back at us, smiling. There remains just enough light on that blue-night road to see by, and in this light Susan's hair is a dark and tangled halo. *Goodbye,* she calls out. *Goodnight. See you tomorrow.*

11.

We knew Pete Schiffer, Joni's lover, by sight only. In the lobby of the Franklin Hotel there was a restaurant that was favored by Ladies' Clubs and lawyers. It was the only restaurant in town that still served a full four o'clock tea, complete with cucumber sandwiches and an assortment of delicate cookies. To have tea at the Franklin Hotel was a sign of both wealth and conservatism; the waiters wore short-waisted coats and bowties. Our mother had once belonged to a Ladies' Club, and would take tea with this group every third Sunday of the month. On one of these afternoons, when Franny and I could not have been more than four and eight years old, we went with our mother to tea. We were helped back into our church dresses and informed of the rules for the outing: no whining, no fidgeting, no running about. We were not to eat too many cookies and above all, our mother told us, kneeling in front of us and straightening our collars, we must not answer questions about our father. *Why?* We might have asked. But she could not explain. *Just don't,* she said, standing up and moving us out of the house through a waft of clean wool and Chanel No. 5.

At the Franklin Hotel, we sat on spindly chairs next to our mother and drank tea clouded with milk and honey. Our waiter was a student of Mother's, a tall boy with a dark, shining face, a boy named Anthony. He liked Franny and me and brought us a plate of little cakes iced with pale green and blue frosting. These we ate carefully with our fingers, nearly trembling with delight and fear, the other women watching us, watching our mother, with slightly sorrowful expressions. As we were leaving, Anthony came up behind Mother to help her with her coat, and they spoke together, laughing. My mother touched Anthony's forearm very lightly. *Tomorrow in class,* she said. *I promise!* Her laughter was clear and soft. *Tomorrow in class.* The other women exchanged looks and cleared their throats. There was a general murmuring of goodbye and thank you, an agreement about next month's reading selection, and the Ladies of the Ladies' Club dispersed. Mother was in high spirits as we walked home (for she was now freed); at the corner of our street she took off her high heels and walked the remaining distance in her stocking feet. *What beautiful little cakes Anthony brought you,* she cried. *Did you have a nice time?* And then her laughter returned. *Isn't it like playing dress up? Like acting in some ridiculous play?*

Yes, yes! We agreed, and asked if we could take our shoes off, too. We adored our mother when this mood overtook her; a humorous and slightly rebellious nature that was equal parts reality and playacting itself. The next month, though, our mother was told that the monthly gathering had been canceled. The month after, she was told there was no longer room for her in the club; a member's sister had recently moved to town and must be given a spot out of loyalty. Mother was flippant. None of it mattered, she declared. She'd never cared for the Ladies' Club anyway; the women were catty and the tea was always lukewarm. Sunday afternoons were much better spent in blue jeans and flannel shirts, taking naps and doing things around the house. And this, after all, was true; our mother preferred to spend her time this way. Still, for a few months after her last tea with the Ladies' Club, when the third Sunday of the month would roll around, she would spend a few moments at her closet considering her pale dresses and sweater sets before pulling on slacks. It was only the ritual that she missed; it was the feeling of preparation and performance, the blessed release when at last the tea was over, and she could walk away, through the revolving glass doors of the Franklin, out into the clean air. Oh, to leave that space! To leave those faces that made her worry and examine herself; to put on her coat and catch up her purse and stride past Pete Schiffer the concierge, stiff and approving in his pressed blue suit; to push out onto the street where she was strong again, and capable of living her life in any manner she might choose. She would walk home with a great energy, her body leaning forward as if to propel herself further, faster, and when she came home she was free, for to feel freedom, of course, one has first to feel caught.

I think of my mother when I think of Joni's leaving Jack. I think of my father. I think of being caught. I imagine Joni putting on a Sunday dress, the soft cashmere that Jack bought for her, and taking the bus from Colt's Neck to town. I see her walking into the lobby of the Franklin hotel one afternoon, intent on proper tea, and catching Pete Schiffer's eye. The decision would have been swift, as it had been with Jack; here was a new form of freedom, a breed closer to the life she was now envisioning for herself. With Pete, there was reason for pencil skirts, ruffled blouses, lipstick; there was reason to go from the house to the road and beyond.

It was only one sympathetic way of looking at the situation. But we were not very sympathetic of Joni; Susan would not allow it. Joni was moving in with him, her concierge. He lived in a set of rooms on the ground floor of the hotel; there was a kitchenette and a large bathroom and a row of windows that let in light and a direct view of Main Street.

In May, Jack decided to move to Oregon. It was something he'd been thinking about for a long time, he told Mother; something he'd been thinking about off and on since Alice had died, truthfully. Alice's parents were in Oregon, and they weren't so old yet; they loved Susan, and missed having someone young around the house. He didn't say that they'd been fighting to get hold of her ever since Alice died, had threatened him with lawyers and custody battles until he'd convinced them otherwise, had agreed that Susan would spend every Christmas with them and two months every summer. Mother knew this though; she remembered late nights when Jack would show up on the doorstep of the nice house, Susan's bundle in his arms, and ask if they could stay there, just for a night, a few days, until things settled down again. Those were nights when Jack and my father sat up late, drinking and playing cards and talking, talking, endlessly trying to configure ways to prove to Alice's parents that Jack was a suitable father, that he could do it alone.

Jack Leroy had grown up with my father, had studied alongside him in college and later in graduate school, though in the History department. He would have gone on for a Ph.D., my mother told me once—told me proudly, as if talking about a husband or a son—but Alice's death had put a stop to that plan, as it had put a stop to many plans. Then came the barbershop. At first, it had been just a part-time job, a way to make money while still in school. He took some teasing for it in classes and among friends—Jack the beautician, Jack the stylist. He just knew how to trim hair, was all; he'd been doing it since he was a little boy. His father liked a neat line along his neck, a neat curve above his ears; he kept a short mustache. Jack's mother had cut her husband's hair for many years, it was a monthly ritual: Sunday nights in the kitchen with a stool and an old tablecloth for a cape. The trembling began when Jack was five, little tremors in his mother's hands and face so that small things—peeling apples, polishing silver, lacing her shoes—became long, concentrated endeavors, and the moments in the kitchen with her husband—running the cold edge of scissors across the nape of his neck, leaning forward to check for evenness, snipping the corners that had got away from her—were no longer possible. It was these Sunday evenings she mourned the most, she once told Jack, the strange intimacy that came with shaping someone's hair. Some days they were only two people running the same household, raising the same son, but when she bent over his shorn head under the bright lights of the kitchen, there was a tenderness between them that appeared in no other moment. The trust was complete; he'd swing the table cloth over his shoulders, perch upon the stool, hand her the scissors, and bend to her, feeling the brush of her body as she moved around him, the warm rush of her breath as she blew loose hairs from his skin.

It was her palsy that made Jack learn how to cut hair; she placed him on an empty milk crate so that he might reach his father's head and showed him how to snip at an angle, how to measure each short layer between his pressed fingers, how to shave the fuzz from the neck. So it was that in college, when Jack went looking for a job, he went to the barbershop first, was given a trial run, and was hired. The job carried him through college, through the few years of graduate school with Alice by his side. When she died and he was left suddenly alone with a baby to raise, the man who owned the shop offered Jack a share of the place. A man had to keep going, after all, he said; a man had to fix himself to get along in this life. In a few years, when he retired, the place would be Jack's. It was a good business, had been going steady for twenty years already, would surely set him up steady for the rest of his life. Jack shook the man's hand and drove out to the house on Colt's Neck that was still being built; the men were inside putting in light fixtures and testing the plumbing. In a week's time Jack would come out with the paint that he and Alice had ordered from the store downtown; they had picked pale blues, warm browns, downy grey like a gosling's breast for the baby's room. The house was a gift from Alice's parents; for your future, they had said, handing over the check. Standing in the house then, the light from the windows catching sawdust still settling in the air, all he saw was a chain around his ankles, an anchor of home and child; the future spread forth with such invisible shape he could scarcely find footing.

For fourteen years he had been successful at keeping them at a distance; Susan was his own, the house kept to his own design, his own liking—at least, kept to the taste he knew Alice would have wanted had she lived. The barbershop was even his own—anchor or no anchor—and with the coming of Joni, the picture of his independence, his ability to be a man in his own right, had been complete. Then came Joni's leaving, and suddenly the picture seemed a farce. Giving in to Alice's parents had always been the looming thing on the horizon, the surrender to be given, and now he had surrendered easily and concretely, with no apparent doubt or hesitation.

The day he told Mother of his plans, the day Mother relayed the news to us, we ate our dinner in silence. For the first time that season we had opened every window in the house, and through the screens there came the interminable sound of no sound at all—only the low rush of wind through trees on the mountain and the distant lumbering of a car engine on the main road. We had not known—or expected—that Joni's leaving would cause such a reaction. To Susan, Joni's leaving, while shocking at first, seemed to have delivered relief, a swift entrance of new freedom and comfort. None of us had stopped to think that Jack might have actually loved Joni, not even Mother. We had taken for granted his acquiescence to her strong-willed ways; we had not counted on his love for purple curlers and porcelain elephants and evening gimlets. She was frivolous and ambivalent and quick-tempered, everything that Jack was not; perhaps this contrast, Mother suggested, had been the thing he'd fallen for. It was one explanation. "When will they go?" Franny wanted to know. At the dinner table, the silence finally broken, Mother shrugged and re-filled her wine glass. She didn't know when. Sometime in late July. Jack wanted Susan to spend August in Oregon, so that she'd at least be accustomed to the new living arrangement before she was forced to become accustomed to a new school. *Grow accustomed,* he'd said, as if she were an animal in a new pen, a plant leaning into a new source of light. "She'll get used to it," Mother said in my direction. "We'll all get used to it. Eventually we'll all be fine."

I left the table then, pushing my plate away. I wanted to look Mother in the eye and declare my hatred for Jack. It seemed the worst cut, the worst blow someone might deliver to Susan. I imagined her walking the halls of some strange school, her thick legs swathed in new white tights, her unruly hair getting caught in the straps of her school bag, her underarms breaking into a cold sweat. Here, we could cling together against the forms we could not mold ourselves into; apart, we would be entirely alone.

That evening Mother drank too much. After dinner, after delivering the news with a steady, almost nonchalant face, she went out onto the side lawn with the newspaper and a glass of bourbon. I heard her stumble in the soft, thickening grass, and her glass fell to the ground with a muted thud. She swore under her breath and came back into the kitchen for a re-fill. She stayed out on the side lawn until she no longer had light to read by, then found the pack of cigarettes she kept in the garage and strolled up and down the drive, smoking and considering the dark, sleeping face of the Leroy house.

12.

Jack was determined—he'd already sold off the business to a pair of brothers, had pounded a 'For Sale' sign into the yielding spring earth of his front lawn, had begun bringing home boxes from the grocery store to organize the contents of the house. If the house didn't sell right away, he told Mother, he'd come back later when it did—when it surely would—and clear any remaining things away. Surely he'd have a buyer by August. But he'd come back once more; once more he'd come back. He said this to my mother with an earnestness of which I had not known him capable.

May beat us all around. Jack lost himself to the task of packing up their lives and began ignoring Susan, so that even if she had raised a complaint or staged a dramatic refusal, he may not have noticed. Mother got sad again, and went back to her days of frantic physical labor—this time digging up an addition to the garden fifteen feet wide. When her classes finished during the second week of May, she took to the earth with shovel and hoe and tore great chunks of grass up and away, lifting the roots of weeds as she'd snap loose irksome threads from an old blouse and piling these clods in great heaps in the wheelbarrow. She cut and dug, cut and dug, rhythmically and neatly as if following a line the ground had prescribed for her, and within two days a wide square of black, dense earth lay before her. Her hair became knotted, her fingernails rimmed with dirt, but Franny and I did nothing to deter her fever; we had seen this pattern before, we knew our mother's best energies and worst obsessions and we let her be, learning again to scramble eggs or fry potatoes when dinner time came and she was still kneeling in the bright dusk of the season, her head bent and shoulders shifting as she worked her way between developing rows. She would become, she declared, a woman known for her garden. She would be that kind of woman. She'd call up Mrs. Tray, declare peace, and ask her for tulip bulbs. (One plants tulips in the fall, Franny told her.) She would win contests if she deigned to enter them, which she wouldn't—she wouldn't be that kind of gardener—but she'd win them had she the interest or the time. The garden would instead be a silent bragging, a final proof that she could take care of herself; she didn't look to any man for advice or labor. "Everyone else is moving on," she said. "So must we." The garden got a new fence: tight wire strung around seven foot poles, tall enough so that the white-tailed deer that sprung from mountain to field at dusk wouldn't even attempt the leap.

Susan became angry. It was to be expected, with a decision like Jack's, but we had hoped that she might simply respond with hysteria, crying and pleading with Jack to change his mind, for anger in Susan was a rigid, stolid thing. From the time she learned of Jack's plans to the moment she climbed into the truck that would take her away, Susan's temper did not waver—to everyone but me, that is. "She's locked herself down," I overheard Jack tell Mother, saying it like it was a thing he'd seen a hundred times before, a characteristic that was so purely engraved on his daughter he may simply have been describing the color of her eyes or the shape of her head. "She'll get over it," he said.

"She'll get over it," Mother repeated him, examining the dirt beneath her fingernails.

Jack stooped to gather the boxes he'd come to borrow. They stood in the shade of the breezeway; it was a fine day, nearly summer. "Or not," he said.

Mother looked up at him. "Or not," she said.

Susan began cutting class. It didn't really matter, she told me; school was almost out anyway. I didn't argue with her. She had never been a focused or studious student; there were a few of those in our class, quiet girls usually, even quieter than us, who walked the hallways alone but by some miracle found one another at lunch, and loitered in a tight group around the main office, nibbling efficiently at the sandwiches their mothers had prepared for them. They took the front seats in class and took feverish notes. They wore their intelligence like angry, rebellious badges and I envied them; they had more courage than I; they learned early to let themselves be who they were going to be.

Susan and I might have been among them, had we the interest or focus to do more than the minimum it took to pass our classes. We were not lazy or stupid; we earned As and Bs, sometimes a C in algebra, but we were more interested in people than in books. We liked to study body language and facial expressions; we were attune to the secret glances given up and down fidgeting rows or struck out boldly in the sea of busy hallways. We watched the fights between the cheerleaders and their latest boyfriends; we knew which boys wore their hair long and courted girls in beads and turtlenecks and about the group who smoked behind the gym at lunch; we smirked at the couple in black who asked the difficult

questions in history class about government takeover and
half-truths that left Mrs. Hawk red-faced and sweating. Susan
and I were observers, above all else, and without realizing it we
had become somewhat known about the school. Our silence
might have defined us, or our constant companionship; our
acquaintance with Ellen Tray no doubt helped put us on that
map of chaos and status, even if our mark was small.

So it was that when Susan began skipping class—leaving
at lunch and not returning—I found myself suddenly and
horribly alone. It had never fully occurred to me that besides
Susan, I really had no friends to speak of. I knew other girls
from classes who were polite and said hello to me in passing,
but when one day I sat down with them to eat my lunch, a
yawning silence fell among them, and after eating they drifted
slowly away in pairs, smiling weakly at me as they left. I went
to the bathroom and locked myself in a stall, the remains
of my lunch an angry wad in my hand, and thought of my
mother, twenty years younger, hiding in a bathroom stall with
a solitary apple for comfort and distraction.

Susan did not tell me where she went when she skipped
class. She got on the bus in the mornings and might, if I made
her feel guilty enough, attend her morning classes before
leaving at lunch. She was always at the school again by three,
ready to climb onto the bus as she always had. "You're going
to flunk," I told her.

"Where do you go?" Franny asked.

Susan shrugged and smoothed her hair. "I just walk
around," she said.

It was a Thursday, a day so warm we brought out our sandals
and skirts, when Franny suggested that we simply cut class
ourselves and follow her. "Spy on her?" I asked. We stood at

the corner of Colt's Neck, waiting for the morning bus. Down the road, heading in our direction, we could make out Susan's bright head.

"Just to see what she does," said Franny, raising a thin arm and waving to Susan in a falsely eager fashion.

At lunch, after Susan had gathered her things and disappeared on the wave of other students rushing from the building, I took up my own bag and slipped out after her, trailing a safe two blocks behind. When I passed the junior high, Franny came weaving from the lunch crowd on the lawn, careful to avoid the eye of the teacher's aid, and we ducked together down an alleyway, edged on one side by the backs of houses and on the other by a row of tall lilac bushes heavy with blossom. The backyards of the houses were alive with warm afternoon work; women hung clothes on lines, small children at their feet; windows and screen doors opened to radios, televisions, the awkward bell-tone of a piano being tuned. Ahead of us, at the junction of alleyway and street, we saw Susan pass by. Franny and I went down the alley giddy with pretended stealth, keeping ourselves in the shadow of the lilacs. A dog barked at us and a woman looked up from hanging a billowing sheet and waved.

Susan walked with purpose. Even from two blocks away we could see the fabric of her blouse darkening with sweat. At a street corner downtown, pausing for the light to change, she gathered her hair atop her head and fanned her neck with a flat palm. She passed the record store and the A&P, the green expanse of the university campus sprawling out at her left. At the block where Jack's barbershop stood she turned and took a sharp right down the alley that ran behind the Felix Diner. This, we knew, would allow her to cut around Jack's shop and come out at the corner where the piano bar and the

Franklin Hotel stood facing one another. We waited, safe at
our two block distance, watching for her to emerge again and
move on, past the hotel and the bar, to keep moving, perhaps
towards the road that led far out from town and eventually
returned to dust, passing old farms and winding its slow,
eventual way to hill and then mountain where it continued,
cutting ruts and curves through thick walls of pine. But when
Susan reemerged in the sun again, the light beating against her
bronzed head, she did not continue on. Instead, we watched as
she approached the double glass doors of the Franklin Hotel,
and with the same purpose that had determined her course,
pulled the doors open and disappeared inside.

Through the wide front windows we watched her in the
lobby, sitting at one of the little tables, a cup of tea before her.
This she drank in shaking gulps, clattering her cup against its
saucer, adding cube after cube of sugar. As she drank, she kept
her eyes on the concierge's desk, at the man standing there.
Pete Schiffer was a slight man, pale in face and eye. Only
his hair made him noticeable; it was a thick shock of black,
combed and folded neatly atop his head. I could only imagine
him in bed with Joni; all that hair for her to run her fingers
through, to grip between her bony, frenzied fists. When he
fixed himself up, Franny said, watching him through the glass,
he must put a kind of wax in that hair. "No one's hair does that
by itself," she told me, nodding slowly, as if the image of Pete
Schiffer, shirtless and freshly showered before the tiny mirror
in his hotel bathroom, a jar of pomade full of his fingerprints
on the sink edge, were a solemn thing to envision.

Pete did not seem to be aware of Susan; he had most
likely never met her, though it stood to reason that he'd at
least heard mention of her name, Joni having lived with
her for long enough, having feigned the status of mother,

welcome or not, to this tall and thickly red-headed thing. It occurred to me, peering through the window at Susan's trembling and awkward figure, her solid build confronting the spindles of the chair beneath her, that I might not know what would become of her after she moved away. On Colt's Neck, the Leroy house would stand empty, would sell, would eventually fill with new life, and somewhere in the world Jack and Susan would continue on as they always had. They would both become older, altering slowly in body and mind, letting their lives carry them places and deliver them things, all of this happening away from us, out of our range of witness and judgment. There was a slight but irrevocable sense of grief at such a thought, a homesickness that came to me in familiar waves. There had been Father. There had once been Ivan. There were rooms through which I'd never again walk; windows that looked out on lost views. There was Mother, kneeling in the dirt, her hair so long it now met the soft curve of her hipbones. Yet none of these pictures, locked in my mind, seemed as full of pity and irretrievable loss as the picture of Susan alone at a table in the lobby of the Franklin Hotel, trying to catch the eye of the man who should not matter to her but did.

I took Franny's hand to pull her away, but not before Susan looked up from her keep of Paul Schiffer and saw us through the clean glass of the window.

13.

Franny and I spent almost every afternoon that summer with Susan, in town at the record store, sitting in booths alone or crammed together, listening to Roy Orbison and The Beatles and The Simon Sisters. Susan still loved Frank Sinatra the best. "He's music for cocktail parties," she said. "For ladies in nice dresses." Her gaze would shift and she'd be lost then to dreaming, her face slack and distant as she imagined what life might be possible to her. It was a dry summer, dusty and unfertile, and the only bearable places were indoors. We went from record store to five and ten to diner steadily before trudging home through the heat. Most days we waited until dusk to start home, and sometimes we'd go to the university to catch a ride with Mother. She taught a summer class that year, an evening class, and we'd sit outside the lecture hall in the pristine grass of the campus, the only place that could force cool green lawn in the midst of fire season, and wait for her to come out, blouse damp and linen skirt wrinkled.

Susan was planning a party for the last week in July. A farewell party, she said. We'd listen to Sinatra and take cocktails on her back lawn, she told me one afternoon as we sat with Franny in a booth at the record store. "And you must dress accordingly," she said, looking over my grass-stained cut-offs. I could almost see her evoking Sedina Harris as she spoke, her eyes bright with pretending. "Cocktails?" I asked.

"Well, fake ones," she said. "Unless we can get Joni and Dad out of the house."

"Joni's out of the house," Franny said. "Joni's at the Franklin Hotel."

Susan looked startled for a moment, as if she'd just woken up.

I glared at Franny.

"I only tell *truth*," she said.

Susan pretended she hadn't made the slip. She shook her head as if to erase the moment and looked at me slyly. "I'm going to invite Charlie Mullan," she said. "For you."

"For me?"

"Don't deny it, Grace."

"Invite who you want, Susan," I said, but I could feel the heat creeping up under my skin and I made some excuse to leave the booth and choose a new record. Franny trailed me, and I felt her jab my side sharply.

"Look," she hissed, busily smoothing her hair.

Standing and fingering through a stack of classical recordings was Ellen Tray.

"Hi Ellen," I said.

"What's happening?" Ellen asked, pulling a record from the stack and studying the cover.

"You listen to classical?" Franny asked.

"I need a present for my dad," said Ellen.

"His birthday?" said Franny. Her eyes roamed over Ellen's lanky frame; today she wore a filmy white dress that hung mid-thigh; her legs were tanned and she stood with one knee bent, absentmindedly kicking her sandal on and off.

"No, just a present." She slid the record back and sighed. "We listen to this stuff together, sometimes, and I figured I'd get him something new, you know?"

"Yeah." Franny nodded, crossing her arms and flipping her hair. "Cool."

"So what's the word?" asked Ellen. She grinned at me. "Sophomore year, huh?"

"Yep."

"What'll you do when high school's done, Ellen?" asked Franny. Ellen would be a senior that year.

"Oh hell, Fran," Ellen said, "don't ask me that." She smiled though, and leaned back against the record bin as if settling in for a longer conversation. She looked over my shoulder, "hello," she said, and I turned to see Susan behind me, red-faced and stiff. Susan was in awe of Ellen Tray.

"Hello," said Susan, locked in place a foot or two out of the circle.

"This is Susan Leroy," I said to Ellen, a sudden sense of boldness washing over me; I was Ellen Tray's friend, she'd said it herself, and Ellen Tray was all Susan wanted to be, in school she watched her as you'd watch a celebrity or a queen.

Ellen leaned forward and extended a hand to Susan, a strange gesture for a teenage girl, a gesture better suited to a grown man, but somehow fitting for Ellen, who had always been a little unlike a teenage girl. "I think I've seen you around school," she said.

Susan blushed and shrugged.

"Susan's having a party," I said. Susan shot me a look, but I kept on. "Week after next."

"That sounds fun," said Ellen.

"Oh, it's not for sure," said Susan. Her face very nearly matched the red of her curls.

"Can I come?" asked Franny.

"Duh, Franny," Susan said.

"Susan has a beautiful back yard," I said. "She lives just down from us on Colt's Neck."

Ellen nodded.

"You should come, Ellen." I turned to look at Susan. "Of course, only if it's okay with you, Susan."

Susan stammered a moment before answering. "Of course it's okay," she said at last. She swallowed and seemed to regain a fraction of poise. "You're more than welcome," she said.

"Cool," said Ellen, grinning. She turned back and glanced over the classical records. "I don't know what to buy him," she said.

"Does he have Mahler's ninth?" This came from Susan, and we all faced her, a little surprised. She stepped forward with her shoulders straight and flipped through the records. "Here," she said, pulling one out and handing it to Ellen. "It's my father's favorite."

Ellen took the record from Susan, studying her face. "I don't think he does," she said slowly. "Thank you."

"Mahler's always a good bet." Susan turned to Franny and me. "Are we going to the diner?" she asked.

"Sure," I said. I looked at Ellen. "Want to join us?"

"I'd better not," she said. "But thank you, Grace."

At the door Susan turned back. "We'll send you an invitation," she called to Ellen. Several other people in the store looked up. "For the party."

Ellen nodded and laughed. "Cool," she called.

In the diner we had to fight to find three stools together. We ate lime freezes and Franny squeezed her hands to her temples and shut her eyes when she got a cold headache. "Are you mad?" I asked Susan. She was sitting with her legs crossed under her pressed white skirt.

"I'm not mad," said Susan.

"It should be a good party."

"She won't know anyone there."

"She'll know us."

"She knows me," said Franny. She tilted her glass toward her face, the last chunks of ice slopping around the corners of her mouth.

"I thought you liked Ellen," I said. "I thought you wanted to be friends with her."

"I do," said Susan.

"Well here's your chance."

Susan shrugged and turned to Franny. "What song do you want?" she asked, and went to the jukebox before Franny could answer.

"She's just embarrassed," said Franny. "Ellen's popular and she's not."

"I'm not popular."

"But Ellen knows us from before, so it's different."

I studied Franny's reflection in the mirror over the fountain; the heat had turned her hair a little frizzy, and her cheeks were ruddy. "We were in Hollywood last year," I said. I don't know what made me say it. "This time last year."

Franny nodded, chewing the end of her straw. She rested her chin in her hand. "I didn't like it there," she said.

A week later I turned fifteen and there was no roadside café, no Father and Ivan across from me in the red vinyl booth, no van to camp out in, and Franny was right, it was better not to be there, it was better to be where we were. We ate cake in the evening, after the worst of the heat, sprawled out on the side lawn. Susan gave me a pale pink sweater and jeweled hair combs, things I'd never wear but exclaimed over anyway, shredding the paper from the box and watching the ribbon blow away in the breeze and get caught, a quarter mile down the road, around some barbed wire fence.

The phone rang at nine and I went to answer it; Father's voice came at me tinny and distant. "So you're fifteen," he said. It was true. "When I was fifteen I decided to run away from home," he said. "I filled a bag and camped in the desert for two nights." My father had spent two years of his life living outside of Roswell, New Mexico; it was a thing I often forgot.

"What did you eat?" I asked.

"Jerky," he answered. "And a loaf of my mother's banana bread that I'd stolen from the cooling rack."

"Did she find out?"

"About the banana bread." *And were you frightened?* I

might have asked, but it wasn't the sort of thing you asked my father.

"I wasn't afraid," my father said. "There were lots of stars," he said, "and coyotes howling, and a great deal of dust. Sooner or later, though, I had to go home." Now, he said, he was calling from a pay phone outside a movie theater in Manhattan, and there were no stars to be seen, no coyotes.

"What movie?" I asked.

"Something called *Attack of the Fifty Foot Woman*," he said, and we laughed.

The evening of Susan's party, Mother had her hair cut. She went to Jack's barbershop in the evening after she'd taught her class, after the barbershop had officially closed, because women didn't frequent Jack's shop, and perhaps weren't really allowed there. I would not have known this had I not been in town by myself that day, having my braces tightened. I was in good spirits because Dr. Rona, our dentist, had told me that I could have my braces off before school began. Instead of riding straight home, I'd gone to campus to wait for Mother so that I could tell her the good news. I don't know why I did it, but instead of waving to Mother as she came out of the lecture hall, caught up in a stream of students, I let her pass me by. I stood behind a tree and watched her walk to the street, where the station wagon was parked. I watched as she opened the back door and threw her books and briefcase onto the seat. She had only her purse then, slung over her shoulder, and instead of getting into the driver's seat she looked around her for a moment; it was an hour before dusk, and the air was soft. There came the sound of lawnmowers going and sprinklers clicking their set paths. My mother was wearing a sleeveless blouse, white and crisp, and when she reached inside the car to take something from the dash—her sunglasses—I could see the brighter white of her brassiere outlined beneath the fabric of her shirt. She settled her sunglasses over her nose and walked down the street. I left my bike behind the tree and followed her, far enough so that she wouldn't feel me. People watched her as she walked by them. She smiled at two teenage boys who stood aside as she passed. She retrieved a little girl's rubber ball when it bounced into the gutter. A white-haired woman, stooped low with arthritis, started out of a store with a package and my mother ran ahead to hold the door for her. I expected her to stop at the diner, thinking that she was going for a hamburger, a malt. She knew that Franny and I would be at Susan's that night. I watched as she passed the diner and then I saw a figure waiting for her, a man's body outlined behind the glass of a door. Jack came around in his white barber's apron; he was very tan and he smiled fully, his head cocked in humorous and tender greeting. He held an arm out to her; she went to him and kissed him on the cheek before going through the door. I stood still on the sidewalk, watching the place where they had stood.

Inside, Jack would draw a cape over my mother's bare shoulders. He would loosen her bobby pins and run a wet comb through the tangled folds that had grown so long, so unruly in all the days since Father leaving that she rarely bothered to brush them anymore; she simply bunched them into place with pins, smoothing the topmost layer with her palms and Franny's boar bristle. The steel of the blade, when its edge met the back of her neck, would be cool. She would not flinch. She would come home with a short bob; waves she hadn't known existed settling softly over her cheeks and ears. "What do you think?" she'd ask, and I'd tell her *beautiful, beautiful,* and think of the way Father, in moments of simple love for her, when he thought no one was looking, would reach out and tuck loose strands behind her ears, would gently grip the loosened length like a rope and pull her to him saying, *Hello stranger.*

I turned and went back to the campus. I rode my bike through town carefully, slowly, but when I came to the long stretch of paved road that made its way out of town towards Colt's Neck, I sped up, pedaling until my thighs ached and I could feel beads of sweat dampening the waistband of my shorts. The road was emptied of cars; everyone was in town at the movies or drinking beer by the river. I slowed and came to a stop in a sidelong ditch that bordered a wide field. This was the only pasture for miles that still held a stone wall for enclosure, stacked up and mortared into place decades before. There were horses in the pasture, and the wall would have been easy for them to clear, it stood no more than three feet, but it seemed they had no interest in clearing it, or perhaps they had simply been alive so long that they wouldn't have known what to do with themselves if they did. I let my bike drop among the tall, dry grasses and climbed the wall, settling myself on the other side where the earth was cool; there was the damp, fecund smell of manure, but also the sweet scent of fertile soil and sage. I leaned back against the wall and let my legs splay out in front of me. The horses, half a mile out, looked up once, then resumed their grazing.

There were places where I should have been, places where I was expected; Susan at her house, dabbing perfume to her wrists and choosing records for dancing; Franny at home in front of her closet, wondering what to wear. Still, I didn't move, and felt almost that I couldn't. "Just go to sleep," my father would sometimes say to me when I was little and would fight with Franny or come home with a bad grade on a math test;

"Just close your eyes for an hour, and when you open them things will be different." It was not always a kindly suggestion; sometimes it was an order, said with exhaustion or dismissal. *Go away and close your eyes, Grace. Come back to me a different person. Come back and the world will be changed.* When I was little I believed the change would encompass my father, too, when I awoke, and sometimes this was true. If I slept long enough, waking sweaty to evening sun, the afternoon napped away, I would find that he'd finished his work for the day and was cooking in the kitchen, the radio tuned to the evening news, the smell of garlic bristling with butter in the pan, his apron smeared with fingerprints, a fresh cocktail resting on the windowsill, the sun coming through the glass and ice cubes, creating patterns of light on the kitchen tiles and refrigerator door. "Welcome back!" my father would laugh, and sip at his drink. "Do you feel better?" *Yes,* I would say, rubbing sleep from my eyes. *Yes, I am better.* Franny would be in the den, humming to herself; Mother would come sweeping through the back door with her briefcase and high heels in hand, calling out to us, *hello, hello!,* and he would have been right, my father; the world was changed.

When we lived in the nice house, my mother would occasionally play a bridge game with the ladies who lived in the neighborhood. Sometimes Franny and I would go along. These women were—firstly—wives and mothers, and my mother's status as someone professional, as a mother and wife who also worked full-time, and at a job that demanded most of her mental capacity, was something of a fascination to the other women in the bridge game, and not always a kindly fascination. "How does David feel about you working so much?" they'd ask her, leaning forward and whispering the question as if asking about matters of sex or money. "Doesn't he mind?"

"He works too," my mother would say, lighting a cigarette. "He works just as much." The women would smile politely, sadly, and shuffle their cards, but they talked about my mother behind her back.

"Those poor girls," they'd hiss when mother would excuse herself to use the bathroom.

"It's the husband I wonder about."

"He's very handsome."

"He's simply never around."

"My husband sees him at the lounge nearly every night."

"Your husband is there, too."

"Business!"

"My Neil says there's something funny about him. Says he always has some young student along with him."

"Well, that's his job."

"That's not what my Neil sees."

"I saw him in a play once, he was quite *good,* you know."

"Still, what can he be doing all those hours away?"

"It's those young students he's courting, those college girls."

"It's not the *girls* my Neil's seen him with."

A hush then, an in-take of breath, a shuffling of cards.

"It's a terrible thing."

"Terrible."

"Poor Nora!"

"Those poor little girls."

"Quiet now, quiet."

These women were not unintelligent women, and at that time I regarded them with my own brand of fascination; they were well manicured and seemingly trouble-free and they made lives out of recipes and sewing bees and gardens. I envied my friends in the neighborhood who went home to mothers like these; they would walk through front doors strung with red and green at Christmas, pink at Easter, hues of gold during Thanksgiving time. My mother, too, was celebratory, but in a slightly forgetful, ramshackle fashion; just as we'd stolen the tiny pine for the farm house the first winter on Colt's Neck, so too were our Christmases in the nice house defined by last minute decorations and bouts of extravagant cooking. When Franny and I would go with our mother to the bridge games, we'd be resigned to a basement or a kitchen or a backyard, served juice and celery sticks on folding tables and told to get along, to play nice with the other children, but Franny and I would usually keep to ourselves, making up our own games or sneaking into the house and hiding where we could hear the gossip, waiting for our mother to collect us and walk us home or to the diner, laughing and rolling her eyes and telling us what ridiculous things the other ladies had done or said. Our mother was a superb actress; she knew how to hold her cards and cross her legs and sip her drink so that she resembled perfectly the women around her. *Mrs. Clarke is upset because her son got a parking ticket,* she'd tell us as we walked home. *She thinks she ought to send him to parochial school! Apparently someone baked a cake for the church picnic and Mrs. Newell found a hair in her slice, long and blonde! Bishop Cather is rumored to take a shot of whiskey before he gives the sermon!* She relayed all these things in a high, breathless voice, her face flushed and full of humor as she imitated the scandalized ladies of the bridge games. Franny and I were just stopovers on the way to Father, though; her real delight lay in telling him the gossip she'd heard, in laughing with him. Our parents loved to gossip, and for a time, a span of years that continued, I believe, even in small ways after Father's leaving, they held between them a deep and impenetrable friendship, a dialogue based both on time and simple cohesion that no third party could ever decipher or enter in to, not even me or Franny. It was this friendship that I suddenly feared for, sitting there against the stone wall, the evening fading around me. What did Mother find in her friendship with Jack? Was it something akin to what she held with Father? A friendship based on history seems the strongest kind—it accounts for all mistakes, all shared stories—and Jack knew my mother's history. He, more than anyone else, came the closest to knowing my mother in the way my father had, as someone once young, grown older but not yet old, as a woman who fought and worked and raised two daughters. And again, here was Jack as someone who knew what my father could not know, because of his absence; Jack knew my mother as a woman left behind. He watched her work the small acreage on Colt's Neck with a fervor foreign to me and thus, I assumed, foreign to Father. Perhaps he had not been watching as closely as I guessed, had not parted the curtains in Joni's smoke and elephant filled living room to peer down the road, morning, afternoon, night, to see what his Nora was up to. My imagination allowed him a great deal, though. I saw him as he watched her raking and burning leaves, jumping away when the flames grew high, smoothing her hair from her temples, from the sweat that had plastered there. He watched her drinking, late at night, the first few weeks we'd been there; she sat in her nightgown on the side lawn, the grass tall and slick and in need of mowing. The winter came and he watched her heal slightly; she stayed inside longer hours, she beat her body less with work, the rakes and paint brushes and buckets went untouched then neatly stacked and put away in the barn. And what might he have heard? Sounds could carry on still, clear nights; there was no town traffic to drown out phone calls taken on the front or back porch, the cord stretched taut and my mother's silhouette crouched small into the receiver, her words low and murmuring and then cracking with sudden laughter. Jack and my father used to laugh together. I learned this late. It was an entire world unknown to me and yet it clung to me, or I to it, because it spoke of a seemingly uncomplicated time, however much it had dissolved in quiet chaos. I could envy Jack's knowledge of my mother and hate him for it at the same time and also, the strongest pull, feel an almost obsessive curiosity over him, over his possible love for both my parents.

I could have fallen asleep there, leaning against the wall, the day's heat rising up and lessening and the ground cool to the backs of my legs; I could have fallen asleep and wandered home at daybreak, my mother sitting out on the front porch in a humming, steady panic, her new haircut a frothy cloud about her head. I had the power to worry her, to frighten her, to abandon her; it would have been an easy thing to do. All it would take would be to stay away an hour too long, to not go back, to go somewhere else instead. Abandonment, I thought, in the physical essence of its execution, was an action both simple and clean. Only when the mind caught up with the body did the trouble begin; you'd have to be a strong sort of person to keep your mind quiet long enough for your legs to carry you far, you'd have to tell all your intentions and guilt and longing to hush up, just this far, just beyond that state line, the last hour of night, just until turning and going back was more of a burden than to keep moving forward. My father had gone that far, after he'd climbed onto the bus and pulled onto the interstate; he'd crossed a line where going back was no longer feasible, where any known way of life would see his return with a turned shoulder of faintest hurt and bemused recognition. To say that my father had gone looking for a better life seemed wrong and contained betrayal. He simply wanted to wake up to a life that was enough, and as it happened, we had allowed him that chance.

The sun cast a burnished, itching glow through the lids of my closed eyes; to open them would mean squinting, would mean stumbling blind through abundant light, but I opened them, and squinted, and stumbled in my standing, because it was what my father would have told me to do. *Welcome back,* he would say. *And are things different? And has the world changed?*

14.

Franny was waiting for me. She was dressed and sitting neatly on the couch, her skirt straight, her hands tucked under her thighs. She looked up at me. "What's wrong with you?" she asked.

"I was at the dentist."

"You've got dirt all over your face."

I lifted a hand to my cheek.

"Well?"

"Is Mother home?"

"She called earlier," Franny said, getting up from the couch and going into the kitchen. She filled a glass with water.

I followed her and stood watching her drink. "What'd she say?"

"That she was having dinner with Jack in town." Franny furrowed her brow and held the water glass toward me.

I shook my head.

"You'd better go change," she said. "Susan was over here looking for you earlier."

"Mad?"

"Of course."

I wasn't used to Franny being so patient with me; there had always been a strain of tenderness within Franny, but it was a hidden side of her personality, one that only revealed itself when she was very tired or very worried. I hadn't seen it in months, not since she'd begun her change, her sudden and sure departure from childhood. "What would you like to wear?" she asked me as we stood in the kitchen, and when I shrugged she took my hand and led me to the bathroom. "Wash your face," she said. She took a clean washcloth from the cupboard and soaked it with warm water. "I'll pick something from your closet," she said. I heard her in my bedroom, switching on my record player and sliding open the door to my closet. I washed the dirt from my face and used Franny's comb. My hair snapped with static and floated in frizzy lines around my head and shoulders; I hadn't used the iron on it all summer long and I didn't bother to now. Franny came in with a purple dress. "This one?" she asked, and I nodded, pulling off my blouse and unbuttoning my shorts. Franny lifted the dress over my head and pulled up the zipper. I let her gather my hair between wet palms and smooth it into a braid. In her makeup bag she had a little brush that smoothed my eyebrows and lipstick the color of coral. I sat on the edge of the bathtub while she hovered in front of me. Finally she stood me up and turned me to face the mirror. "Okay?" she asked. We were the same height, Franny and I; it had happened without us knowing. We left the house together and walked down the road to the Leroy house.

The big front door stood open, and we could see through the screen into the dim of the hallway and the living room beyond. There was a din of voices coming out at us, shrieks and laughter and the high-pitched whine of a record turning. We looked at each other and I started to push through the screen without knocking, the same as we'd done all summer when visiting Susan, but Franny stopped me and rang the bell. "It's a party," she said, grinning and waving at Susan's figure coming toward us.

"Well Christ!" Susan cried when she saw us. "What are you ringing the damn bell for?" She reached for my hand and pulled me toward the living room. "Can you believe it?" she hissed, looking around at the crowd.

"Susan," I said, "what about your Dad?"

"He's out for the night, I told you. I told you that before."

Franny and I followed her to the kitchen, bumping and weaving and smiling awkwardly at every face. The kitchen counter was a sea of dirtied glasses and sticky brown bottles. "Try this," Susan said, fishing around a cupboard for something clean to drink from. She filled two coffee cups with pink liquid from a punch bowl.

"Ugh," Franny said, holding her cup away, "what is this?"

"Vodka Kool-Aid," Susan said. She took a long swig. "Come on girls," she said, leaning against the counter sloppily, having to reposition herself when one elbow slipped in a pool of something spilled. "Loosen up already." She glared and drank.

"Who are all these people?" Franny asked.

"People I invited!" said Susan. She turned to me. "You said you'd be here at seven."

"I had a dentist appointment."

"Until seven?"

"It looks like you've done fine without me," I said.

"What if your dad comes home?" Franny asked.

"He's out."

"Who's he out with?" I asked.

"Joni."

"Why is he with her?"

"She wanted to see him."

"He's out with our mother," Franny interjected.

"What?" asked Susan, her anger faltering for a moment.

"Our mother," Franny said.

"Why would he be with her?"

"They're friends," said Franny, shrugging. She sipped her drink and cringed. "This is really disgusting."

"I don't think so."

"No, it really is," said Franny.

"I don't think they're together." Susan was almost yelling now. She looked at me, her eyes wide. "He was going to talk to Joni."

"Maybe they're all doing something together," said Franny. She squealed then, and clamped a hand over her mouth. She grabbed my arm. "Look," she said, pointing toward the front hall.

Susan and I turned in unison to see Charlie's blond head peering through the crowd. Susan sighed and went to greet him, gathering her drink and swaying around the counter that separated the living room from the kitchen.

"I thought Susan wasn't popular," Franny said, sniffing the contents of her glass.

"She's not."

"She promised beer," came a voice, and Franny and I turned to see Ellen Tray coming into the kitchen. "On the invitation," she said, and I realized I'd never opened mine; I'd let it rest unread inside my book bag. We watched Susan through the crowd; her bright red head bobbing back and forth, her laugh and excited squeal cutting through the din. "I'd watch her," Ellen said; she had an open beer can in hand. "She's been drinking that punch all evening."

I only half heard this last from Ellen; Charlie Mullan was waving at me through the crowd, and I felt my throat and ears grow hot.

"Your boyfriend?" Ellen asked, and Franny grinned, but Charlie and Susan had reached us before I could answer.

"Look Grace, its Charlie!" Susan said, a false expression of excitement on her face.

"Hello." I took a drink from my coffee cup, forgetting what it contained, and began to choke.

Franny slapped me on the back a few times.

"Want a beer, Charlie?" Susan asked.

"No thank you," Charlie said.

"Oh pooh," said Susan. She opened a beer can and thrust it toward Charlie.

"No," said Charlie, his hands in his pockets, "but thank you."

"It's a party, stupid," Susan said.

"He doesn't have to drink, Susan," I said.

"Don't tell me what to do," said Susan.

"I'm not."

"You were an hour late for the damn party anyway."

I looked away from her.

"You could at least apologize," Susan said. Her hand was still outstretched, holding the beer for Charlie. She seemed to have completely forgotten where she was; her gaze was fixed on me.

"She had an appointment, Susan," Franny said.

"I'm not apologizing," I said, looking at my feet; my

whole body was taut. I could feel Franny looking sidelong at me, her face wary.

"Susan," Charlie said, and she looked at him. "I'll take the beer."

Susan looked at the beer in her hand. She shook her head. "No. You don't want it." She turned and slammed the can on the countertop; beer foamed up and over the sides, pooling on the linoleum. There was a silence then; in the living room the record began to skip and there was a clattering as someone stood up to change it.

"This is fun," said Ellen, and Franny laughed.

Susan turned to her, her brow furrowed. "What's funny?" she asked.

"Nothing."

"You laughed," said Susan. She pointed a finger at Franny. "You were laughing at me."

"No I wasn't."

Susan eyed Franny. "How old are you anyway?" she demanded. Franny flushed.

"Susan," Ellen said, "maybe let's talk to some of the other guests."

But Susan was shaking her head slowly; her arms were crossed tightly and her jaw was clenched. "I've got a rule for the night," she said, tossing her hair from her face. She looked from me to Franny between narrowed eyes.

"A rule?" I asked.

"No sisters tonight," she said.

Franny and I looked at each other.

"That!" Susan cried, pointing. "I'm sick of your little looks." She stalked to the punch bowl and filled a new glass to the brim. "My party, my rule. No sister shit." She was looking at Franny again, and Franny, for all her growth, for all her satiny hair and fringed boots, seemed to shrink under Susan's gaze. "You're just a little tag-along, aren't you?" Susan said, and took a drink. She snorted. "I don't even know how old you are."

"Stop, Susan," I said.

"Oh you," Susan laughed then. "She knows I'm only joking."

Franny turned away from us, dumped the contents of her cup down the drain, and went through the back door to the yard.

"Oh boo-hoo," said Susan, laughing still.

I stared at her.

"What?" she demanded. She shook her head. "You girls," she said.

"What the hell is wrong with you?" I asked. I could feel Charlie watching me.

Susan looked at him; she knew I wouldn't lose myself in front of him.

"Just a party, Gracie," she said.

"You invited Franny."

"I don't think so." She raised her eyebrows and met my eyes. "You two just come as a package." She straightened and smoothed her dress. "I have other guests," she said, brushing past me and weaving her way into the living room. Few people looked up as she walked by; they were, none of them, her friends. Someone had turned the turntable up to a deafening volume and beneath this there was the sound of something breaking, someone laughing. Susan turned back and looked at me at this sound, her face struggling between stoic anger and panic.

I stared at her, my face still, and after a long moment she turned, stumbling against someone and spilling her drink, and staggered down the hallway. We listened as the door to her bedroom slammed shut.

"She's drunk," said Ellen.

No one stayed very long. After the beer was gone people began to leave, streaming out of the house and down Colt's Neck, their cars billowing dust into the air. No one asked after Susan. Only a few people said goodbye or thank you or asked where they might find a garbage can. At ten there was still blue light on the western horizon. I found Franny lying on the back lawn, Susan's big white cat Felise purring on her chest. "Want to go home?" I asked. She didn't look at me. "I'm sorry about Susan," I said. I stood over her. "She's drunk, Franny." When she still didn't answer I started to walk away.

"What does it matter if Jack and Mother were together tonight?" she called after me. I turned back. In the heat of Susan's anger I'd almost forgotten about them. The barbershop, the haircut, the dark earth of the field and the stone wall—all of it seemed very far away and faint. I looked down at Franny. She was slowly stroking Felise, her knees up and her feet bare.

"I don't know," I said.

"You know."

"I don't."

Franny was silent.

"I'm going to check on Susan and go home. Come with me if you want," I said, then waited. "Are you coming?" I asked.

"I know where home is," she said.

I didn't wait for her, but I didn't go inside to check on Susan. I walked around the house, tearing the skirt of my dress when it caught on overgrown bushes. At this time of night, on these clear and warm nights, sound carried easily, and with windows opened it was easy to hear a neighbor's phone ringing or a sudden burst of laughter. There was a telephone ringing somewhere across the road, and I headed towards our house following the sound. Franny and I had forgotten to leave any lights on, but the back door stood open, and I made it through the screen door and the dark kitchen to the telephone before the final ring. I remember saying hello, breathlessly, thinking that it would be Mother, thinking of bad things though I did not know why, but thinking them nevertheless. Sleepy drivers and careless summer roads. How quick escape would be when a lover was there to flee with you, or somewhere waiting for your arrival. When I answered the telephone, my father's voice was on the other end.

"You're there," he said.

"I'm here."

"I'm so glad," he said.

When my mother came home that night, it was to find Franny and me sleeping in her bed, the sheet kicked away against the heat. I woke to watch her shed her dress and lay beside me in her slip that seemed to glow in the blue night coming through the window. She smelled of cigarette smoke and bourbon. "Did your father call?" she whispered. She put her hands to her neck, smoothing the bare skin, the suddenness of her exposed throat and shoulder. She said nothing of the late hour, the new haircut, or Jack.

"He invited us for the last part of August. Franny and me," I said.

My mother was quiet for a long time; I watched her face, thinking she might have fallen asleep, but her hands kept a steady smoothing motion, first on her own arms and then on mine. "August then," she finally said, then sighed her deep sigh and turned to pull the sheet up over the three of us.

The next day I went across the road to check on Susan. She answered the door in her nightgown, squinting into the bright sunlight; her hair was bound back by a set of purple curlers that Joni had left behind, and I could hear the television going in the living room. She stood aside to let me in without a word.

"Is your dad home?" I asked, surveying the living room. It was spotless. Not a sign of the night before remained. Susan just shook her head and slumped back against the couch cushions. An upright fan stood in the corner and churned the air listlessly. I sat down in the rocker and pushed myself with the tips of my toes. On the television, a man and a woman were exchanging angry looks; the background music swelled and then cut away for the commercial. "Well," I said.

Susan glanced at me.

"Did he get mad?"

"He didn't find out. He came home late."

I just nodded. "What's with the curlers?" I finally asked. "Your hair's already curly."

Susan gave me a tired, amused look. "For a more perfect curl, of course," she said.

I rocked harder, the spindles of the chair creaking every time I let my full weight against them.

Susan flung the blanket away and stood up; for a moment I thought she was headed towards me, ready to force the chair still, but she passed me on a waft of hairspray and went to the kitchen. On the television, the angry man and woman were back.

"Remember that game we used to play?" I called to Susan. "When we'd shut the volume off and make up the lines?"

From the kitchen came the sounds of drawers opening

and slamming shut, the rush of water, a clatter of ice cubes in a glass.

"Remember?" I called again.

Susan came back to the living room with a wet cloth in her hand and a glass of ice water. She swallowed two aspirin before leaning back again, the cloth spread over her face. "You were good at that," she said, her voice flat.

"At what?" I asked, forgetting what I'd even asked in the first place.

"The lines game. At that. You were good at that." She spoke without removing the cloth from her face, so her words came a bit muffled.

We were silent for a while. I watched the soap opera; Susan might have fallen asleep. Then she spoke again, startling me. "Of course, you would be," she said. "It was your game to begin with."

I waited.

She leaned forward, the cloth falling from her face, and reached for her water glass. "You must know all about making things up like that. From him, I mean."

"My father didn't talk about his work much," I said. It seemed a diverting, adult thing to say.

"Not him," said Susan. On her face there was a taunting, trapping grin. "The other one," she said. "His boyfriend."

I stared at her. There was a long silence in which she dunked the cloth in the water glass, wrung it carefully to avoid getting the carpet wet, then positioned herself more comfortably on the couch, stretching herself full length as if preparing for a long sleep. She folded the cloth and placed it back over her eyes.

I thought of all the afternoons and evenings when Mother would eat too much and take one too many cocktails and end up prostrate in bed or on the living room couch, her shoes off and her nylons twisted, her hairpins scattered. She never asked for it, but I'd bring her aspirin and a cold washcloth and a pillow for her feet because I had seen Father do this for her, I'd seen him become tactful and soft when the moment called for it. Mother's drinking had subsided greatly since the first spring on Colt's Neck; whether this was due to healing or happiness or sheer, guttural responsibility I did not know; the importance lay in her calmer ways. Rarely now was I shaken awake at midnight by a mother who wanted simply to talk, a slur on her breath, or greeted in the afternoon by a mother asleep on the couch, dust on her clothes, straw in her hair and a sweating, half-empty cocktail glass on the coffee table. My mother was not a drunk, but she did like to drink, sometimes too much, and watching Susan now, suffering her hangover, I saw how life with my mother had stifled any trace of what might have been a frivolous teenage streak within me, had made me angry and impatient with behavior that had no credible purpose, behavior that might be deemed ridiculous. This impatience was the result of living as half-child, half-adult with a mother who was at once loving and frivolous and deeply sad; it was also, I knew, a direct link to my father, a piece of his genetic code made manifest within me.

Watching Susan, something within me fell swiftly and fixedly into place. I felt completely spent. It seemed to me that I had lived the past year of my life being very, very good, and very patient, and I was exhausted. It had not made one bit of difference, this being good. Time had gone forward just as it always had; around me decisions had been made, changes secured, houses emptied and left and new life found.

Despite the fan in the corner, the air in Susan's living room was muffled and close. I had been in this room too many times to remember, had spent sleepovers and study sessions here and countless hours consoling Susan when Joni made her cry. Susan's life was not difficult; she had a father who doted on her and loved her, a well kept house with food in the refrigerator, a television, a room all her own. She did well enough in school; teachers liked her; she was entrusted. Even Joni had entrusted her, worried over her, asked her what she'd like for dinner and wept when Susan slammed doors in her face.

I stood up quickly and walked to the front window, pulling back the curtain. The room flooded with afternoon sunlight.

Susan sat up, the washcloth falling to her lap. "What's wrong with you?" she said. She stood and pulled the curtain closed again. "I don't feel well," she said.

"Clearly," I said. "I've never seen someone so unwell."

"I'd like you to leave now." Susan crossed to the television and switched it off. With her back to me, she began unwinding the curlers from her head, setting them in a neat row atop the television.

"You know, I don't feel sorry for you," I said to her back. "I don't feel sorry at all."

Susan mumbled something low beneath her breath, and continued to slowly untangle her hair.

"Can't hear you," I said.

She set the last curler in its place and turned to face me. Her hair was a massive web of dark, half-damp waves. "You don't know me," she said.

"I do know you, Susan. And I know when you're being ridiculous."

"You don't know a thing about me," she said, her voice still nothing more than a low monotone.

"I know a few things," I said. "I know how you went to the hotel to spy on Pete Schiffer."

Susan turned crimson. "Get out of my house," she said.

"What do you even miss, Susan?" I tried to catch her eye. "Joni? You hated her, at least you pretended to." I paused, kept on. "Your mother? Do you miss her? You never even knew her." It was a surprisingly easy thing to say, a sliding down through still water, a thing I'd always wanted to say.

There was a trace of something other than anger in her face then, a subtle weakening in her jaw line, and I feared I'd gone too far. I had begun to sweat; I could feel the beads rolling between my shoulder blades. Susan was staring at the coffee table with a pale, blank face.

I swallowed. "We're only fifteen," I said. "I don't see why it has to be so heavy." But it was heavy; already I could feel the weight of what I'd said filling the dim room. I didn't know what else to do but leave. I was turning to go when Susan's voice came at my back, her words so low I had to strain to hear.

"At least she didn't choose to leave," she said.

I stood still, not turning around, studying the carpet at my feet; a mossy green so recently swept it still held vacuum lines. At the nice house, my father had always taken care of the vacuuming. Sometimes he whistled while he did this job, loud enough to be heard over the running motor. Sometimes he was silent. My father worked with his shirtsleeves rolled up. He worked seriously and with devotion, a man who knew his calling. He drank bourbon in the evenings. He was quick to anger, quick to make a joke; often he was remarkably good, remarkably kind. One day he went away, and I began to forget him.

I went away from the house without saying goodbye, without looking over my shoulder. It would be the last time I would speak to Susan Leroy for more than fifteen years.

15.

What had I expected? For Mother and Jack to fall into some desperate, secret affair? To find them embracing in the dusty and dim corners of the old barn? Perhaps. I might have imagined it that way. Their not-so-secret admiration had an entrancing quality to it; there were moments when I could make them a story the way I'd made stories for all of our neighbors—Sedina and Joni and Charlie Mullan. Jack and Mother were just another part of the landscape of the place, victims of past sorrow and the variety of life they now lived, a life cut off from town concerns. It had been true: in town, our secret lives could be both known and hidden; we were surrounded by the troubles of other human kind. On Colt's Neck we lived in a bubble of story; our histories and our current longings were our character; they helped us know more fully where we stood on the stage. Of course my mother should carry on some indefinable romance with the man whose wife she'd once known and loved, the woman whose death she still sometimes felt, in the contours of her innermost grief, that she'd had a divine hand in. Of course. It was a leading role. More than that, it was a role she could write for herself; this time, the ending was known: the man would be leaving. She could prepare herself accordingly; cut her hair and slave over the garden and make a show of strength to all who watched her.

I am too hard on my mother. In my memory of her, that year after my father left, I see that many times she was teetering on a precipice and that many times she was standing on solid ground. When she teetered I had the shameful desire to reach out a flat palm and push her, for I had the notion that where she fell might be a place of greater truth; she would

shed whatever shroud she'd picked up the day of his leaving
and return to the mother I'd once known dearly, sweating
earnestly over canned goods in the kitchen and writing love
poems to tuck inside my lunch sack. She was different now,
that was all. I both saw this plainly and plainly riled against it;
there was not much more I could do.

Summer. Franny and I sleep as late as we can, before
lawnmowers and barking dogs and the encroaching, insistent
heat forces us from our beds. We wake and Mother has left
hours before, driven the dawn road for town and her work
there. Franny cuts slices of bread, toasts them in the oven,
spreads them with butter and honey. She fills a thermos with
coffee; she has taught me to want coffee upon waking. Still in
nightgowns, we take our picnic breakfast into the woods on
the mountain behind the house. It is cooler under the canopy
of trees, and we know well the path to Charlie Mullan's
hunting shack. We often find him there; he's been awake since
dawn, shotgun in hand, apple cores at his feet, on his cheek
a red welt where he's rested his head against the doorframe
to sleep for a few minutes. Charlie seems older than us, and
we take comfort in his quiet ways; he demands nothing and
never questions our company. We have made toast for Charlie
too; we have considered him when measuring coffee.

There was a morning when I went alone up the mountain
to see Charlie. The early day was shrouded in a low mist;
the dry grasses of the field held dew at their tips as I passed
through them; all the other houses were sleeping.

When I reached the shack that morning, Charlie had
already shot two grouse, and they lay in a neat, soft bundle at
his feet, their delicate ankles tied together with a loop of string.
He pointed to them when he saw me, and I nodded, though

I hated the sight of them, the way their ashy breasts merged with the leaf and earth where they rested. That morning, I'd made egg sandwiches wrapped in foil, the yolks still warm and runny. Charlie said that his own mother didn't know how to cook eggs properly. They always came out grey and gritty, he said, too tough.

"I made these eggs," I told him. "Not my mother."

He nodded, then took a bite. I had the sudden urge to defend my mother's habits, to explain away any curiosity over her daily absence, over the fact that Franny and I woke to an empty kitchen and cracked the shells of our own eggs, buttered our own toast, drank coffee at twelve and fifteen, and on summer days often didn't change from our nightgowns until very late in the day. These were not such unusual things, but Charlie, I knew, woke to a coddling mother, and perhaps expected a different sort of life, though he escaped from that coddling quick enough, came up here to shoot at soft birds and take handouts from the neighbor girls.

I sat beside him then, the neighbor girl, in my nightgown, my bare feet stuck into unlaced tennis shoes. If Susan had seen me she would have sighed with deep disapproval. At least I'd combed and braided my hair and gargled with a gulp of mouthwash from Mother's bathroom shelf. At least I'd cleaned the sleep from my eyes. All this done with competing purposes; for a time there had been the intimation that Charlie might feel a particular way about me, and that I might return this feeling. As such, it seemed plausible that on one of these mornings—a morning when we were alone, such as this one—it might become necessary for Charlie to kiss me. When and if such an event took place, I did not want my breath to smell of ten hours sleep; I did not want my hair to be matted and snarled. I had a vague idea of how

I'd like to appear if such a moment were to present itself: certain, passive, slightly paler than I was, slightly smaller. At the same time, there was a part of me that did not at all welcome the idea of kissing someone. In truth, the idea struck me as ridiculous and embarrassing, an act that would surely just prove my ineptness and naivety and that would forever ruin my comfortable regard of Charlie. After kissing a boy, it became necessary to consider many worrisome details with which I did not want to bother: dress, body, fingernail shape, conversation style, type of underwear, brand of deodorant, one's personal limits and brand of bravery. I liked the current state of my friendship with Charlie; I did not feel that I needed to try very hard to be accepted in a complete way. So it was that I often went about our breakfast hours in a state of half-preparedness, breath clean, hair combed, my summer nightgown hiding what it could of my unshaven legs.

Charlie seemed to notice nothing about my appearance. He was a clean, quiet dresser; Mrs. Mullan washed, dried, pressed and folded every article of clothing he owned, set out daily ensembles for him, looked him over when he came to the breakfast table to face his overcooked eggs, and sent him out into the world with either a gentle brow of affection or a tight-lipped frown of worry. So Charlie told it. At one time, when he was younger, she might have told him to go back upstairs and change if she disapproved in some way of his appearance, but his father had put a stop to that. If it wasn't for his father, in fact, Charlie doubted if he'd ever be allowed outside. We were curious about Mrs. Mullan, Franny and I, though a sense of propriety and something else—a dim fear of her, perhaps—kept us from asking too many questions.

We asked Mother what she knew of Mrs. Mullan, who had once belonged to a book club that Mother had attended when we'd first made the move to Colt's Neck. This club, for women only, met in the library of the Catholic High School that stood at the juncture of town and country, where one could see street lights and livestock within the same radius. Mrs. Mullan had invited Mother to the club as a kind of feminine and neighborly gesture; it was more than a book club, she'd explained in her nervous, slightly assuming manner. More like a women's club. They met twice a month to discuss books of course, but also to swap recipes and sewing patterns. Sometimes, Mrs. Mullan added, the club was helpful for discussing family troubles. A balm, she'd said. A balm for difficult times.

My mother had agreed, desperate only to be rid of Mrs. Mullan whose healthy hips, bound tightly by the sturdy cotton of her rust-colored dress, filled the doorframe with determination. "What could I bring?" Mother asked. "A bottle of wine?"

Mrs. Mullan blushed and took a step away, finally retreating. "Oh nothing but your lovely self," she'd said. "We're not really a wine-drinking bunch."

Mother had stayed with this club for two months, longer than we'd predicted. She must have found what Mrs. Mullan had said to be at least partly true; there was comfort in the company of women, even if you cared little for sewing patterns or fruitcake recipes. A balm; perhaps my mother did find this there. Perhaps those two months had been strangely healing. Eventually she'd returned to her evening routine of cocktails and silence, in those early days after everything had changed and she'd found herself to be a single woman, pitied by curious neighbors, invited out for evenings of well-mannered gossip in which she was expected to reveal something of herself and her situation. Family troubles; yes indeed.

That morning on the mountain, Charlie finished his egg sandwich in four large bites and wiped his mouth with a neatly folded handkerchief. He glanced down at the dead grouse and gave the bird a nudge with his boot. "Your turn for a story," he said.

I looked at him, confused, my own sandwich still half-eaten in my palm.

"Your father," he said. "Your mother. Their story."

I stayed silent, staring at the bound feet of the hunted birds. For a moment, a long while it seemed, I could not recall their story. I could not remember what had happened. I shook my head, hoping for some jolted clarity. "Why do you want to know?" I asked.

"Do you ever feel shame?" He asked the question politely enough, but I saw then what he was after. He already knew our story.

"Shame," I said, repeating the word; it made a funny shape in my mouth. It occurred to me that I'd never stopped to look at it in such a way. I did not look at it in this way when I saw them standing behind the piano together, long ago in the nice house. I did not want to tell his story openly, my father's, and of course this could be the action of shame, this keeping of secrets, but it didn't feel this way to me. I didn't tell that story because if you tell a story it becomes somehow more material than it had been before, it gathers life and starts running ahead of you. If I stayed silent, I could still keep him within reach; if I stayed silent, there was still the distinct notion that one day we'd look up and find him tapping at our window, asking to be let back in.

The mountainside had become hot on my return trip home. I didn't run, though the thought of it crossed my mind; it crossed my mind that I could crash through the underbrush, that I could make a more dramatic exit. But I didn't. I just stood up and walked away, my bones doing the things I told them to do. I would have liked to stay sitting beside Charlie Mullan. I could have so easily become addicted to the pursuit of his attention. Something deeper drove me though; a nauseating homesickness, and a longing to once again be a very little girl, still outside of greater knowing.

The day with Charlie Mullan on the mountain was also the day that Franny got her first period, and I came back to the house to find her bloody and only a bit tearful, sitting on the bathroom floor. It was the day Mother stopped in town and bought our train tickets to the east, coming home in the evening to hang them with false excitement on the refrigerator door, a talisman to our going and a blind faith in what would gather us at the other end of the line. These things happened, and yet I cannot remember any changed emotion in us. I can no longer recall the sound of Charlie's voice or the exactness of his final words to me. I see him fingering the soft breast of the dead grouse. I feel my own movement away from him and down the edge of the mountain, my nightgown catching on the low branches of infant trees. I know Franny's blood to be the color of ink; I see us wadding up the stained bathmat and tucking it deep into the trashcan by the roadside. What did we do for the rest of that day? We must have felt very spent; there must have been a kind of welcome weariness to be relished. Perhaps we made a lunch and ate it together in the basement where the afternoon heat could not reach us, where the bare backs of our legs pressed against the cool cement floor. Our mother came home to us and presented the tickets with flourish, her face pale and determined. "See!" she might have exclaimed. "You're really going." She had spoken with

Father; money had been wired, plans arranged.

Most likely I slept in Franny's bed that night. Had she told Mother about the day? Had we gone to the grocery for sanitary supplies and aspirin? Had we celebrated in some way? Was my mother the type of woman who would have celebrated such events? I can remember that I did tell Franny about what Charlie had asked me.

She shifted her hips on the mattress and kicked the sheet away. The room, even with both windows opened wide, was heavy with trapped heat. "I could tell you were upset," she said. "You came down from that mountain pretty quick." There was a long silence then, as heavy as the air.

"Are you ashamed of Father?" I finally asked, and I felt Franny's face turning towards mine on the pillow. But she didn't answer. She wouldn't have anyway; Franny did not like to talk about Father in unsure ways. The known situation, its visible contours—this was truth for Franny, this was understanding, and the known situation was that Father had gone away, was living with Ivan, and that we had begun, however unwillingly, to grow accustomed and even comfortable in his absence; we had woken up one day to realize that we did not want to return to the nice house and the life it once contained. "I want to stay on Colt's Neck forever," Franny had said to me once as we'd been walking home from the river and its buried swimming holes. In town this same river flowed dirty past dirty houses. Upstream, nearer Colt's Neck, it was clean and deep and clear. We walked and the sun of that country spread reams of light in every direction; we walked feeling blessed simply for knowing a wider space than any we had known before.

I moved so that my face was a mirror of Franny's against the pillow, the tips of our noses nearly touching. "Do you suppose that Father and Ivan kiss?" I asked.

"Of course," said Franny.

"How?" I asked.

"Like this." She put her palm against my cheek, sticky and small, and met her lips to mine.

In all my dreams of Father, we are no longer in the nice house. We are out here on Colt's Neck and Father comes and goes like a live-in guest. Sometimes I dream that I wake at night and he is in the kitchen, making tea and reading. "Good to see you," he says, and I join him and ask for honey. He reads to me from the newspaper or from a script, if he's in the middle of a project. "What's wrong with it?" he'll ask. "How should we play it?"

I'll tell him how. "Make her more courageous," I say. "The female lead."

He refills my teacup and listens, intent.

"She needs to be louder," I say.

He nods, a slow grin spreading across his face, and it is the best feeling, this saying of something that pleases him.

Sometimes, after our tea, we sit on the top rails of the fence and look over the nighttime field. Father's got a glass of something in his hand and he offers me a taste. Vodka. But how do I know this? It doesn't seem to matter; it's just a taste I deduce like any other and it's part of the dream. My father looks in the direction of the Leroy house and takes a drink. "I was friends with Jack," he says. "We were very good friends."

"His wife," I say. "She died."

"Yes. That was a sad day."

"He's leaving," I say of Jack. "He's going away too." I look sideways at my father and see that he is very tired and very sad. There are blue circles under his eyes and he needs a haircut. Jack could cut his hair for him, I say. I want to know how long he's been here. I don't mean on the fencepost. I mean this time, this visit. How long? And why do you only come at night? Mother would be so glad to see you.

My father shakes his head. "I miss him," he says.

"Ivan's all the way in the east," I remind him. "You've come out for a visit, remember? You can go back and see him soon; he'll be there." I lay a hand on my father's shoulder. He is crying. His face bunches like a crumpled cloth; he has dozens of lines around his mouth and eyes from years of laughing, from every emotion felt. "You'll see him soon," I say, patting his shoulder as if he were a little boy.

He passes a hand across his face and suddenly he is calm again. "Are you friends with Susan?" he asks.

"Yes."

"I asked you to be friends with her."

"I am. I remember."

"What's she like?" he asks. Now we are sitting in the grass. My father is wearing black trousers and a day-worn white dress shirt. He reaches and unfastens the buttons at his wrists to roll back his sleeves; his arms are tan and slender. His shoes are polished. "I stopped for a shine before coming," he says. "At the place by the diner."

"The Felix Diner," I say.

He nods. "Alice Leroy had flaming red hair."

"You could see her on the stage."

"Clear from the balcony."

"And then she died."

"Then she died." We are quiet and the morning comes. I wake up sweaty, the sheets warped around me. I am fifteen. We live in a farm house. We live a strange half-life of outside work and modern convenience, and we spend our days going between house and barn, hillside and field; we do these things as if we were born to them. We spend our days wondering about the lives in other houses. We spend our days trying to imagine what he is doing. We spend our days waiting for her to return home, and every time she does we are secretly, wondrously relieved.

16.

Beyond Colt's Neck, at the end of dirt roads and smaller farm homes, one is met abruptly by a wall of forest. Through this wall runs a thin and overgrown path, though it is discernable enough for following. Take this path, and you'll come across dark parts of the river, the same that has cut its way clear from the middle of town and earlier than that, even, earlier back to other woods and other towns, to places we've never seen nor heard of. The dark parts of the river are deep, and ideal for swimming. On Sunday afternoons, when they are not bound by their work, the sons of ranchers can be found here, naked, tanned to collarbone and elbow, pale as new babies on stomach and buttocks and thigh. They jump from rocks, doing somersaults in the air and hooting at each other, holding cigarettes between their wet lips as they sprawl and dry out on the riverbank where the sun cuts through the tops of the trees and pools its heavy warmth.

We were afraid of these boys, Franny and I, our early summers on Colt's Neck, afraid of these almost men. We had some idea of what they could do for us, and would do for us, in later years when we would become braver and practiced in certain things. We might have been afraid of the swimming boys, but we snuck along the path through the woods listening for them, hiding ourselves where we could watch and not be seen. One we liked best. He was dark, with a square chest and a brilliant red scar that ran the length of his left calf. He swam gracefully, diving from rocks rather than somersaulting, studying the scene about him with patient and pleasant interest.

One day, watching him, Franny got brave, and stood up from behind our hiding place. She waved. The one with the scar stood upright on the far shore, atop a massive rock black and shining with wet. He was naked head to toe, and he was waving back. As we watched, he reached up and placed a hand over his heart. He looked at Franny as if she were two feet in front of him and began to whistle; a clear, heavy sound that crossed the still water and seemed to encircle us. Franny turned and bolted and I followed, tripping on exposed roots and the knotty scabs of dried underbrush. We ran until we reached the cut off between forest and field and were immersed in full, sudden light. Franny was gasping, laughing. She hugged herself then reached out and caught me roughly under the arms, tickling me. I pushed her away and we walked on.

Here we could see the train tracks that snaked through expanses of alfalfa getting their second cutting of the year. It was Franny who remembered; it must have been the tracks that made her remember, or the fields, and she asked if I remembered too, the drives we'd sometimes taken with Mother and Father when we were very young. I said yes but had to work hard to bring it back; the view from the deep passenger seat; the open windows letting in the hot summer air; the steady shapes of our parents in front of us, and a bronzed forearm resting against the car door. A new car. I remembered this. The smell was new. There had been some excitement at the purchase, for there had been several months with no car at all. Cars borrowed from friends and relatives. The old car reminisced over like a beloved pet; that old boat.

What had happened to her? She'd died, of course. She'd died when Alice Leroy had died. She'd limped away with blood pooling at her floorboards, caked in her upholstery. The new car held no residual blood and my father drove carefully. We would drive the very road that bisected Colt's Neck. Maybe we would stop to see some people we knew, a little girl and her father. More often we would just keep driving, no real purpose; just a Sunday drive to see the harvest, to watch for the passenger train, to lean out our windows and wave, trying to get the engineer to blow his horn.

Franny and I followed the fence line west, towards our home on Colt's Neck. No train passed through for us to see.

We were waiting for the day when the Leroys would leave us for good. Mother was waiting. She did her work—driving in to town in the morning and coming home in the late afternoon to dig in the garden—but even that distraction could not calm her waiting. Garden digging was interrupted every few minutes by the careful watch of the Leroy house across the road, its now curtain-less windows lit up from within.

One evening Jack arrived at the back door, carrying with him a box of assorted things: combs and razors and scissors; a framed photograph of Susan and a potted plant that he thought Mother might care for. She set the clay pot on the ledge below the kitchen window. "Do you like your hair?" Jack asked her.

Mother nodded. "Oh yes," she said, like a little girl, smoothing a lock behind her ear. At the back of her head, her hair rose in a sculpted cloud from her thin neck. "Oh yes," she said again.

"I'm so glad," Jack said. He lingered for a moment before leaving, looking as if he had forgotten something very important but could no longer recall why it had meant so much.

They left us on a clear Sunday morning. Franny and I stood at the end of the drive and watched Jack test the latch on the trailer that was hitched to his truck. Susan sat in the passenger seat, staring away from us. Jack shook my mother's hand then bent as if in afterthought to kiss her cheek. He did not meet her eyes, though she searched for a look from him, her face wan and childlike. She watched him climb into the truck beside Susan and slam the door. As they pulled away, Susan turned to look out the rear window of the cab and she watched us retreat in this way, bumping down the washed-out road, the outline of her wild hair receding slowly until she was just a dark shape in the back of a truck, sitting beside an upright man.

In the days before we left for the East, my mother became a frantic woman. She decided last minute that we weren't at all prepared for such a trip, let alone for an entire month with a father we'd not seen in a solid year. Preparing for the trip meant trailing after Mother through the Woolworths and Army-Navy stores downtown, buying new underwear and socks, shampoo and Pepto-Bismol, flashlights and stiff green canvas duffels, suited for soldiers heading off to battle, that would hold our clothes and books and shoes. "It's only for a month," Franny said, fighting with Mother over the number of nightgowns she should pack. "Don't they have washing machines in New York?" She opened the wide mouth of her duffel and showed us how she could fit her entire body inside.

Mother tied the drawstring over her blonde head. "Fine," she said. "We'll ship you like that."

She was businesslike in her mania, but as the days passed and the time for us to leave drew nearer, she became more and more forgetful and plaintive; many mornings we'd wake to find her watering the front lawn flowers, staring dumbly across the road at the silent Leroy house, the hose forgotten in her hand and soaking the earth around her. The night before we left she stayed in the basement until two, ironing skirts and blouses, packing and re-packing our bags. She'd brought the little kitchen radio downstairs for company, and through the vents in our bedrooms Franny and I could make out the faint echo of dance-hall music. This memory is so clear to me that I can close my eyes and exist within it; it is a great regret of mine that I did not extract myself from whatever form of teenage self-absorption I was then shrouded by and get up from my bed, walk through the darkened house to the basement stairs, and go down those stairs to keep my mother company.

Often, caught in some memory of my mother as she was in that aftermath year, I am a bit startled to realize that she was a lonely woman—not only during that year, but during many of her years. My mother too was surprised by her own loneliness. The very fact of it—of being alone, being left, as it were—had hardened itself in my mother until she came to regard it as something outside herself, an enemy that must be looked in the face, recognized, and then either destroyed by strength of will or ignored with a steadfast purpose. There was simply no time for public wallowing. There was laundry to be folded, dishes to be washed, lessons to be planned. There were two daughters to be raised in some fashion. A womanly figure to be kept intact. Good times, too, must be penciled in.

Since Jack and Susan had left, it seemed that a crack had developed in this locked resolve, and my mother became desperate, preparing in every corner of her body for the next departure, the next person to leave her. We would leave her.

We would come back, of course; of course we might not. We might choose him. We would go away, and she would be a single woman in a farmhouse. I imagined her standing in open doorways, walking through cleaned and emptied rooms, kneeling between the shooting growth of her garden, watching the days pass in their reserved and silent manner as if caught in a trance. It was a dramatic imagining—though suitable for my warbled, fifteen-year-old sorrow—and probably inaccurate. Still, it was a role my mother—someone who was secretly drawn to the power of dramatics—might just perfect for the sake of perfection.

I climb aboard an eastbound train with my towheaded sister. We are already clinging together, fearful of strangers, of the days-long journey, of eating in the dining car, of the place we are going to. We embrace our mother; her face is pale but calm, any trace of anxiety worked away by exhaustion. She stands on the platform in overalls and cardigan, her short hair smoothed behind her ears, her hands tucked into her pockets. She looks like a young girl, and other women in skirts and heels glance at her as they walk by; they see a working woman too busy to bother with lipstick or nylons or drawn-out goodbyes at train stations. Her gaze remains locked on the train after we have boarded, moving along the row of windows until Franny and I have found our sleeper car towards the very back and pulled down the top pane of glass so that we can lean out and call to her. We fight until we have managed to each squeeze our heads out the window. She smiles finally, and waves. Other people point and laugh at us as the train begins to pull away from the station. Franny hoots like an owl and crosses her eyes until Mother laughs too. She laughs and then just as quickly clasps a hand to her mouth in a gesture of disbelief, as if she's learned something astonishing. This is our last view of her before she vanishes from sight; a small woman in working clothes, her hair a little too fluffy about her head, a neatly callused hand held to her face as if to keep from crying out. The train moves on, gathering speed, until the station is only a fragile shape behind us.

I kept my head out the window, squinting against the wind, feeling that I would have given anything to be back on that platform beside her, to shake her and remind her of the car key in her pocket, of the drive home through the summer morning, of the day that lay ahead. I would plead with her. *Get in the car,* I would say. *Go home now.* Go home. You've eaten nothing, I saw you. You are hungry, and things are bad when you are hungry. Make toast and tea; keep the radio on for company; carry it from room to room. Go outside. Spray the garden with the hose; there are growing things there that need you. Go about your day. Pet the cat. Make your dinner. Remember your work. The house is quiet. The windows are wide open to the season. It is summer and you are alone; this only means that you are free. You sleep and wake alone. You have this time to think, and it is possible to imagine another life for yourself. Think of it in a neat, linear way—no complications.

We are at the house on Colt's Neck, you and me and Franny and Father too. There has never been any other house but this one. The big house and its trouble, its hollow nights and choreographed parties are but dreams, scenes from some play we went to see. We all went together. Father was directing. You took us to this play, all dressed up and clean, and Father was waiting for us in the wings of the theater—an important man, commanding and kind, and he belonged to us. There are familiar things here; the smell of heavy velvet curtains, the din of voices in contained space, the feel of the stage floor worn dusty and soft as skin, the contours of Father's face and neck as he speaks and listens and laughs. You are watching him. We go home after the applause, and together you and Father take cocktails on the front porch. Franny and me, we're sleeping on the side lawn; we've made a nest of blankets and pillows. There's the smell of split wood in the air—wood that Jack came to cut with Father. Jack. He's still around too. He's across the road in the house with all the windows lit. He lives there with his daughter called Susan and his wife, called Alice, who has a head of flame-colored hair. She is your friend.

On the porch, Father is reading to you from a new script. He's been working at it for a while now, smoothing out the oddities, the clichés and kinks, and the job is almost done so his spirit is light. "Nora," he says. I hear him speaking your name. "Nora, I think I've almost got it right." He reads to you, acting out the parts. One part belongs to you. When he's finished he'll hand you the pages to be typed up, click click, on your typewriter in the basement room with the warm paint and all the old school books. You type in the early morning when the light is coming through so heavy it hurts your heart. The script is a small sheaf of paper and in time, after many readings, it will become soft and worn so that you can fold it and keep it in your pocket. You can carry it with you wherever you go, and even when you can't see it, you know by heart which lines are yours.

The End

ACKNOWLEDGMENTS

I would like to thank Deirdre McNamer, Debra Magpie Earling, and Bryan DiSalvatore, writing mentors and champions of the highest degree. Thanks also to my writing friend Abi Maxwell, who (unbelievably) liked the things I wrote. The MFA 'novel group' read, critiqued, and celebrated the very early drafts of this book—I'm indebted to them for that time and support. I must also thank Chris Cauble, my editor with Riverbend Publishing, for offering his insights; any good piece of writing is a product of writer and editor, and this book was made much cleaner thanks to Chris's advice. I'm also grateful for the Sterry family's generosity, and in particular, for Nedra Sterry, who believed in Montana women writers. This book is the result of many years of sometimes dedicated, sometimes scattered work. During that time, my life was made immeasurably better by the friendship of Lauren Leslie, by the boundless love of my sisters, Anna and Sally McHugh, and by the ever-present support of my parents, Robin and Sarah McHugh. Jonathan Driggers, who lets me be myself and loves me anyway, gave me the final courage to send this work out into the world. Finally, I want to thank Melvon, Blakely, Sarah, Firman, and Margery. It is a blessed thing to be counted as one of your own.

ABOUT THE AUTHOR

Beth Hunter McHugh, 31, was raised in Helena, Montana, and is a graduate of the University of Montana where she earned a B.A. in English (2006), an M.F.A in Creative Writing (2009), and an M.Ed in Curriculum and Instruction (2015). She taught writing at Bitterroot College and currently teaches English at Hamilton High School. Her work has appeared in literary magazines, including *Orange Quarterly* and *Writing Tomorrow.* She lives in Hamilton, Montana.